GREEN *as* GRASS

Books by Mary-Celeste Ricks

A Stage for Harriet

Green as Grass
(Sequel to *A Stage for Harriet*)

GREEN *as* GRASS

MARY-CELESTE RICKS

SWEETWATER BOOKS
An imprint of Cedar Fort, Inc.
Springville, Utah

ISBN 13: 978-1-4621-4160-9

Published by Sweetwater Books, an imprint of Cedar Fort, Inc.
2373 W. 700 S., Springville, UT 84663
Distributed by Cedar Fort, Inc., www.cedarfort.com

Library of Congress Control Number: 2022930457

Cover design by Shawnda T. Craig
Cover design © 2022 Cedar Fort, Inc.
Edited and typeset by Valene Wood

Printed in the United States of America

10 9 8 7 6 5 4 3 2 1

Printed on acid-free paper

To Brian, my very favorite nerdy gentleman

Chapter One

September 30, 1813
Lady Norbury's card party

"Miss Louisa! There you are. Do tell me what you think of my bespoke new fob! Isn't it marvelous?" Beau asked.

Louisa looked up to see Mr. Brummell descending upon her in all his evening finery, and she could not reel in a smile. "Which one, sir?"

He gestured to a small bird-shaped bronze medallion hanging from a blue ribbon at his hip. She smiled when she saw it. "I am quite partial to birds, sir," she said. "So I am not a reliable judge, but I do like it."

"I am aware, Miss Grenfeld. That is why I asked you in particular." He gave her a small wink. "Now let us see. Whom do we have here this evening?"

Louisa turned and surveyed the elite assembly alongside her dear friend, Beau Brummell, that esteemed icon of fashion. They had become good friends the last season, and she was proud of herself for earning his approval.

"What do you think of that one, there?" Mr. Brummell asked her.

"Hmm?" She glanced in the direction he indicated. There, entering the drawing room, was a starry-eyed young man who had to have just returned from a tour. The look of overt interest in his eyes ran decidedly counter to the practiced expression of boredom worn by most of the pink of the *ton*.

Louisa giggled. "He's come straight from a home tour, my dear Brummell. Can you not see? Far too sure of himself to be fresh from Oxford and practically bursting at the seams to tell everyone of all the beautiful countryside he's seen in the Lake District. He may even recite a poem or two."

Mr. Brummell chuckled lightly. "Whatever else he may be, he's certainly green as grass, isn't he?

"Indeed, but who knows—he may become all the rage once the season sets in. It's dreadfully early for such predictions, you know."

"If anyone were to know, it would be I. Or you, perhaps. You're becoming quite the arbiter of fashion too, you know."

She playfully slapped his wrist with her fan. "You flatter me, Brummell. I could never presume my opinion could carry as much weight as yours."

"Hmm. Perhaps not. But *I* am fond of your opinions."

Louisa rolled her eyes heavenward for an instant but smiled.

"Really, though," Brummell continued. "What devilish awkward hands! Quite a decent coat. It looks like Weston's work. But that neckcloth! Looks as though he had his valet do it. Do you know who he is?"

Louisa shook her head. "No. I'm certain I can secure an introduction, however. Look there—he's talking with Mrs. Clavendish."

When Louisa turned back to Brummell there was a wicked glint in his eyes that she knew all too well. She smiled curiously. "What is it, Brummell? You've just had an awful idea."

He smirked at her. "He looks green enough that I'd wager you could make him fall in love with you by the end of the evening."

She flushed. "Nonsense! Not by the end of the *evening*, in any case. I'd need at least a few weeks to do that."

"So you admit you could do it?"

He had been baiting her! She glanced back at the young man for a moment and stood her ground, pursing her lips. "Of course I could. But it doesn't follow that I ought to."

"Don't be missish—it's all in good fun. How about a little wager?" he said. "If he comes for a morning visit within the next two days, you win. If he doesn't, I win. Is that fair?"

She shook her head and laughed. He would find anything to bet on. "I suppose. What is at stake, pray?"

"Fifty pounds?"

Her heart pinched nervously. That was almost all of her pin-money for the entire quarter, and, although she was fairly confident she could win, Brummell shouldn't be betting so heavily if he were in as much debt as the rumor mill claimed he was.

"No," she said. "Just one pound."

He pouted at the small stakes but nodded and they shook hands.

They were interrupted just then by Lady Stanfield, an older woman in a silver gown, jewels and feathers nestled in her graying hair, who latched herself to Mr. Brummell's arm. "My dear Brummell, you *must* assist me! These young snips are tearing me to pieces at speculation, and Mrs. Hayes has utterly refused to partner with me again!"

Mr. Brummell smiled indulgently at Lady Stanfield and joined the table, but not before casting Louisa a meaningful glance toward the green young man.

Louisa closed her fan and allowed it to dangle casually from her wrist. She nodded at a gentleman her father's age as she made her way to the young man's vicinity.

As she walked toward that end of the room, she passed a large mirror on the wall and verified that she was just as pretty as she had been upon arriving at the party. Her auburn hair was piled high in a fashionable style of curls and braids, adorned with pearls. Tiny cream satin slippers peeped from beneath an impeccably cut dress of deep blue. Her lips were reliably plump and pink, her cheekbones high, and her eyes a dark, shining brown beneath perfectly arched brows. She walked toward the door, as if to leave, but paused meaningfully next to the conversing pair for a moment. Sure enough, her method worked.

"Oh, Miss Grenfeld!" Mrs. Clavendish said. "Do come here. I want to introduce you to Mr. Andrew Brougham. He's recently returned from a grand tour of the north country!"

"It's not really a *grand* tour, madam," Mr. Brougham sounded mildly uncomfortable. "Travel to the continent is nearly impossible at the moment for those not enlisted."

"This is Miss Louisa Grenfeld, Mr. Brougham." Mrs. Clavendish barreled on heedlessly, "And I am certain you two will find *much* to speak of. Oh, Mr. Farnsworth! You must excuse me." The lady hurried off after Mr. Farnsworth, leaving the pair alone.

"A tour of the northern country sounds fascinating!" Louisa said, carefully hiding her sarcasm. She'd listened to so many stories about such 'tours' lately that she was quite tired of them, but she also knew it would inevitably surface later in the conversation if she did not initially inquire. "Where did you visit, sir?" Louisa opened her fan again and peered from behind it in a way calculated to spark interest.

Sure enough, roses bloomed in the young man's cheeks. "Oh, all the usual places, of course. The Lake District, and some of the more famous lochs and forests in Scotland. We made it as far as the Scottish highlands before we needed to return. Fascinating wildlife."

Louisa raised an eyebrow. He hadn't mentioned a single ruin, poem, or famous individual, unlike how most others did. Was he really so dotingly fond of the outdoors?

"Do you hunt, sir?"

He laughed nervously. "I'm a terrible shot, but I do enjoy being out on horseback, especially through wooded country. I tend to get distracted, however, so it is no longer easy for me to find hunting companions." He smiled in such a cheerfully self-deprecating manner that Louisa found herself warming to him despite her original intentions.

"Indeed?" she laughed. "And what is it that so distracts you, sir?"

"Birds, mostly."

She blinked a few times. The proper response from a young lady of her social caliber was to laugh carelessly at this confession—birdwatching was far from a popular topic for the drawing room. But she couldn't help herself.

"Is that so?" she asked. "And are you an avid avian scholar?"

Mr. Brougham smiled. "I do love birds, though I do not consider myself an expert. I have a pair of birds as pets here in town, but I prefer the ones in my dovecote or that live wild on my estate."

Louisa's eyebrows raised in interest. He had already come into his own estate? But he was so *young*. "Tell me of your dovecote. You keep doves and pigeons, I expect?"

"Mostly," he admitted, "though I have encouraged a few wild varieties to roost as well. And I also enjoy training birds."

"Hawking?"

He nodded. "Also pigeons, doves, and an African parrot. Enough about me though, Miss Grenfeld. I fear I am boring you. I would love to learn more about you."

Louisa smiled at him. She was far more intrigued by him than she had bargained for, and more interested in birds than she was willing to let on to the rest of the *ton*. High society was not kind to bluestockings, and she had noticed that men did not like women to be *too* talented. Drawing a pretty bird or flower was all that was required. A perfectly accurate rendering seemed to only make gentlemen look at her strangely. She'd very quickly learned to hide her talent.

But this Mr. Brougham certainly did have nice eyes—of a soft gray-green hue. The color went nicely with the chestnut of his hair, which curled on the edges in a fashionable style that parted to the side and fell into his forehead.

"Oh, there is not too much interesting about me, I'm afraid," she said dismissively. "Like all young ladies, I enjoy attending balls and parties and the theater, and I'm no more accomplished than most young ladies can boast." She had learned, while still in her first season, that the more she encouraged others around her to speak instead of herself, the more attractive she would be, and the more gossip she would overhear.

Mr. Brougham nodded. "Are you musical?"

"A very little," she said. "I sing, when pressed, and I play the piano only enough to accompany my song. My artistic talents lie in a more visual direction."

Mr. Brougham raised his eyebrows. "Do tell me more. What do you most like to draw?"

Scientific drawings of birds, she thought. But she would never actually admit to that. She smiled innocently. "When did I say that I drew, sir?"

He was taken aback. "I beg your pardon! I only assumed . . . is it needlepoint? Do you cover screens?"

She laughed. "I was only quizzing you! Yes, I do enjoy drawing. And painting, too."

"And what sorts of things do you draw?"

She cleared her throat and turned her attention for a moment to a passing gentleman. "Mr. Saunders, I did not know *you* would be here this evening!"

The man smiled. "I would not miss it, knowing you were likely to be here, Miss Grenfeld." He bowed over her hand. "Perhaps you will join my table for a hand of cards as the evening continues?"

"I should be delighted to."

As Mr. Saunders left, Louisa turned her attention back to Mr. Brougham. "Now, Mr. Brougham, you were telling me more of the sights you were able to see while in the north country."

Mr. Brougham frowned curiously. "I believe I was asking *you*, Miss Grenfeld, about the sorts of things you enjoy drawing."

Louisa's jaw grew tense. He'd remembered! He was a far better listener than most young men she'd met.

She laughed lightly. "Indeed I was. How clever of you to remember, sir," she said, embarrassed her attempted change in subject had not gone unnoticed.

Mr. Brougham smiled at the carpet. "I . . . don't much like talking of myself."

Louisa brightened at the opportunity. Flattery was one of her favorite talents. "But a gentleman of such address and consequence as yourself really ought to put himself forward!"

Mr. Brougham looked back into her eyes, and the warmth she saw there surprised her. "I would like to speak with you more, Miss Grenfeld, but I would hate to bore you at a party such as this when there are so many others who wish to claim your attention. Might I make a morning visit to your home during the course of the week?"

His sudden shyness was not unbecoming. "I would be disappointed if you didn't," she said encouragingly, unable to hide a genuine smile at the thought of winning her bet.

He smiled. "Excellent. Now . . . we are at a card party." Mr. Brougham said. "I see Mr. Saunders is part of a new whist table being formed. May I escort you to the table?" He held out his arm.

"Of course! I should like that very much," Louisa said, taking his arm.

They hardly spoke during the rest of the evening as they played cards at separate tables, and since Mr. Brummell left early, after demonstrating clear frustration at the low stakes offered at his table, she was not able to make a full report to him, either.

She passed an enjoyable evening feeling every bit the bright young socialite she was. And it only added to her delight that every few minutes she caught Mr. Brougham watching her curiously from across the room only to quickly glance away whenever he was caught.

Chapter Two

October 1, 1813

Mr. Andrew Brougham reached for his coffee without looking up from his book. Misjudging the distance, he knocked the cup over and immediately tore his eyes from the page.

"Blast," he muttered, only to see that his overturned coffee cup had long been empty and made no mess. He looked around his study. Papers were strewn everywhere. Bewick's *History of British Birds* and several other books on wildlife and biological reference manuals lay open on the table, while his forgotten estate ledgers had been unceremoniously piled atop a small roll top desk in the corner.

"How long have I been at it?" he murmured, leaning back in his chair to catch sight of the clock on the wall. It was nearly eleven. "Late!" Andrew leapt out of his chair, letting it fall to the floor, and rushed off to his chambers, hastily instructing his valet to help him dress for a morning visit.

"Why the sudden urgency, sir?" Henry asked, matching Brougham's apparent haste as he stripped off his master's house coat and retrieved fresh linens.

"I had determined to make a visit this morning, and the morning is nearly over," Andrew said, and smiled to himself in the mirror as he remembered the charming way Miss Grenfeld's eyes had caught his in the candlelight last evening. Could it be she found him as interesting as he did her? Or did he hope too much? Reading the thoughts and feelings of others had never been a talent of his, and he did not trust himself to gauge Miss Grenfeld's interests accurately.

Henry nodded. "Shall I fetch your blue coat, or the gray?"

"What think you of the green one?" he asked.

Henry nodded. "I think it suits you very well, sir." As he retrieved the coat and prepared to carefully insert Mr. Brougham into its precision fit, he casually asked, "Are you . . . off to see a young lady, sir?"

Andrew sighed. "Is it that obvious, Henry?"

Henry shook his head, but his not-so-carefully hidden smile gave him away. "You simply seem a trifle more agitated than usual, sir."

Andrew looked down with a nod. "I am agitated. The young lady in question . . . she's unlike other young ladies I've met."

When Henry remained determinedly silent, Andrew cleared his throat. "Do you have any advice for me, Henry?"

"I shine your boots to a mirror sheen. It isn't my place to make social recommendations."

Mr. Brougham narrowed his eyes at Henry and frowned. His valet was normally a fountain burbling with advice on proper comportment, and his sudden silence concerned Andrew. "Tell me, Henry. Is it not your duty to try to keep me from embarrassing myself where you can help it?"

Henry did not require much convincing. He smiled proudly. "Very well, sir. How long ago did you meet the lady?"

"Only last evening, at Lady Norbury's."

Henry's lips tightened. "And did she flirt outrageously with you, sir?"

Andrew thought back to the night before, to the way Miss Grenfeld's dark eyes had sparkled at him from behind her fan. "I have no idea. How do I tell, Henry?"

"Did she ask you to visit her?"

"Well, no. I offered, but she did graciously welcome me to do so."

"Did you specify you would come today?"

"No. Yes. Well, I asked if I could come today or tomorrow. Does that matter?"

Henry set down the brush he had been using to ensure Mr. Brougham's suit was completely free of lint. "Sir, if I may speak plainly?"

"When don't you?" Mr. Brougham mumbled to himself.

"Young gentlemen who too eagerly approach a young lady of interest may unintentionally . . . frighten her away. Young ladies often prefer men of mystery, who school their feelings and keep them hidden."

Mr. Brougham was mildly disgusted. "You mean I ought to let her think I don't like her?"

"Exactly, sir," Henry said proudly.

Andrew sighed. "I . . . but what if she *does* like me, Henry? If I am too aloof, she may think I don't care two straws for her and set her cap at the next young fellow to come along."

"Then perhaps the young lady is not worth pursuing," Henry said lightly, starting to tie his employer's cravat.

Mr. Brougham thought back to Miss Louisa. She had earned his admiration by appearing genuinely interested in what he had to say. Not by ignoring him or pretending not to care. From what he was able to tell, she spoke to everyone that way, and he liked that about her. He liked it at least as much as the way her auburn hair and dark eyes had shone in the candlelight.

"Oh, I'm certain she's worth any effort," Mr. Brougham said quietly, distracted by the vision in his mind.

Henry stopped in the middle of tying and looked Mr. Brougham in the eye. "Be sure you aren't taken in by an enterprising fortune-hunter," he warned. "There are plenty of young ladies of questionable virtue who would be easily lured by your fortune."

Andrew shot Henry a sharp look. "Henry, please. I am nervous enough as it is. Lady Norbury surely doesn't invite young ladies of ill repute to her evening card parties, and Miss Grenfeld was well-liked and well-known by everyone there—even Mr. Brummell."

Henry raised his eyebrows and nodded, impressed despite himself.

"And I'm told I ought to imitate him as much as possible. At least, Weston tells me that whenever I'm being fitted. The point is, Henry, that I already know full well she's a respectable young lady and, unless I gravely mistake the matter, she seemed to enjoy conversing with me!"

Henry had looked away at the beginning of the tirade, and now looked cautiously back. "Your cravat shall need to be redone, sir. I apologize." He silently began repairing the flustered damage Mr. Brougham had wrought to the carefully executed knot.

Andrew sighed. "I did not mean to offend you, Henry."

"It is not my place to take offense, sir," Henry sniffed, as he finished the knot and stood back to inspect it.

Mr. Brougham said nothing further, but as he left the room he noticed his cravat was tied a trifle tighter than he normally liked it.

October 1, 1813

Louisa sighed. Her aunt was in one of her moods, it seemed.

"What about Mr. Sheffield? He had a house in town," Aunt Frances said.

"He only ever breathed through his mouth," Louisa said, wrinkling her nose. "And his breath smelled terrible!"

"Come now—it couldn't have been that bad."

"*You* never needed to dance with him."

Her aunt shook her head. "Honestly, Lou. Of all the shallow reasons . . ."

Louisa turned to her needlework with a sigh. "He was never a serious candidate for me, Aunt. Even if there had been any natural attraction between us, he had *no* conversation. Physical imperfections I can overlook, but I need to at least be able to speak to my husband, don't I?"

Aunt Frances grumbled assent and continued covering her screen. "Wasn't there also James Mendon?"

"In a manner of speaking. No formal proposal, but there was interest."

"On your side?"

"Heavens, no. He quoted out of the Bible too much."

Aunt Frances set down her needlework. "Louisa, really! You need to settle down, and sooner rather than later."

Louisa frowned and turned away.

"You do not want to be an old maid, do you?" Aunt Frances asked quietly. It was a sore subject for her. She had been considered a spinster for as long as Louisa could remember.

Louisa groaned. "Of course not," she said. "But I had rather be an old maid than end up in an unhappy marriage arrangement."

Aunt Frances sighed. "What are you hoping for? What will it take to make you finally agree to settle down with someone?"

"What would it take *you*?" Louisa asked.

Aunt Frances glared at Louisa. "I beg your pardon, Louisa? We are talking about your marriage prospects! This is a serious discussion."

Louisa set down her needlework and watched her aunt intently for a moment. "Oh, I am serious, Aunt. Deadly serious. Why did not *you* ever get married? And why can I not be like you?"

Aunt Frances shook her head. "I cannot believe I am hearing this."

"What of Colonel Compton? He is still a handsome man, and well set up. Did he not single you out for a visit not so very long ago?"

Her aunt's cheeks were flushed. "Yes, he did, and I assure you I was flattered, but I am *not* interested in contracting a marriage at this point in my life, Louisa. I am forty-five years old!"

Louisa sensed a certain something in her aunt's tone that warned her away from pressing further, but she could not help herself. "But you are a very beautiful forty-five, Aunt. You would be an excellent wife for any older gentleman."

Aunt Frances's eyes narrowed to slits. "Louisa, we are *not* talking about me," she said tightly.

Louisa sighed and allowed her lower lip to protrude. She had no desire to be married at present, but perhaps her aunt was right. Louisa needed to focus on what sort of husband she wanted to find eventually if she were ever going to find him. An excellent marriage was the greatest hope of every young woman in society. With marriage came adulthood. Respectability. Influence. And in some ways, greater liberty. Ideally marriage could also be happy as well as sensible, and Louisa had long been ambitious.

But a goal could not be met until it was made.

"Oh, all right," she grumbled. "What do you wish me to do?"

Aunt Frances chuckled. "You speak of marriage as though it were on par with cleaning the stables. What sort of man do you wish to marry, darling?"

Louisa paused in thought. "You know I'd love a house in town," she finally said. "Of my own. A permanent establishment."

Aunt Frances smiled, her eyebrows rising, clearly eager to turn the topic of conversation back to Louisa. "But Mr. Sheffield and Mr. Mendon both had houses in town!"

"I hadn't finished! He'll also need to have a good bearing, a good wardrobe, and a neat appearance."

"I suppose those are reasonable requirements," Aunt Frances conceded.

"And we need to be able to have pleasant conversations."

"Yes, yes, Lou. All of that *sounds* very reasonable, until you begin to notice that no one seems to meet the exacting standards you set for both fashion and intellect. If you find such a man, will you be able to snap him up?

"Yes," Louisa said firmly. "Yes, I am quite certain I could. Now can we please talk of something else, Aunt?"

"Very well," her aunt said. "Have you had any letters from Charlie recently?"

"Not for three weeks! I'm afraid my brother is not quite as devoted a correspondent as we had thought he would be. But in his last letter he certainly seemed contented enough with Oxford."

Aunt Frances chuckled. "He's always made fast friends. And he *is* a good correspondent, my dear! I had a letter from him only last week."

Louisa scowled and shook her head. "No fair, Aunt! He ought to have written to me too."

"I'm certain he will soon. What is for luncheon?" Aunt Frances asked.

"Ham with boiled potatoes and leeks. What has that to do with anything?"

"Oh, nothing. But I'm famished," her aunt said, a hand pressed to her trim waist.

The butler knocked twice and entered. "Mr. Brougham," he announced.

Louisa tossed her needlework to the side with a smile. She had won her bet! Her brief moment of triumph was followed by an inward cringe. That means poor Brummell had lost yet another bet. He had been finding himself on the rocks more and more lately with his heavy gaming habits, and only seemed to dig in more deeply in response. He would surely face ruin if he did not begin to mend his ways soon.

She stood to greet her guest as Mr. Brougham shyly walked into the room, his hair askew where his hat had been removed in a hurry.

"It is good to see you, sir," she said with a smile. "How do you do, Mr. Brougham?"

He smiled at her. "Very well, Miss Grenfeld. Very well, indeed."

"May I introduce my aunt? Miss Frances Bickham. Aunt, this is Mr. Andrew Brougham."

"Honored to make your acquaintance," Mr. Brougham said with a bow.

Aunt Frances glowed. "A pleasure, Mr. Brougham," she said, as they all sat down. "And how did the two of you meet?"

Louisa piped up. "At Lady Norbury's card party yesterevening, remember?"

"I had not had the pleasure then," Aunt Frances said. "Mr. Brougham. It is very good to meet you. Tell me, where do you stay in town?"

He seemed a bit taken aback, and Louisa frowned at her aunt's forwardness.

"I've a house on Hill Street."

Aunt Frances shot Louisa a significant glance. "Ah, Hill Street! Yes, we know it well. An excellent neighborhood. You are very fortunate, sir."

Mr. Brougham looked uncomfortable at this effusion and Louisa quickly interjected, "We have no permanent establishment of our own here in town, you see."

She flashed an irritated glance at Aunt Frances and wondered if she were trying to make the situation awkward on purpose.

"Mr. Brougham, tell me more of yourself," Aunt Frances said warmly.

"Erm . . . there isn't much to tell, really."

"Have you also a seat in the country?" she pressed.

"Aunt, really!" Louisa said, her cheeks flushing. "I am certain Mr. Brougham's situation is none of our affair."

Aunt Frances turned on Louisa. "A gentleman's estate is hardly a private matter, my dear!"

Mr. Brougham cleared his throat. "I do have a seat. In Suffolk."

"Beautiful, to be sure. And not too terribly far from Louisa's father's estate, in Kent! It is, again, lovely to make your acquaintance, Mr. Brougham. I wonder if I might prevail upon you to join us for luncheon?"

He hesitated. "I had not . . . that is, I do not have other plans."

Louisa glared daggers at Aunt Frances, who ignored her. What was she trying to do to the poor man?

"Excellent!" Aunt Frances said. "We are very pleased to have you join us. I shall speak to the cook directly." She abruptly stood and walked out of the room, leaving the pair of them momentarily stunned.

Left alone, Louisa allowed herself to bask in the momentary relief of her aunt's absence. She was almost certainly trying to play matchmaker, making it seem as though Louisa regarded their guest far more highly than she really did. What a shambles! Louisa turned to Mr. Brougham and smiled, happy for the opportunity to regain control over the situation. "Mr. Brougham, only yesterday you were telling me about your visit to the Northern Counties before we were interrupted by the card tables' forming. Do tell me more."

Mr. Brougham smiled hesitantly. "Perhaps we had better talk of something else. I do not wish to bore you."

Louisa was pleasantly surprised by his social chivalry, and her smile broadened of its own accord. "You have never bored me, sir!" she said. "I would not have asked if I did not wish to hear you speak of it. Tell me about some of the wildlife you saw there."

Mr. Brougham smiled and began describing the birds of prey he had seen in Scotland. "The Golden Eagle was my favorite, when I managed to spot one. It was perfect athleticism and grace as it dove to catch its prey. I suppose it did not hurt that the scenery was lovely. The eagle that I saw swooped down over the shimmering waters of Loch Ness and caught a fish in one easy motion. Incredible."

Louisa found herself leaning forward, cheerfully entertained and enjoying the enlightenment and the brightness in Mr. Brougham's eyes.

Chapter Three

October 1, 1813

Andrew glanced up as Aunt Frances re-entered the room a few minutes later.

"It will be a few minutes yet," Aunt Frances said, upon reentering the room. "Louisa, would you be so good as to favor us with a song while we are waiting?"

Miss Grenfeld stared at her aunt long enough to blink a few times. "I am sure Mr. Brougham would much rather converse. He knows such interesting things about birds, Aunt!"

"Indeed, I *would* like to hear you play," Andrew said eagerly.

"There. You see now, Louisa? Please indulge us."

Miss Grenfeld smiled stiffly and Andrew felt suddenly guilty. He did not want to be put on the spot again, but felt bad forcing Miss Grenfeld to perform if she did not wish to. She took her place behind the pianoforte and began to play a simple Italian piece he had heard several times before. Her voice was sweet and light while still strong. He found her quite pleasant to listen to, and he heard no errors in her playing, either. He would have been happy to simply sit there and listen to her sing, but Miss Bickham leaned over to whisper in his ear.

"Louisa is quite accomplished, you know—she draws and paints, and can sew the most charming little things!"

Mr. Brougham nodded politely, but continued listening instead of responding.

"And she is quite fond of you already, sir. I hope that we shall continue to see a good deal more of you in the future!"

Mr. Brougham glanced over in Miss Grenfeld's direction, suddenly conscious of how tightly his cravat had been tied that morning. "She is?" he asked, not quite daring to believe her. "Well . . . I am happy to visit as often as I am welcome."

Miss Bickham nodded cheerfully.

Miss Grenfeld finished her song, gave a polite curtsy, and hurried back to her seat on the sofa.

"Very well done, Miss Grenfeld. You sing very well. And I wanted to tell you that I . . . very much enjoyed meeting you last night."

She smiled at him. "As did I, sir."

"And there's something I've been meaning to ask you since then—what sorts of things do you enjoy drawing and painting?"

She froze for an instant before laughing. He loved the sound of her laugh. It was no polite society titter, though he knew she was perfectly capable of one. At her home, though, her laugh was sincere, honest, and a mite louder than most.

"I like painting all sorts of things," she said, "though I'm not usually brave enough for portraiture."

"Everything but people, then?" he asked.

"Nearly," she said with a smile. "Trees, flowers, squirrels, birds . . . even fruit."

"Did you say *birds*?" He couldn't restrain a grin. She only grew more and more interesting.

Her cheeks flushed. "Yes."

"I don't suppose you'd let me see any of your artwork?" he said. "I would very much like to."

She looked down at her hands. "Perhaps on another visit, Mr. Brougham."

He frowned and licked his lips. Was there anything he could say to make her change her mind? He could tell she was uncomfortable, but he was burning with curiosity and could not resist asking. "I really would very much like to see some of your work, Miss Grenfeld."

She sighed. "No, sir. I have put myself on display enough this morning and I wish to be let down from my pedestal!"

Andrew laughed in surprise. *Humble and clever, too? She's really quite perfect.*

"I am, however, very interested to learn more of *you*, sir. You cannot be unaware that your estate's reputation precedes you."

Mr. Brougham froze and his mouth settled into a frown. "Does it?"

"I cannot help but notice also," she added, "that despite this you seem rather unfamiliar with the manners and workings of society here in London. I know *I* have never seen you here before."

He felt the heat rise in his face. "Yes, it's my first season in town. I couldn't avoid it any longer."

"Why were you avoiding town?"

He laughed nervously. "Perhaps that is the wrong choice of words. I've simply always found elsewhere to be during the season until now. Am I really so green?"

"Oh, dear. I didn't mean . . . yes, you are! But it doesn't follow that that's such a very bad thing," she insisted. "Only that you'll need to accustom yourself to some things. Like others speaking of your property as if it's already half theirs, for most mean no offense! Secrets, especially about the worth of one's fortune and estate, are rarely kept for long here."

Mr. Brougham nodded. He could feel himself relax. Miss Grenfeld came from a thoroughly respectable family—she was no danger to him. "I have already been warned to steer clear of fortune hunters," he said.

Miss Grenfeld quirked an eyebrow. "The important thing to avoid isn't necessarily a fortune hunter, Mr. Brougham. I would argue that nearly everyone participating in the marriage mart is a bit mercenary to one degree or another. The things to really avoid are low birth and bad breeding. Disreputable connections can easily ruin one's standing in society, regardless of one's fortune."

"Well-connected," he said with a nod. "Like you."

She nodded and smiled. "Yes, like me. I am also not entirely without fortune, though in London mine is considered rather modest."

Mr. Brougham wondered to himself why she was being so suddenly open with information about herself. She had appeared more reluctant to talk of herself the evening before. Was she advertising herself as a worthy candidate for marriage? His pulse sped up.

"And I?" he could not resist asking.

"Hmm?"

"I am of tolerable birth and fortune, am I not?"

"Oh, yes! Indeed. In fact, I am absolutely certain there will be no end of young ladies setting their caps at you this season."

But are you *one of them?* he wondered. He smiled. "Well, now that we've established that we are both perfectly worthy candidates for matrimony, shall we discuss something else?"

She laughed, and he found himself wanting to do anything he could to hear that sound again. He wished he were clever enough to find a ready response. They were briefly interrupted as Miss Bickham slipped back into the room and picked up the screen she had been covering earlier, silently commencing work on it.

Louisa turned back to their guest. "Tell me more of your tour of the north, Mr. Brougham. I have hardly ever traveled beyond London and Kent, where my father's estate is."

"I suppose, if it really does interest you . . ." He began describing the different locations he'd visited. He talked for several minutes, and Miss Grenfeld made a perfect audience, probing him with additional questions whenever he fell silent.

". . . Not only Windermere, which, placid and lovely though it is, I found almost crowded. I could hardly go for a walk near the lake without coming across someone who tried to introduce themselves."

Miss Grenfeld nodded and smiled in all the right places, and laughed occasionally at Mr. Brougham's most persistent attempts at wit. When he had exhausted his English escapades and moved on to the Scottish ones, his voice grew even more animated and his gestures more emphatic.

"The capercaillie was the most exciting find, perhaps. They have to be rather good at hiding because of their large size, but they are beautiful birds, though not the only colorful ones in the region."

"Yes, you mentioned the capercaillie last evening. What other birds did you find?"

Mr. Brougham paused, embarrassed. "I . . . I am sorry, Miss Grenfeld. I have forgotten myself. How long have I been speaking?"

"It can't have been longer than about half an hour."

"Half an hour?" Andrew could not remember a time when someone had ever allowed him to speak for fully half an hour without interrupting him or claiming that he was boring them to tears. "I must be boring you, miss. I'm terribly sorry."

Her eyes widened. "You weren't boring me! Whatever gave you that impression, sir?"

"I've always been told that I ought never to speak more than ten minutes together or I am likely to be a bore."

Miss Grenfeld raised her eyebrows and nodded. "That is generally true. Not for you, of course, but for other young gabbers. I must confess that, although I have occasionally told polite untruths to protect another's feelings, I am not telling one now. I like what you have to say, Mr. Brougham. Most young men inevitably talk of their own self-importance and are willing to go on for far longer than half an hour in doing so, which does indeed make for very dull conversation. But not you. Tell me, have you always been so unselfish?"

Mr. Brougham blinked in surprise as Miss Grenfeld told him the opposite of what his mother had always told him. This was turning into the most unusual conversation he'd ever had. "I have never considered myself unselfish."

Miss Grenfeld shook her head with a smile. "You were telling me of some of the wildlife you saw in Scotland, sir. Please go on, if it doesn't displease you."

Mr. Brougham continued where he'd left off after a brief hesitation and another encouraging glance from Miss Grenfeld, describing the variety of color in the Scottish crossbill, and the difficulty of distinguishing its species from another without inspecting the slight hook in the rather large beak.

Andrew hesitated after glancing at the clock. Miss Grenfeld's chaperone had been silently working at her needlepoint for some time now and he was beginning to grow uncomfortable. Was he boring her? He could read nothing but interest on her face, but perhaps she was good at feigning it. His mother had told him time and again not to bore young ladies with talk of wildlife. She insisted it would drive the good *ton* away.

He paused after describing two Ospreys soaring through the air together with motions as graceful as a dance.

"I beg you, Miss Grenfeld. I feel I am speaking more than my fair share. I know you have interests of your own and I would love to hear about them."

Miss Grenfeld blinked in surprise, but she smiled. "Very well. I like society," she said simply. "*People* interest me. They are all so different, and yet alike. The more I learn about people the more I find odd similarities in the most unlikely places."

"Oh? What sorts of similarities?"

Louisa shook her head. "I ought not to reveal secrets, sir. But rest assured that I like all I have been learning about you so far."

Andrew felt his heart jump into his throat. He swallowed hard. "Do you? I . . . I cannot imagine why, but I am glad."

Louisa frowned at him and shook her head. "My dear Mr. Brougham, you must develop a bit more self-confidence! A handsome, polite, intelligent young man like you should never be made to feel small. Who taught you to doubt yourself so?"

It was likely a rhetorical question, but a face sprang to his mind. *Mother*, he thought to himself. She was a good woman, but anxious and eager to find faults in him to fix, supposedly for his own good. He had realized long ago that fixing what was wrong with a person was her method of showing love, and he appreciated the sentiment, if not the actions inspired by it.

In the midst of this brief reverie, a maid entered the room. "Luncheon is served."

He cleared his throat again. "Wonderful," he said, "Thank you again for extending the invitation."

As he watched Miss Grenfeld gracefully rise to her feet and walk to the door, he realized he was likely already more than halfway in love with her.

Chapter Four

October 1, 1813

They had a rare evening at home that night, and Louisa was enjoying the brief respite between parties. After supper she went straight to her bedchamber and was helped out of her gown. She sighed as her stays were released and relished the cool, fresh linen of the nightgown she pulled over her head. It was only after she had crawled into bed and cuddled under her blankets that she realized her candle was low and she had forgotten the book she had been reading in the sitting room. She sighed and reluctantly climbed out of bed, slid her feet back into her satin slippers, and pulled on a robe.

As she tiptoed down the hallway with her candle, she passed her father's study. The door was slightly ajar, the glow of the fireplace barely visible, and two voices were talking.

"Two hundred pounds on ball gowns?" Mr. Grenfeld grumbled.

Louisa froze outside the door and listened carefully.

"That is not terribly immoderate for a member of the *ton*, you know," her Aunt Frances reasonably said. "Most women spend far more to look far worse!"

Louisa smiled at the compliment, but a worry line still formed above her brow.

"But my daughter is spending as though she has double the portion that is hers! If this is the cost of every season in London and if Louisa remains as reluctant to marry as she has been the last three seasons, I simply . . . I cannot indulge her this way forever, Frances."

Louisa felt sick. She *had* tried to economize in her dress, but there were some things that couldn't be helped. Her position in society dictated that she simply *had* to have at least half a dozen new formal ball gowns per season to avoid becoming an object of ridicule. She had never chosen the most opulent or expensive styles, instead deferring to Mr. Brummell's wise suggestion to exchange finery for a fine fit, but nevertheless, some expense was required. "I have been trying to persuade her to give more serious consideration to the young men who express interest in her."

"And I thank you for that, Frances. Truly. A girl needs a mother, especially when she reaches this age, and I am grateful Louisa has you to care for her."

"I'm lucky to have her too," Aunt Frances said quietly.

"You might know better than I, then," Father said. "Why has she rejected all these men? I thought for certain that Mr. Sheffield's asking my permission was a formality. I was most disappointed when nothing came of it. He is a thoroughly respectable man and I believe he married another young lady last year when Louisa rejected him."

"Yes," Aunt Frances said. "It is true that Louisa did not like him. She initially gave a superficial reason, but when pressed she admitted the true reason was that he lacked conversation."

Louisa heard a nearly silent noise that could have been hands thrown into the air in frustration and landing with a muffled flop.

"Conversation takes *time* to grow. Heaven knows that Georgiana and I did not always get along, but . . ."

"Sir, that was different," Aunt Frances said gently. "You two were decidedly in love before you were married."

Silence reigned for a moment, followed by a sigh. "Yes."

"Louisa did enjoy a pleasant conversation today with a fellow named Brougham who came by."

"Brougham, did you say?"

There was silence, and Louisa could only assume her aunt was nodding. She held her breath.

"It might just be the same one," he murmured. "Terrible story. His uncle had been trustee since his father died and apparently he'd been embezzling from the estate! Was the devil of a business to sort out last year, or so I heard."

"He *is* already come into his estate, then?" Aunt Frances clarified.

"Yes, in Sussex. Or was it Suffolk? And it's a fine one. Houses in town and Brighton, too. I wasn't aware you'd made his acquaintance." Mr. Grenfeld seemed very pleasantly surprised, which lifted Louisa's spirits.

"Louisa made his acquaintance at Lady Norbury's card party."

"Now *there's* a connection I can approve," he said cheerfully before his tone changed. "Unless he's a rackety sort of fellow. I've never actually met the man, after all."

Louisa smiled at the thought of someone calling the awkward, bird-loving Mr. Brougham *rackety*, but her stomach twisted at the way they referred to him—as a marriage prospect. Mr. Brougham would likely make some young lady very happy someday, but she did not necessarily think that she was that young lady. Besides, she hoped to make it through at least another season or two before needing to find a husband.

"I don't think you'd disapprove of her acquaintance with him. In fact . . . I think you would like him very much. I was disappointed when you did not join us for luncheon today, for he was there!"

"Is that so?"

"Yes, he was quite enraptured by the tea—he said it was the best cup he had ever had."

Her father chuckled. "Then I am very sorry I missed it."

"I do not think you will need to worry for long on that front," Aunt Frances said, "for he seemed quite taken with Louisa, and I believe she could grow to like him, too. He will likely visit again soon."

"And he isn't rackety?" Father said hesitantly.

"Not at all!" Aunt Frances said. "Perfectly respectable. Rather green, in fact."

Mr. Grenfeld seemed pleased. "Oh, I like that. Yes, not like that irresponsible Brummell fellow."

Louisa scowled in her hiding place, but thoughtfully raised her eyebrows only a moment later. It was a fair criticism of Brummell.

Aunt Frances laughed in some shock. "He's the leader of fashionable society, sir. More influential even than the regent! There is little to gain by offending him."

"I have very little interest in fashionable society. Or in being in London at all! I would much rather return to Thorngrove and have done with the whole season!"

"But you know Louisa would be miserable left in the country year-round with a personality as social as hers."

"Then why does she not get married? I've had at least two gentlemen—each with a London house of his own, mind you—approach me for Louisa's hand. Two! But she refused them! And I ought to remind you that while London offers many pleasures for you ladies, for me it does not!"

"I am sorry for that, sir."

Mr. Grenfeld sighed. "*Sir,*" he repeated bitterly. "Won't you call me Arthur, Frances? We are practically brother and sister."

Louisa bit her lip and held her breath as she listened. Her mother's elder sister, Aunt Frances, had lived with them and been close to Louisa for as long as she could recall. She had more or less taken on the office of governess when Louisa was little, to the extent that she'd lost more than one formal educator who had been offended by Frances's involvement in the schoolroom. But since her mother had died six years ago, she had also taken on the role of trusted confidant and guide. Louisa would be lost without her.

"I . . . do not like to forget my place," Frances murmured.

"Your place is here, with us," Mr. Grenfeld insisted. "We are a family."

Frances was quiet for a moment. "I am sorry . . . Arthur. Perhaps it's only dear Georgiana's loss that makes it difficult for me."

Louisa drew away then, tiptoeing across the hall to the sitting room. She felt guilty for eavesdropping on what was clearly a private conversation she wasn't meant to hear.

Her heart pounded as she hurried to pick up her book from the side table where she'd left it. She clutched it to her chest and took a deep breath. Could it be true? Father had asked Frances to call him by his given name! Was it out of mere brotherly affection, or was there the hint of something more than friendship between her father and her aunt? Oh, she hoped there was! That may have been why her aunt was so reluctant to talk of her own prospects.

It would naturally cause a scandal if their feelings were ever made known—they shared a roof! But it was a pity, for Louisa could not think of anything wrong with the match. They were not brother and sister, after all—Frances was her mother's sister. And her mother and Aunt Frances had always been close friends, so it had been a natural solution for Aunt Frances to join their household when she was unable to form a good match of her own. She had been with them for years, and Louisa had even more precious memories with Aunt Frances than she did with her own mother.

She remembered the way Aunt Frances cared for them after her mother had died when she was a little girl. Frances had been as miserable as either she or her brother, but she had put their needs before her own and tenderly cared for two grieving little children and a heartbroken widower. Aunt Frances took care of Father when he was sick and made him laugh when Louisa had thought he might never even smile again. She also remembered her father making Aunt Frances giggle despite herself and cast burdens off her shoulders that she was never meant to carry in the first place.

Louisa smiled. She remembered her father carting her about the house on his back when she was a little girl while Aunt Frances carried Charlie on hers, the four of them laughing all the while. Aunt Frances was, as her father had said, *family*. Just as much as her mother had been.

What would happen when Louisa married and left to establish a home of her own? Frances could not possibly stay and care for father alone. She would need to come live with Louisa and her husband, whomever he turned out to be. Or . . . Louisa sighed. Would it not be wonderful if Frances and her father could marry?

Louisa paused on the steps before climbing upstairs. If she were left a spinster, would *she* be willing to stay on as a household companion or a governess to her younger brother's eventual wife and children? She wrinkled her nose and shook her head. Perish the thought! Poor Aunt Frances. She was so very good, and she deserved far more than the hand life had dealt her.

Chapter Five

October 2, 1813

Andrew's mother was home when he came down the stairs in the morning, which was unusual.

"Andrew! How have you been, darling?"

He frowned. His mother, Lady Margaret Brougham, generally only used that tone when she wanted him to do something difficult or embarrassing. He braced himself.

"Hello, Mother." He kissed her cheek quickly. "I am well. How are you?"

"Very well, indeed. Where have you been?"

Andrew sighed. "I have been upstairs working on a . . . project," he hedged. His ledgers were more or less up to date, but he had been ignoring them in favor of writing down more of what he remembered about capercaillies. Fascinating birds.

"What sort of project?"

He knew her well enough to know she would only tease or berate him if he mentioned his wildlife notes. "What is it you needed, Mother?"

The corners of her mouth turned down and she lifted her chin. "I've just been by to see dear Ruth—you know, Her Grace the Duchess of Dorset."

Andrew raised an eyebrow. That was a name he had not heard before. His mother loved to name-drop, but this was likely the first duchess she'd managed to acquaint herself with on such terms. He tried his best to seem as impressed as he should be. "Oh?"

"Indeed, and her daughter is recently returned from a *long* summer holiday in Brighton. I'm told it's done her a world of good. Would you like to meet her? I was hoping to introduce the two of you to one another some morning this week."

"I . . . perhaps," he said. He hated being dragged about for morning visits with his mother. She could have painted his likeness on a wooden board and carried it about with her for all the good his presence did. Morning visits offered only weak tea and silly gossip. The tea he was served at Miss Grenfeld's was a notable exception. It had been brewed perfectly and was served on a simple but elegant tea service.

Besides, his mother was forever going on about titles, and he tended to prefer the contents of a person's mind to their lineage. Some of the most vain and ignorant people he had ever met came from noble families.

His mother pressed him. "Why not come with me today, my dear? This morning!"

He struggled to come up with a proper excuse. "I have morning visits of my own to conduct, you know."

His mother frowned suspiciously. "Who is it you can have cause to visit? You've hardly been introduced to anyone at all since you've been in town."

He raised an eyebrow. It certainly felt as though he had made the acquaintance of at least a hundred new people so far. He cast his mind about for a single name his mother wouldn't find objectionable.

"Lady Norbury," he finally said, "has said she wants to introduce me to her niece. So really, if you don't mind, I am quite occupied. I also have plans to dine away from home this evening, Mother, so do not wait for me."

He left the room, put on his coat and hat, and grabbed his walking stick, hurrying out the front door before his mother could say another word.

Once outside, he sighed. He needed to work on having better excuses, but his mother's conversation tended to overwhelm him. He wondered how long it would take his mother to see past his misdirection and discover the whole truth of his budding interest in Miss Louisa Grenfeld. He could never keep secrets from his mother for long. It wasn't that she coaxed him into confessing, either—she was simply a well-practiced gossip who could piece together a concealed reality with nothing but suspicions, observations, and a single hint.

His appointment to visit Lady Norbury was, of course, fictitious, but he did not believe the lady would mind a visit from him, and it was a fine autumn morning. He walked in that direction, hoping he would recognize the house in daylight and that the lady would be home and willing to welcome him. He was not even certain which hours she kept. It seemed a bit of a presumption, but the rules of society were so completely arcane to him that he could never be sure if he were correct or not. Everyone else he knew seemed to make morning visits with impunity, so he decided to take the risk.

As he walked down the street, he nodded politely to a flower vendor, whose eyes lit up. "Hello there, sir! And a very good morning to you!"

He nodded again, unsure of how to reply, and continued walking.

"Which flowers have caught your eye, then?" the enterprising lady asked him. "I have some 'specially pretty lilies here today."

"I had not . . . that is—"

"What about this bouquet right here? Any lady would be thrilled to be on the receiving end of this one." she pressed, thrusting the flowers under his nose for him to admire.

It was a pretty bouquet, and Andrew felt flustered. "It is pretty," he admitted. He wasn't accustomed to asserting himself. In fact, if living with his overbearing mother had taught him anything, it was to always err on the side of polite surrender when he could. He had begun trying to change that in recent years but had made far less headway than he would have liked.

"Only a shilling, sir! Just imagine the look on the lady's face!"

The flowers tickled his nose and he sneezed. He had already stood there too long, paralyzed by this fear of offending others. He reached into his pockets to see if he had any spare change and located an errant shilling, which he used to purchase the rather large bouquet of flowers from the ambitious vendor.

"An excellent choice, sir!" she said with a gracious smile. "Good day to you!"

As he continued, he wondered to himself how he ought to dispose of the embarrassing flowers until he saw that he had wandered to the corner of Park Street. His heart thudded in his chest as he thought of visiting Miss Grenfeld again. Henry would certainly say it was too soon.

The memory of her sparkling brown eyes as they caught the sunshine through the window lit his mind, and he took a few steps up the road before he caught himself.

He had visited her only yesterday, he reminded himself. Henry thought him a slow top already, and he had no desire to prove his valet correct. He surely could not visit Miss Grenfeld again so soon. Perhaps she would be at the party that evening. He'd received an invitation to a soiree. Henry had reminded him that morning of his commitment to attend while tying his cravat, but he couldn't remember the name of the hosts for the life of him.

He continued walking slowly down the street as he thought, not wishing to look foolish for appearing to lack a destination. Perhaps he could simply leave the bouquet with Miss Grenfeld's butler and continue on his solitary walk. Lady Norbury lived in Grosvenor's Square, which was not at all far from here. Yes, that's what he would do. Leave the bouquet. And if he caught a glimpse of Miss Grenfeld through the window as he left the flowers with the butler, all the better.

His heart was in his throat when he walked up the steps, but he did not allow himself to hesitate. It *was* a lovely bouquet, and he hadn't anyone else to give it to—fresh flowers tended to make his mother sneeze.

He knocked.

The butler answered almost immediately and held the door open wide. Andrew held out the flowers to the man, but he found himself swiftly shepherded through the door despite himself. "Welcome back, sir," the butler said smoothly. "I shall inform the misses Bickham and Grenfeld that you have arrived."

"I—"

Andrew was left standing in the vestibule, still holding the large bouquet, as the butler disappeared to announce his arrival. He flushed, and meekly allowed a footman to take his coat, hat, and cane as he awkwardly juggled the flowers from hand to hand. A moment later the butler returned and gestured for Andrew to follow him. Feeling extremely foolish, he complied.

It was too late. He had been announced. He wondered if he was dooming himself. What exactly was it that happened if you gave a lady more attention than she desired? Henry hadn't been terribly specific. Andrew swallowed.

"Mr. Brougham!" Miss Grenfeld's aunt stood and cheerfully received him. "Are these beautiful flowers for my niece? They are lovely indeed. How very thoughtful of you! Please come in and do be seated." Miss Bickham called for a maid to come and arrange the flowers in a vase.

Andrew barely had time for a polite nod of acknowledgement before he found himself seated in a chair opposite Miss Grenfeld, completely overcome.

She was clearly surprised to see him, but nodded in welcome. "How do you do, Mr. Brougham?" she asked.

"Well enough," he said. Something in her eyes gave him a bit of heart, and he tried to compose himself. "I had intended to simply leave these with your man at the door," he said, "but he was most solicitously welcoming."

Miss Grenfeld gave a pleasant laugh. "Yes! Phelps is very good."

"I do not wish to impose," he said.

"You do not impose, sir," Miss Bickham insisted. "As a matter of fact, Mr. Grenfeld has expressed a desire to meet you himself. He had intended to come and visit you sometime this week, but you have saved him the trouble. I will go and fetch him here at once."

"That is not necessary, Aunt. Surely Mr. Brougham has other engagements to uphold."

"I have no other engagements, but—" he said.

"Excellent." Miss Grenfeld's aunt smiled at him once more before disappearing, leaving him feeling out of his depth and alone with Miss Grenfeld and a footman.

"I know it has only been a day," he said. "But I do hope that you have been keeping well."

She laughed again. "Indeed I have, sir. Very well indeed. And you? How have you occupied your time away?"

"Oh, with this and that. I've done nothing out of the ordinary. Have you any interesting stories to tell?"

She laughed. "Oh, nothing out of the ordinary," she echoed pointedly, giving him a mischievous smile.

He shook his head. "Are we, both of us, so determined not to speak aught of ourselves?"

Miss Grenfeld surveyed him silently for a moment with a sparkle in her eyes. "Perhaps you are right. Perhaps we are destined only to speak of far more interesting things than ourselves throughout our friendship."

"And you *would* say that we are friends?" he asked softly.

She radiated quiet confidence. "I certainly consider you a friend, sir, and I very much hope you think of me that way too."

Andrew felt warm from head to toe. "That I do. A very good friend already, Miss Grenfeld."

His mind eased. She did not seem unhappy to see him at all. Could it possibly be she would welcome his continued attentions? He could only hope. "If you must know what I have been occupied with of late, I was writing a bit more of what I remembered seeing while in Scotland, and I read what little I could find on the capercaillie."

"Yes, you were telling me about them yesterday," Miss Grenfeld said. "Tell me more!"

Andrew hesitantly told her a few basic details about them, noting when he had observed something different in the wild than he had previously read about them. Only a few minutes later, Mr. Grenfeld entered the room, clearing his throat. Andrew stood immediately.

"Good day, sir," he said with a formal bow.

Mr. Grenfeld looked Andrew up and down and then nodded approvingly before returning the bow. He smiled and gestured for Andrew to be seated.

"I have heard good things of you," the older gentleman said, taking a seat himself.

Andrew frowned in confusion. "You have the advantage of me then, sir."

"Forgive me. I am Mr. Grenfeld. Arthur Grenfeld of Thorngrove Hall, in Kent."

Andrew nodded. "Andrew Brougham of Hillside Manor, in Suffolk."

"None too far from Kent," he said approvingly. "Yes, very good." Mr. Grenfeld looked expectantly between Andrew and his daughter. Miss Grenfeld eyed her father warily and the two of them spoke to one another with their eyes for a long moment before Miss Grenfeld finally sighed.

"Did you need something, Father?"

"Yes, very thoughtful of you to ask, my dear. I would very much like a private word with Mr. Brougham. If he would oblige me?" Mr. Grenfeld said.

"Of course," Andrew murmured, taken aback.

Miss Grenfeld stared at her father for a second, her mouth set in a firm, disapproving line, before taking a deep breath and following her aunt out of the room. The door had hardly closed when Mr. Grenfeld started in.

"I hope I am not too forward in asking you what your intentions toward my daughter are, Mr. Brougham."

Andrew blinked a couple of times. Mr. Grenfeld did not beat about the bush, did he? "Erm . . . I hadn't . . . that is, I—"

"Because my hope is to see her very soon engaged."

Andrew flushed. "Oh. She is courting someone, then?"

"Not yet," Mr. Grenfeld said, giving Mr. Brougham a significant look.

Andrew pretended not to notice. He felt so uncomfortable he wanted to crawl out of his skin and run away. What was he supposed to say? "Well, I . . . I hope that Miss Grenfeld and I can continue to be friends," he said.

"You have my leave to consider becoming more than friends."

Andrew stared at Mr. Grenfeld for a moment. He had never had a conversation like this in his life.

He hadn't dared consider that Miss Grenfeld could actually like him, let alone consider marrying her. What would it be like to marry Miss Grenfeld? Her laugh sprang to his mind, and he saw her smiling brown eyes. He thought of how easy it was to talk with her.

"I . . . am honored," he finally answered.

"Excellent," Mr. Grenfeld said. "I'll leave you two to it, then. She might show a bit of resistance, but don't let that stop you. She doesn't always know what is best for her!"

Andrew could only stare at Mr. Grenfeld as the older gentleman stood and walked out of the room with the air of someone who had just completed a task he had set out to accomplish.

Chapter Six

October 2, 1813

"Men can speak more directly one to another than women can," Mr. Grenfeld insisted later that afternoon.

Louisa's face was still in her hands, and Aunt Frances was furious. "I'll count us fortunate if you haven't frightened him away entirely! I want Louisa to marry him as much as you do, but openly soliciting his courtship yourself is not the way to go about it!"

"It's the response I would've liked to see from my own father-in-law," Mr. Grenfeld said stubbornly.

Louisa sighed heavily and sat up, surprising both of them by beginning to laugh. "You two are *both* ridiculous," she finally said. "When did I ever say I wanted to marry Mr. Brougham? It is my decision every bit as much as his, and you two cannot make it for me."

Her father's brow furrowed. "You have never sought my ire before, Louisa," he said. "Do you wish to begin now?"

Louisa shook her head and assumed a solemn expression. "Not at all, Father," she said gently, "but as I am the one who needs to live with the consequences of this decision for the rest of my life, I think it only right that I be the one to make it. Not you."

Mr. Grenfeld surveyed her with an unreadable expression. Louisa held her breath. At long last, he said, "I suppose you are right."

The corner of Louisa's mouth lifted hopefully.

"But," he continued, "I do need to draw a line somewhere, and I'll not be held hostage by your failure to decide, Louisa. This is the last season in London that I will provide for you. Make of that what you will. I hope you will choose to contract an eligible match that will give you the future you desire. As for myself, I only wish to return to Thorngrove and remain there year-round for the rest of my days."

Louisa's heartbeat was the loudest thing in the room, pounding in her ears.

Her father stood and walked over to her, taking both her hands in his. "I do wish to see you happy, my love," he said, "and I agree that the decision will be a much happier one if it is your own. However, refusing to make a decision is a decision unto itself."

He kissed her forehead and left the room, leaving Louisa dizzy as the weight of this speech settled on her shoulders.

"I believe your dark blue waistcoat suits you the best, sir," Henry told Andrew as he helped him into it. "For an evening soiree, at least."

Andrew nodded. "Thank you, Henry."

Henry finished the last few details of Andrew's ensemble and reached for the pomade.

"Not too much this time, Henry," Andrew said. "It has a rather greasy feeling if there is too much."

Henry nodded and continued working.

When he was finished, Andrew acknowledged him. "Thank you very much," he said politely.

"Where are you off to this evening, sir?"

"A soiree at another home on Hill Street. I believe the Admiral's wife is hostess."

"Very good, sir."

Henry finished styling Andrew's hair (with far less pomade than usual) and presented him with a small selection of fobs for his consideration. Andrew chose a single small fob and attached it, allowing it to dangle just below his waistcoat. Henry seemed to be waiting expectantly for something, and Andrew could no longer pretend to ignore what it was.

"Miss Grenfeld will likely be there," he said.

Henry had been displeased to learn that Andrew had not only visited her the day after meeting her, but had visited the next day as well and brought flowers, too! He had only been stopped from making a speech of thorough disapproval with a direct order of the sort that Andrew hated to give, and Henry had been sullen about it ever since.

Henry pursed his lips. "I trust you know what you are doing," he said.

"Did I tell you that her father welcomes my attentions to her?" he asked.

Henry raised an eyebrow. "You did not."

"He does," Andrew said. "And I still have no idea what to make of it."

"Perhaps her reputation has been tarnished, sir, and her father is desperate to find a husband for her."

"Henry, that is an awful supposition." Andrew snapped. "There is no evidence of that."

"I apologize. Perhaps it is good that her father approves of you. After all, a lady must be subject to her father until the day she is subject to her husband. If you desire her as a bride, then her father's approval is essential."

Something about Henry's speech rankled at him. Andrew frowned until he realized what it was. "I don't particularly want anyone *subject* to me," he grumbled.

Henry swallowed a smile. "I am subject to you, sir."

Andrew nodded, but a frown remained on his face. "I suppose that is true, as are the rest of the people in my employ or whose land I own. But I do not . . . how do I put this?" he wondered aloud. "I have never wished to lead with brute strength, coercion, or fear."

"No one would ever mistake you for a brute, sir."

Andrew nodded. "And I would not have them do so. My father was a very gentle man, and I wish to be as kind as he was. But I also . . . I also recognize that if I am *too* kind, I can be taken advantage of." His mind leapt to his uncle, whose mismanagement of his affairs before he had come of age had been a nightmare to untangle.

He had been fortunate to have his mother fight for his cause as formidably as a bulldog, but too often, her protection of him had more closely resembled control.

Henry nodded. "I see your dilemma. It is one that many face."

"There is a difference, though, I think, between standing up for oneself and being domineering. I think now I would rather fail to advocate for myself than subject others to my will through any sort of unfair coercion. But perhaps I ought to learn to walk the line more closely."

Henry looked unusually thoughtful and quite pleased. "Very well said, sir."

October 3, 1813

Louisa smiled as she was greeted enthusiastically by her hostess and made her rounds about the room, flitting from one conversation circle to the next, taking care to greet everyone she was acquainted with by name, and speaking for a few extra minutes with any new people she was introduced to. She had a responsibility to uphold as a young leader of fashion.

Her father was comfortably wealthy and respectable enough to allow her entry into all but the most exclusive events reserved for titled patrons, but her real position in society was of her own careful making. She owed her popularity to being friendly to all but the least deserving members of society—those embroiled in scandal—and her taste in matters of ladies' dress was so exquisite that her opinion frequently became the rule.

"Brummell!" she said, walking over to her friend.

He smiled and swept her a bow with a little flourish.

"I like the way you've styled your hair this evening, sir," she said with an approving nod.

He preened for a moment and Louisa let out a giggle. "Well?" he asked. "I believe you and I had a wager."

Louisa smiled. "Indeed we did. You owe me one pound, sir. And hard-earned it was!"

"Oh?" Brummell asked, anticipating a story.

"Miss Grenfeld!" a voice spoke from behind her and she turned to face the source.

"Oh. Mr. Brougham," she said, and her smile flickered for a moment as she greeted him. "How do you do this evening?"

"Very well," he said with a polite bow. "I am pleased to see you as always, Miss Grenfeld."

Brummell let out a small chuckle behind her. "You seem to have your hands full, Miss Grenfeld. I will come by for a visit soon."

"Do!" she said to his retreating back.

When she turned she saw Mr. Brougham still standing next to her, awkwardly taking in the rest of the room. She nodded politely and moved to speak to another person behind him, but he moved with her.

"Do I ask too much to sit next to you during the musical portion of the evening?" he asked.

"I had not . . ." She admitted to herself she was impressed at his sudden boldness—he seemed like such a sheepish individual. "I would be delighted to oblige you," she said when she could not think of an excuse not to. "Pray, excuse me."

She walked over toward another conversation grouping and was only able to exchange a few words with her friend Miss Norris before Mr. Brougham was once more at her side, smiling silently. When she turned to him in question, he simply said, "May I get you anything, Miss Grenfeld?"

She smiled weakly and demurred, but it was from that moment that she spent the better part of the evening trying, and failing, to subtly rid herself of Mr. Brougham. He clung to her side like a barnacle. As long as she had an eligible bachelor as a public hanger-on, she could not exactly entertain a romantic connection with any other gentleman. She very nearly lost her composure a time or two and eventually had to escape to the retiring room for a brief respite.

During this visit, she overheard a conversation between two giggling young ladies chattering behind a screen.

"Did you see that Brougham fellow? Miss Grenfeld doesn't seem to want anything to do with him."

"I wonder what awful scandal he's been a part of," the other girl wondered aloud. "She is never that rude to anyone that hasn't been terribly naughty."

"Perhaps his feelings are simply not returned," the first girl said. "How embarrassing! I wonder what cause she has to discourage his advances. Not wealthy enough, perhaps? I've heard nothing of his fortune, have you?"

"It can't be that—he is quite wealthy from what I have heard. Full of juice. And he has a house in Brighton!"

"He's not unattractive, either."

"No, he's rather handsome, in fact. And his suit is well cut."

"Perhaps she's holding out for a title."

"Why should she?" the first girl asked. "She is pretty enough, of course, and very stylish, but not nearly wealthy enough to tempt a titled gentlemen when there are plenty of titled ladies to go 'round. Bit arrogant of her, I should think."

"If anyone could do it, it would be Miss Grenfeld, though."

Louisa had heard quite enough. She swept out of the retiring room, her cheeks flushed. The nerve! She tried to be very careful in her gossip never to say anything hurtful or presumptuous about others, but the reminder that others did not always do the same was never pleasant. *Something* had to be done about Mr. Brougham if she did not want these whispers to grow worse. He wasn't a bad fellow, but he was embarrassing them both! She sighed. There was nothing for it. She would simply need to gently guide his attentions toward some *other* young lady. Then she could begin forming an eligible connection for herself.

"Miss Grenfeld! There you are," Mr. Brougham said.

Louisa took a deep, steadying breath. First, she reminded herself, she had to survive this evening.

"Lady Margaret Brougham is here to see you, miss."

Louisa and Aunt Frances glanced at one another in confusion before standing to greet the imperious woman as she swept into the room.

Lady Margaret Brougham glared at Louisa through beady, critical eyes, and it was all Louisa could do to remain calm. The woman surveyed her with a gaze that made her feel about two feet shorter, but Louisa's rigorous training and experience in society had taught her to maintain her composure under circumstances far worse than these.

"Lady Margaret, have we had the pleasure of a formal introduction?" Louisa asked. She was almost certain they had never been introduced.

"Of course we have," the lady said, "I am well acquainted with Mrs. Norris."

Louisa struggled to keep a pleasant expression. She was almost certain they had never been formally introduced—she never forgot a name or a face.

"May I introduce my aunt, Miss Frances Bickham?"

"How do you do?" the lady said formally.

Aunt Frances responded politely, but seemed ruffled by Lady Margaret's prickly demeanor.

"Miss Bickham, may I request a brief private audience with your niece?" Lady Margaret said.

Aunt Frances looked back and forth between the two of them, and Louisa tried her best to seem composed and confident. "As you wish, Lady Margaret," she said, standing up and walking out of the room with a concerned backward glance.

Louisa turned to face the lady's unwarranted ire.

"Miss Grenfeld, I am sure you are aware of my son's handsome fortune and respectable position in society. I am sure you have also heard that my late father was the Earl of Derby. Mr. Andrew Brougham is not without connections."

Louisa inclined her head and continued to listen in respectful silence.

"I have nothing but his future happiness in my mind, and I have the highest hopes that he will form a most eligible match with a titled young lady of fortune."

"Any loving mother would," Louisa replied, maintaining her calm.

The lady's eyes narrowed. "And to see him pounced on by the first sophisticated young London lady he lays eyes on is not what I had in mind!"

Louisa blinked but did not allow her face to betray her emotions. This was going to be harder than she'd thought. She swallowed back her pride and strengthened the polite facade guarding her true feelings from Lady Margaret's view. "I am aware your son is, shall we say, rather green in the face of London society and its numerous rules and deceptions. Your fear is not unfounded, my lady."

"Then you admit to laying a snare to entrap my son!"

Louisa's eyes snapped shut at this insult and she took a deep breath inward. Her heart was beginning to pump harder with anger and annoyance at these false accusations. "I have done no such thing, my lady," she said firmly but calmly.

Lady Margaret's nostrils flared. She was clearly not maintaining her temper as well as Louisa was. "Well, know this—my son would never seek out a match that displeased me," she said boldly. "My opinion carries far more weight with him than you seem to realize, Miss Grenfeld. And I, for one, do not approve of you."

Louisa's blood was boiling, but she did not show it with more than a twitch to her lip. Surely the lady had said more than enough to drive her point home. She had to be nearly finished by now.

The lady's sudden smile made Louisa's hair stand on end. "Well. I am gratified by your silence, but I would prefer a demure apology and a promise to keep your distance from my son. Can you oblige me in this, young lady?"

Louisa stared at Lady Margaret. She had never been spoken to this rudely. "Lady Margaret," she said, "I am well aware my family is untitled, but we do not lack respectability and influence. I agree that, in title and fortune, your son could perhaps do better than I." She gave a meaningful pause. "But he could also do far, far worse, and I think you would do well to remember that."

The older woman's eyes narrowed into slits. "Was that a threat, Miss Grenfeld?"

Louisa somehow refrained from groaning. "No, my lady. I have no intention of seeking your son's attentions."

Lady Margaret narrowed her eyes as she surveyed Louisa. "And will you promise me not to seek his company to excess?"

Louisa fought the urge to roll her eyes at the woman's absurd paranoia and instead took a calming breath. "I never intended to do so.

But Lady Margaret, your son is a gentleman with the power to make any choice he likes. And I, too, may make my own choices. You have no authority to limit my movements in society."

"Then you admit to trying to sink your hooks into him!"

Louisa's nostrils flared. "Absolutely not. As a matter of fact, I intend to request that he cease his solicitous but uninvited attentions the next time he visits."

"You claim he is pursuing you, then?"

Louisa was growing tired of this. "If he were not, why else would you come here to lecture me?"

"What arrogant *cheek*!" The lady's face turned red.

At the sight of Lady Margaret's anger, a rational voice within Louisa reminded her that, despite the titled lady's unpleasant nature, it was best to eventually find a way into her good graces. Louisa had no desire to create enemies. She inwardly sighed and regathered her composure, sitting down. "I have no wish to either frighten or offend you, my lady," Louisa said with exaggerated calm.

After a long moment of silence, Lady Margaret hesitantly sat back down across from Louisa, her eyes still narrowed suspiciously.

"Lady Margaret, if I am not mistaken, you have two primary concerns—one is that your son simply hasn't experienced enough of the world or of society for you to believe him capable of making the best decision on his own."

The woman's anger seemed to dissipate at this assertion. She nodded, her lips pursed, and allowed Louisa to continue.

"The other concern is that a sophisticated and designing young female may draw him into a marriage he would later regret."

The woman's eyes narrowed. "And are you admitting that you are such a young woman, Miss Grenfeld?"

Louisa sighed. She was growing tired of this. "Certainly not, my lady, as I have already said. If I am to marry, it will only be into a mutually agreeable situation."

"And may I have your word on that?" the lady asked.

Louisa worked to keep her eyes from rolling heavenward as she responded. "Yes. I have no desire whatsoever to entrap a man into marriage against his will."

The lady's face relaxed and a self-satisfied smile curved her lips upward. "Then it would appear my fears are unfounded, Miss Grenfeld. Forgive me for supposing you wanted to marry my son. However, it sounds as though you could make a very useful sort of friend for him, to help introduce him into society. I am told your circle is very extensive, indeed."

Louisa was inwardly flabbergasted by the lady's resolute conclusion that she could never be considered an acceptable marriage prospect for her son, but if this assumption curbed the lady's animosity, Louisa was willing to nod and smile.

"Lady Margaret, it would be an honor to help your son form desirable connections in society. I am happy to assist in any way you think I can."

Lady Margaret nodded approvingly. "You move in very exalted circles for an untitled young woman, and you seem to always secure invitations to the most exclusive parties."

Louisa nodded, encouraging this line of thought. "And my taste in fashion and in friends is rarely questioned."

Lady Margaret smiled and stood, extending a hand to Louisa. "I thank you very kindly for your most obliging offer to introduce my son to some *eligible* young ladies, Miss Grenfeld. And I bid you good day."

As the lady was leaving, she stopped and turned. "And if you are seeking an appropriate suitor for yourself, Miss Grenfeld, might I suggest my brother's younger son, Mr. Alfred Stanley, whom I believe is currently in search of a wife."

Louisa immediately recognized the name and barely kept calm at this offensive remark. "Good day, my lady," she managed at last.

It wasn't until the woman left that Louisa allowed herself a shudder at the effrontery of the suggestion that *she* might like to be courted by such a stain on the tablecloth of polite society as was Mr. Alfred Stanley.

Chapter Seven

October 3, 1813

Louisa was still overheating with indignation after Lady Margaret's visit when she saw her aunt quietly enter her father's study. Louisa tiptoed toward the partially open door to be sure she didn't interrupt anything by coming in. She stopped and held a hand over her mouth to silence her breath as she listened.

"What are you reading, Arthur?" Aunt Frances asked.

"Nothing," her father said quickly.

Aunt Frances chuckled lightly. "Why do you hide it? You know I would never tease you if you did not wish it."

Mr. Grenfeld grunted in a noncommittal fashion but a moment later, Aunt Frances was exclaiming, "Ah, Miss Austen's work! I had not thought you would be interested in reading *Sense and Sensibility*."

Louisa's father cleared his throat, sounding a bit embarrassed. "I know you and Louisa were both quite fond of it, and since you said there wasn't anything of monsters or spirits or the like in it, I figured I would try it. I must confess for the most part I find it quite dull, aside from the shocking lapses of propriety shown by some of the characters."

"I hope, of course, you are referring to Mr. Willoughby."

"Willoughby? I was thinking first of Miss Marianne Dashwood, who does not always mind her tongue."

Aunt Frances tutted her disapproval. "Now, sir, she does nothing *terribly* untoward."

"She showed a decided preference for a young man who had made no promises to her."

"He willfully deceived her!"

"The rules of propriety are abundantly clear for young ladies."

"Oh, and these rules ought not to apply to young men?" Aunt Frances said, her tone inviting an argument.

Mr. Grenfeld sounded flustered. "No. Er—That isn't what I said! They ought to. The rules of propriety ought to be followed by all. They support and encourage Christian principles and virtues and are essential to maintaining a proper society."

Aunt Frances calmed herself before she spoke. "I do not disagree with that, sir. Only that Miss Marianne Dashwood ought first and foremost to be pitied and not harshly judged."

"Mr. Willoughby made her no promise."

"But he acted as though he had," Aunt Frances countered. "Is that not even more reprehensible than showing an unrequited degree of affection?"

Louisa thought she heard a note of pain in her aunt's voice and it stung her own heart. Is that the way Aunt Frances felt toward Father? An unrequited degree of affection? Could Louisa possibly find a means of bringing the two of them together?

"Yes," her father replied, "But his behavior should not excuse her improper behavior."

"No, it shouldn't. I agree that Marianne's behavior was not quite proper—her own mother and sisters could see that—but she bore the brunt of the punishment and humiliation for that offense, while he escaped completely unharmed from the encounter. That is why I focus my judgment on Willoughby and my sympathies on Miss Marianne."

Mr. Grenfeld was quiet for a long moment. Louisa found herself strangely invested in their conversation, even though she knew she ought not to listen in like this.

"You are correct, of course, as always," her father finally told her aunt. "But my influence over my daughter is far greater than any influence I can claim over the young men who seek her favor. I cannot control how they treat her or behave around her, but I can encourage her to act with prudence for the sake of her own interests."

"Arthur . . ." Aunt Frances petered out. "You are an excellent father," she finally said quietly. "And as her almost constant companion, let me reassure you that Louisa is a model of propriety."

"But that Brummell fellow . . ." her father protested.

"No," Aunt Frances said. "Leave the man be, sir. She can see him for exactly what he is—a clever, tasteful arbiter of fashion with an unfortunate gambling addiction and a great deal of pride. She knows her limits well, sir, and would never imitate him in any way that could harm her."

After a long pause, Mr. Grenfeld said, "I do trust her, but I still worry. She is very fortunate to have you guiding her, Frances. We both are."

"And I would be lost without her, sir."

Louisa's heart was warm and her cheeks were flushed. She clearly was not meant to overhear this conversation. She hurried back to the sitting room, where she stared out the window and meditated on her unpleasant conversation with Lady Margaret. Something had to be done immediately to lay the lady's nasty assumptions to rest.

A moment later, Aunt Frances joined her. "What did Lady Margaret wish to speak with you about?" she asked.

"Nothing of consequence," Louisa said, staring out the window, her mind rudely thrust back into that unpleasant conversation.

Louisa had already not wanted to commit to courting only the enthusiastic Mr. Brougham, and meeting his mother had only reinforced this determination. There were other gentlemen she ought to consider before arriving at a decision, and there had to be some with more pleasant mothers. Distancing herself from Mr. Brougham by making him self-sufficient in society would keep him occupied, appease his mother, and—most importantly—allow Louisa to welcome the attentions of other young men. Aunt Frances and Father may be disappointed, but it was for the best. Mr. Brougham only wanted a bit of polishing and some more confidence to move forward on his own, and she wasted no time before planning how best to accomplish this.

"He'll need some training," she murmured to herself as she considered what would have to be done. He mentioned he would also be in attendance at Mrs. Norris's next card party, and that is where she would change his course.

Louisa wasn't cruel. Careful, clever, and self-possessed, but never cruel. She knew Mr. Brougham had taken an interest in her, so it was only reasonable that she see that interest carefully turned in another direction before she could be free of him with a clear conscience. And most importantly—free of his *mother*. She shuddered lightly as she recalled the titled lady's insufferable presumptions. Indeed, this was all for the best.

She did not see Mr. Brougham again until the start of the party the following evening.

Mrs. Norris approached her soon after Mr. Brougham joined the party. "Louisa! I am so glad you were able to extend the invitation to such a handsome and eligible young gentleman! Would you do me the honor of an introduction?"

"My friend Mr. Andrew Brougham," Louisa said. "And this is Mrs. Norris, the mother of a good friend of mine—Miss Catherine Norris."

Mr. Brougham inclined his head in a polite bow. "Honored to have been extended an invitation, madam."

Mrs. Norris beamed at Mr. Brougham and Louisa smiled as she gently pried him away from Mrs. Norris and set about telling him about the different people in the room.

"There is Mr. Fitz-Herbert. He was widowed a few years ago and now the younger ladies tend to avoid him—he started trying to court again last season but won't look at a lady older than about twenty-six."

"But he's so *old*," Mr. Brougham murmured in mild disgust.

Louisa chuckled. "Yes. So, you see, any young lady you rescue from his clutches will swoon with relief and appreciation."

Mr. Brougham frowned at this, and Louisa quickly but subtly redirected his attention to a young lady across the room.

"And there is Cate—excuse me—Miss Catherine Norris, in that pretty pink satin affair. I will introduce you to her in a moment. Lovely girl. And Mrs. Morton, there in the deep blue gown. She throws some delightful parties, but one needs to take care, because occasionally she finds herself on the fringes of a scandal. Sometimes her parties are to be avoided. And Miss Inge, there . . ."

Louisa hurried through the background information on each individual of import. After a while, she found she was thirsty and caught a glimpse of Robert Dalton near the punch table, so without further ado she took Mr. Brougham over to where Miss Cate Norris was sitting and introduced the pair of them. Even Lady Margaret could never find Cate objectionable, and although she was untitled, she was first cousin to the Viscount of Hereford, so that might count for something.

Thinking of Lady Margaret for even a moment was enough to sour her expression, so when she went to the punch table, Robert Dalton greeted her by saying, "Well, good evening, Miss Grenfeld—who's set up *your* bristles?"

Louisa laughed lightly. Robert Dalton was a delightfully ineligible young bachelor of eight-and-twenty who gambled heavily, flirted freely, and made easy friends wherever he went. "It is as good to see you as ever, Mr. Dalton. Whatever leads you to believe I am angry?"

Robert gave her such a skeptical expression she almost had to laugh again. "Tell me, then, Miss Louisa. Who is responsible for that look on your face? Need I call someone out?"

She giggled once more. "Call out a widow? I should think not!"

"Is she a wealthy, young widow? Because I just might pay her a call. None too plump in the pocket at the moment, you know." He winked.

Louisa's eyes sparkled with her smile. "You never seem to be, Mr. Dalton."

He accepted the rub with a grin. "What is the latest *on-dit*, then, miss? From what little *I've* heard, that Brougham newcomer seems set to make you an offer already!"

She could feel her cheeks flush, but only smiled. "I don't know about that." She glanced about to be sure she wouldn't be overheard before saying, "His mother asked that I introduce him to some more *eligible* young ladies, and even suggested that I set my cap at her nephew, Alfred Stanley."

His mouth fell open and he shook his head. "You cannot be serious," he said.

"I'm afraid I am serious, Mr. Dalton," Louisa said, taking a sip of punch.

"Alfred Stanley? Does she *know* who you are?"

Louisa flushed with pleasure at the implied compliment. "Far too respectable for the likes of Mr. Stanley?" she said hopefully.

"I should say so! You are a diamond of the first water! *He's* a . . . a loose screw too short on blunt to afford bachelor fare!"

One or two older ladies looked over at him when he made this exclamation, clearly scandalized. He nodded a brief apology to them before shaking his head at Louisa. "I should lower my voice, but 'tis a shocking outrage. What did you say to the woman?"

Louisa looked heavenward. "What could I say, Mr. Dalton? I am a young, unattached woman of no consequence in her mind, and she the widowed daughter of an earl who refuses to recognize me as a respectable young lady, let alone as someone to be emulated. It would've been useless to contradict her."

Mr. Dalton shook his head. "You didn't answer my question, though, Miss Grenfeld. Are you setting your cap at that Brougham fellow? He's said to be full of juice and very well-born, but I've never seen him at Watier's! You never really know a man until you play a game of Faro at his side."

"Let us hope, for the sake of his fortune, that he is *never* seen at Watier's," Louisa said with a smile, her mind flashing to their friend Mr. Brummell's embarrassing gaming debts.

Robert narrowed his eyes at her. "Fine then, miss. You keep your secrets, and I'll keep mine."

She laughed at this. "When have you ever kept a secret, sir?"

He wiggled his eyebrows. "If I told you, it'd never be a secret now, would it?"

She heard a throat clear behind her and was surprised to see Mr. Brougham there.

"Er . . . hello, sir," she said. "How was your conversation with Miss Norris?"

"Very pleasant. She's a fine young lady," he said cheerfully. "May I fetch you a cup of punch?"

She blinked at him once or twice. She was already holding a cup, but it was nearly empty. She weakly held it out to him and he took and filled it, handing it back to her before continuing to stand quietly at her side. She watched him for a moment before shooting a confused glance at Mr. Dalton, who looked as though he were trying very hard not to laugh.

"Mr. Brougham? Would you like me to introduce you to Miss Mary Berkeley, there? I think the two of you would find a fair amount in common."

"I would be delighted." Mr. Brougham nodded politely to Mr. Dalton before offering Louisa his arm.

She took it, wondering what on earth she was going to do if his preference for her remained as pronounced as it was in that moment.

Even as she led Mr. Brougham to Mary Berkeley's side and offered them meat for conversation, Louisa felt a sense of foreboding that they would not speak for as long as she had hoped, but it was even worse than she had feared—he was at her side again less than five minutes later.

"I believe they're playing at cards in the next room," Mr. Brougham said when he approached Louisa again. "Would you care to join me for a game?" he asked her.

She shook her head. "Mr. Brougham, you really ought to seek introductions to more people," she chided. "You know hardly anyone here."

He looked disappointed. "Very well," he said, with all the air of a child asked to complete more lessons.

He came willingly enough to make the acquaintance of all of the eligible young ladies and young bucks of fashion, but he did not remain in conversation with any of them for longer than a few minutes, and did not offer to visit any of the young ladies, offending one or two of them who blatantly invited him to do so.

After an hour of forcing introductions and polite conversation, Louisa was already exhausted, and willingly submitted to playing cards with Brougham, doing all she could to ignore the whispers and titters she kept hearing about his excessive attentions to her.

It was one of the longest evening parties she had ever attended. This was going to be more difficult than she had thought.

Chapter Eight

October 4, 1813

"Oh, Aunt, it was *mortifying*! And heaven knows, Robert Dalton is probably off spreading the gossip that the only reason Mr. Brougham hasn't already made an offer is because his mother disapproves. Oh, what was I thinking when I confided in him?"

Aunt Frances said nothing, instead she stroked Louisa's hand in silent sympathy and tried not to laugh until a knock at the door announced a visitor.

"Ugh," Louisa groaned. "I do not know if I can face him gracefully right now."

"Louisa, really. How can you even know if it is Mr. Brougham?" her aunt asked.

"Knock, knock!" a familiar voice said, as an elegant presence swept into the room. "Sorry I didn't wait to be announced."

"Brummell! How good it is to see you!" Louisa said, relieved.

"Here are your winnings, Miss Grenfeld," Mr. Brummell said, handing her a single guinea with a flourish. Then he clucked his tongue. "Now, what is the matter with you, my dear? This is the nearest I've seen you to having a fit of the vapors!"

"Don't tell me you haven't already heard," Louisa said.

"Heard what? That Brougham is clearly besotted with you or that his mother rang a fine peal over you for ensnaring him with your feminine wiles?"

Louisa groaned and hid her face in her hands.

Brummell tutted sympathetically. "Of course I've heard. My sources are very diligent, my dear. This time it was Dalton. But I thought it was all fudge until I saw your face. Quite blue deviled! Come now, what is it? You can't let one angry old tabby cut up your peace so easily."

Aunt Frances gave Louisa's hand a final pat before turning to their guest. "Lovely to see you as always, Mr. Brummell. Louisa, now that you've another source of comfort, there were some things I wished to speak to the housekeeper about."

As she stood to leave and a footman joined them as a chaperone, Louisa turned to Mr. Brummell with a laugh. "Oh, you are just the person I wanted to see now. I *am* upset that Lady Margaret thinks so ill of me. She's wrong, of course, but that doesn't mean I enjoy being called a low-born, grasping fortune-hunter!"

"No, indeed. And surely her accusations are entirely baseless. After all, are you setting your cap at her son?"

"Of course not!" she snapped.

Mr. Brummell's eyebrows raised skeptically and his lips pursed. "I've never seen you so flustered before, Miss Louisa!"

She sighed. "Forgive me, but it isn't entirely without reason. I've been informed I need to marry by the end of the season, Mr. Brummell, for my father won't be hiring the town house again next year. If I am to remain a part of London society, I have no choice but to marry a man with a house in town of his own by the end of the season. But that doesn't mean I had decided on Mr. Brougham, let alone set my cap at him."

Mr. Brummell came to sit next to her on the sofa, clicking his tongue gently. "My dear Miss Louisa has needed to turn mercenary? I'm dreadfully sorry. But surely it needn't be to this green, young fellow with the awful mother. There are others who might suit."

Louisa shook her head. "I hope you are right. But who else might?" she asked, only half-serious. "Mr. Brougham hasn't a single scandal on his record, unlike most of the pinks of fashion *you* run with, Brummell. And as much as I like you and your company, I must admit that I think I might prefer someone a trifle more . . . respectable? And cautious? . . . than your usual crowd of Corinthians."

Mr. Brummell had the decency to pretend to be offended. "Me? Not respectable?"

She laughed. "Well, in any case, not always prudent!"

He conceded this point with a nod. "Fair enough. You know, this Brougham . . . he cuts a fine enough figure. And he sees Weston! So he cannot be completely hopeless. I am certain you, at least, could make something of the fellow. Perhaps he would not be so terrible for you after all."

She raised an eyebrow at this, and the corners of her mouth crept upward into a slow smile at his flattery. Only a moment later, however, she grimaced. "But his *mother*, Brummell!"

He wrinkled his nose. "The Lady Margaret? Indeed. I cannot stand to be in the same room with the woman." He shuddered again, and Louisa laughed at his overly dramatic reaction.

"She is not completely hopeless either, you know!" Louisa always seemed to feel the need to defend the attacked no matter how much she desired to join the offensive. "I have reason to believe she at least thinks my tastes and connections are of value to her. She has asked me to introduce Mr. Brougham to more *eligible* young ladies, you see."

"More eligible than you?"

"Yes. Titled ones. Preferably wealthy, too."

He snorted. "Well, that should not be too difficult. Who cares a fig for a title nowadays?"

Louisa looked down at the ground. Brummell hadn't been quite the same man since he and his former best friend, the Prince Regent, had gone their separate ways a few months before.

"All you have to do," he continued, "is introduce them both to a passel of titled *pigs*, and both of them will very soon see reason. He has already come of age, hasn't he? And he controls his own fortune."

Louisa nodded. She didn't have time to say more, however, because just then a knock at the door announced another visitor.

"That sounds like my cue to visit the next house," Brummell said with a cheeky nod, standing. "I shall leave you now, but do take care,

Miss Louisa. I am certain you will find a way out of this mess—you always seem to."

With a final nod, he swept out of the room as Mr. Brougham entered. They exchanged a quick bow over the threshold before the door closed behind Mr. Brummell, leaving Brougham standing there awkwardly, waiting to be invited in.

"Please have a seat," Louisa said, after just long enough a pause to make the young man uncomfortable.

Mr. Brougham was frowning as he carefully assessed her features. He watched Louisa carefully as he slowly sat on the sofa next to her. "I . . . I cannot help feeling that you are upset with me, Miss Grenfeld. Have I done something to displease you?"

Louisa barely resisted the urge to rest her face in her hands. Her temples could use a massage—he was giving her a headache. "Mr. Brougham, I am upset. We are not courting, sir!" she said bluntly. "And last evening, at the party, you refused to either mingle effectively with others or to allow me to do so! I've rarely seen a pair of lovers cling to one another so stubbornly, and never a pair of mere acquaintances!" She paused, breathless. Her temper, which she normally controlled so carefully, had gotten away from her.

"Acquaintances?"

Her stomach dropped with sudden shame at the look of disappointment on Brougham's face. "Friends, I mean," she corrected.

Mr. Brougham hung his head. "I wondered if you were irritated with me last night. I am never . . . I'm never sure what to do or say at parties like those."

She sighed, his humble contrition making her feel guilty. "I know. It isn't really your fault."

He nodded. "I am most comfortable on my own, or in small parties."

Louisa groaned. "Yes, Mr. Brougham, but you can still learn the skills you need, and can use them even if you aren't comfortable."

"And where am I to learn such skills?" he asked mournfully. "They don't exactly offer courses of study in fashionable behavior at Oxford." He paused, and his voice sank to an almost sullen murmur. "Nor do they teach you how to make love to a woman. Henry was right."

Louisa's heart surprised her by beating a jagged rhythm in her chest as he mentioned love. He was only talking about flirtation in general. He couldn't already *love* her. Could he? And why was she so affected by the thought? He clearly admired her already. She wasn't developing feelings for him, was she? Because if she were, they would completely upset her plans.

She mentally shook her head. Whether he cared for her or not hardly mattered. She had a task before her and an idea that could help him.

"They don't teach those things at Oxford," she said gently, "because most people either figure them out on their own, or they suffer the consequences."

"Consequences?" he asked weakly.

"Yes. A lack of social skill leads to loneliness, spinsterhood, friendlessness, and in extreme cases, utter ostracization."

Mr. Brougham's face had fallen until it was almost comical. She smiled gently. "But that will never happen to you, sir!"

Brougham gave her a questioning glance.

"You see, Oxford may not teach those subjects, but *I* am an expert! I will teach you myself."

Hope brightened his features. "*You* will teach me? Really?"

She smiled at his slight disbelief and inclined her head. "I truly will. You have always felt more comfortable in a classroom or in front of a book, have you not? Consider me your tutor."

"Very well. What must I do?"

Louisa smiled at his compliance. "I will have several lectures, and we can follow each lecture with some practice."

"What are these lectures about?" Mr. Brougham asked with interest.

Louisa returned his smile and, after a moment of thought, said, "Unwavering politeness in the face of rudeness, charm, maintaining interest, discerning thoughts through careful observation, and, most important of all, discovering the motivations of others."

Mr. Brougham seemed a little surprised by her response and the smile disappeared from his face. "You are quite serious," he said.

Louisa swallowed a giggle. "Did you think I was only pretending? I intend to do you good, you know."

Mr. Brougham laughed, but there was a serious expression in his gray-green eyes. "I believe you, Miss Grenfeld. I do not believe you would ever do me harm."

Louisa smiled briefly before regaining her formal air. "First you can practice with me, and then we can practice at the parties you will need to attend."

He had been smiling and nodding, but frowned at this last concept. "Parties I *need* to attend?"

Louisa nodded, giving him a look of sympathy. "But never fear—I shall teach you things you can do to feel more comfortable."

He shrugged. "If you tell me I *need* to attend parties, I will."

Louisa shook her head. "The request is more from your mother than it is from me, but I intend to help you please her."

The smile was wiped from his face. "My mother has been to see you?"

Louisa should not have been surprised that he had no idea of the encounter. She debated with herself how many details to include. Finally, she said, "She only wants what is best for you, Mr. Brougham. She very much likes the idea of my helping you to feel more comfortable in society . . . and of assisting you to make the acquaintance of marriageable young ladies."

He stared at her in silent horror for at least half a minute before sinking his head into his hands. "I did not know she had tried to interfere, Louisa. I am so sorry. I know she can be quite . . . I am sorry."

Louisa had flushed enough for the day and was determined to change the subject. "It is no matter! Let us begin our lesson on politeness with what makes appropriate subject matter for small talk, shall we?"

Chapter Nine

October 18, 1813

Andrew respectfully inclined his head to Lady Gregor as he passed her on the pathway along the Serpentine. Hyde Park was full of people at this time of day. He came to walk at the fashionable hour at Miss Grenfeld's urging, and to avoid his mother finding him at home. Both ladies always seemed pleased when he made an effort to strike out and socialize on his own.

The past two weeks since Miss Grenfeld had become his social tutor had flown by in a whirlwind of social engagements, lessons, and visits. Miss Grenfeld truly had a gift for helping Andrew wrap his mind around concepts difficult for him to understand on his own. She explained things in a clear, polite manner, and her observations were never wrong. He grew to trust her more and more deeply the longer she taught him, and the more carefully he listened, the better he learned.

Andrew had become quite practiced at small talk, and at reading the body language of those with whom he conversed. His conversations with others had grown from five minutes to ten minutes, to twenty minutes with ease, and time began passing more quickly and comfortably for him at parties, even when he was careful to converse about things of more general interest than rare wild birds. Trying to make others laugh became an enjoyable challenge for him, and he relished setting up the conversation so that he could surprise his listener with a perfectly placed pun or just the right cheerfully self-deprecating comment.

A white swan gracefully landed in the water before him and he paused to admire its smooth progression down the Serpentine. When he finally glanced about him at the other passersby, he could see that no one else on the pathway had paused to watch the beautiful creature. He inspected the people walking by. Some of them were talking animatedly to one another, some of them were pretending to admire the scenery while giving sidelong glances at the people on the walkway, and some of them were lumped in pairs blatantly staring at all of the sprigs of fashion around them, whispering furtively to each other. He frowned. He was certain Miss Grenfeld, at least, would enjoy watching the swan with him if she were there.

When Miss Grenfeld had first told him of his mother's visit and made it clear that she had no thoughts of entertaining his suit, he had been terribly disappointed. He had thought that perhaps she was as interested in him as he was in her, but he began to see, through the course of their lessons, that she treated everyone about her with the same kind consideration and interest and was just as pleasant a listener and conversationalist with nearly everyone she met. In other words, he could not be anyone special in her eyes. Perhaps she would only have enjoyed watching the swan to humor him.

The first day he'd recognized this, he'd been bitterly disappointed, seeing the world about him darkly, through a fog. But gradually the fog had begun to lift, and he was now able to enjoy his time spent with nearly everyone, not just Miss Grenfeld.

She stubbornly remained his favorite, however, no matter how obediently he sought to ingratiate himself to other young ladies.

What exactly was it he *did* like about Miss Grenfeld? It was difficult for him to put it into words. Was it mere infatuation that kept her at the front of his mind? He thought of the way her burnished hair shimmered red in lamplight, and the way her expressive brown eyes caught and threw back light when she smiled. Her beautiful face had caught his interest at first, certainly, but as he'd gotten to know her better, he began to have the odd sense that they had always known one another. He felt so comfortable in her presence, as though he had finally arrived at home after a long journey. He couldn't explain it, even to himself.

"I must be a case for Bedlam," he murmured as he picked up his pace and continued walking.

When they had first met, speaking even for a few minutes at that party, he had almost immediately felt this connection with her. She listened to him in a way no one else ever had—with sincere interest. Her laughter never sounded forced. And she may have known how to move about in society with perfect grace and skill, but she didn't give him the same predatory feeling he got from others. Yes, he liked her very much, no matter how much he tried to urge his attentions elsewhere.

He wasn't at all ready to give up his feelings for her, and was not certain he could even if he tried to. There was still a chance that she could be convinced to like him, after all, and as long as there was a chance, there was hope. The longer he looked for someone else, the more he doubted he would ever find another woman to make him feel half so happy as Miss Grenfeld did.

Finding another woman he could be happy with, who would meet his mother's exacting standards, and to whom he could bear to make an offer would be far more difficult than tearing down the obstacles that stood between himself and Miss Grenfeld. To make her fall in love with him, to make his mother see reason . . . Herculean tasks, indeed, but still easier than finding someone else he could love.

Yes, *love*, he repeated in his mind until his heart was thrumming with purpose in his chest. He may not know what he was doing, but he knew his own mind. That didn't make the tasks before him any easier, however.

"Oh, what am I going to do about my mother?" he moaned in exasperation.

October 27, 1813
Lady Gregor's ball

Mr. Brougham was not accustomed to seeing so many richly dressed people in one place. There were countless young ladies bedecked in satin and jewels, their hair carefully curled. Dowagers wearing silk turbans and enormous ostrich feathers. Young men dressed in their finest skin-tight suit coats and breeches, spangled with fobs, their shirt points starched and their white neckties frothing out of the tops of their waistcoats like piles of whipped cream. It was a truly glamorous affair, and he had never felt so alone.

He wandered the room, careful to maintain an attitude of placid disinterest rather than one of outright fascination or fear. As he looked about, he noticed several young people who were apparently not making these same efforts. One young lady was staring so openly at the finery surrounding her that she jostled directly into someone and had to stammer out an awkward apology while blushing furiously.

"Poor thing," he murmured.

"What was that?" his mother asked.

"Nothing."

They continued walking about the room until his mother's attention was happily seized by a woman in a white silk turban, leaving him on his own to seek out young people of his acquaintance.

It took him only a few minutes to find someone he knew. Unfortunately, that first person was Miss Clavendish. "Hello, Miss Clavendish. How are you this evening?"

"It is *so* wonderful to see you here this evening, Mr. Brougham. I do hope that you will ask me to dance!"

He forced a smile to cover his dismay. Her admiration of him was obvious enough to make him uncomfortable, and had been for some time. "I shall certainly do so," he said. "Would you mind introducing me to your friend?"

She turned back to the young gentlemen she'd begun ignoring. He was about Mr. Brougham's age—perhaps twenty-four or twenty-five, and was a veritable tulip of fashion. His collar was starched so thoroughly that he could barely turn his head.

"Pardon me!" said Miss Clavendish. "Mr. Brougham, this is Mr. Philip Palmer. Mr. Palmer, this is Mr. Andrew Brougham."

"It's a pleasure to meet you, sir," Mr. Palmer said, sounding perturbed.

"Your cravat is tied to perfection," Mr. Brougham said. "What do you call it?"

"It's the regent's knot," he said, smiling begrudgingly.

It only took Mr. Brougham another ten minutes of conversation before both Miss Clavendish and Mr. Palmer were both completely at their ease. He mentally thanked Miss Grenfeld a thousand times for teaching him what to say in awkward exchanges like these to render them pleasant.

As it often did, her voice replayed in his mind. *"Always ask about their interests first, and then add—now, this is important!—a very* short *piece of your own on the subject, just enough to make them feel comfortable discussing more. They ought to open right up if you show enough interest. Encourage them here and there and smile and you've made yourself a new friend!"*

Mr. Palmer made a little joke and the three of them all laughed heartily.

"You're a capital fellow!" Mr. Palmer said as soon as Miss Clavendish's attention was claimed elsewhere. "If I don't ask too much, I'd like to introduce you to a few of my friends." Philip brought him to a group of young men all standing together.

"Brougham, this is Joseph Drayton, Michael Heron, and David Upton. Gentlemen, this is Mr. Andrew Brougham."

They all seemed rather pleased to meet him, and one of them even complimented the fine cut of his coat. They seemed a pleasant bunch of fellows, and Andrew was grateful they did not seem mad for gaming or sporting. He really wouldn't have known what to say to them if that had been the case. Through his new acquaintances, he was able to meet several other young ladies and gentlemen. As soon as the dancing began, he did not find any difficulty in securing partners, though he feared he did not pay enough attention to any of them—he was too busy scanning the dance floor for Miss Grenfeld.

After dancing for perhaps half an hour he finally saw her, and he had to catch his breath. He nearly missed a step. As soon as the dance was over, he gave himself leave to admire her. She was wearing a ball gown of cream-colored crepe, with golden leaves embroidered on its edges. Her auburn curls were piled on her head in perfect coils, there were golden leaves and pearl drops scattered throughout the whole coiffure, and pearls gracing her ears and neck. He had never seen her look so lovely. She danced with an enviable fluidity, and gave her full attention to her partner. He had never wanted to dance with anyone so much in his life. He maintained his sight of her as he walked around the dance floor, and was ready, as soon as the dance began winding down, to capture her attention before she could be swept up again.

However, before the dancers broke the set and he could talk to her, a fan rapped his shoulder. "I believe that is your mother, is it not? She's been calling you these three minutes at least," an irritated young lady said.

"Andrew!" he finally heard her call. He grimaced with embarrassment, turned to look at her, and forced a smile onto his face as he walked over to her. It was not easy.

"Yes, Mother?" he asked once at her side.

"Oh, *there* you are!" She immediately began leading him toward a magisterial woman and a pretty young lady. "I'd like you to meet Lady Virginia, the daughter of the Duke and Duchess of Dorset."

His eyebrows shot up. He had not been looking forward to this. *Now?* "The Duke of Dorset?"

"Yes," she said as they arrived before the pair and smiled at them. "This is my son, Mr. Andrew Brougham. Andrew, dear, this is Lady Virginia."

The duchess lifted her chin with a little smile and casually fluttered her fan. "I am delighted, Mr. Brougham. Perhaps the two of you might like to dance?"

Poor Lady Virginia seemed humiliated. "Mother, can you not wait for Mr. Brougham to ask?"

Andrew filled with pity for her, and quickly held out his hand. "It's a pleasure to make your acquaintance. I am at your service and I would be honored if you'd dance with me, Lady Virginia. If you'll have me for the next?"

"I will, sir."

His mother cleared her throat meaningfully and whacked the small of his back with her fan. He forced his smile to grow wider.

"And perhaps the one after that, as well?" he asked tightly. "If you are not engaged?"

He led the obliging young lady toward the dance floor and held back his irritation that this introduction had kept him from Miss Grenfeld's side. He forced himself to continue making polite conversation as they rushed to join the next set of dancers forming.

Lady Virginia may have moved in the highest of circles thanks to her mother's lofty position in society, but she seemed a trifle awkward and anti-social. Andrew caught a glimpse of their mothers talking feverishly behind their fans. He sighed. It was obvious that his mother would much rather he courted Lady Virginia. And perhaps if he had not met Miss Grenfeld first, he could have even made himself like her.

But he *had* met Miss Grenfeld. And he did not want Lady Virginia to fall in love with him. That would render it virtually impossible for him to escape an attachment that both mamas clearly seemed to desire. His mother had been trying to get him to meet her for weeks, and the duchess seemed no less enthusiastic. He sighed. But when he heard Miss Grenfeld's voice in his mind this time, he grinned.

"And it may not be a good idea to discuss wildlife quite so much as you often do. Although ***I*** *certainly find it interesting, many do not."* This gave him an excellent idea.

"I quite enjoy London during the season," he said. "Although the variety of birds one can find in Hyde Park is not nearly so good as it is near my estate!"

Lady Virginia smiled weakly, and Andrew felt an inward surge of triumph. It was going to work. All he had to do was be himself and forget what he'd learned thus far about moving seamlessly about in polite society. He had long been aware that his natural personality made him a bore at parties. He wondered to himself if Miss Grenfeld considered him a bore. She didn't seem to, but sometimes she kept her true thoughts and feelings more shielded than he would like.

He subtly glanced toward the dance floor, and he thought he caught a glimpse of Miss Grenfeld disappearing behind another gentleman in the crowd of people mingling at the edges of the ballroom. He hurried to lead Lady Virginia into the set.

Throughout the country dance, as they bobbed up and down, Mr. Brougham looked over at Miss Grenfeld as often as he could manage, and never once did he catch her looking back at him. He grew more gloomy. When the dance ended, he lost sight of Miss Grenfeld entirely while he was leading Lady Virginia off the floor for a rest. He looked for her, but she was nowhere to be found. Could she have left early? Perhaps for another party?

He stayed near Lady Virginia's side for some time because he would much rather have her company than his mother's. When the lady began to look comfortably bored, Andrew remembered something Miss Grenfeld had told him a dozen times if she'd told him once. He'd been chagrined to learn that there had been something to his valet's advice after all.

"Take care not to show too much interest in a young lady early on unless she gives you proper encouragement! It may scare her off entirely!"

He grinned inwardly. Another bit of advice he intended to try to violently ignore.

As she was responding to a question he'd posed about what sorts of things she enjoyed drawing, she wistfully answered, "the sea."

He did his all to stare soulfully into her eyes, exactly in the manner Miss Grenfeld had urged him *not* to try. "I do like the sea," he echoed.

She looked away. "Have you traveled upon it?"

He smiled. He had found a way to transition to his *favorite* subject. "I am shortly returned from a brief tour of Scotland and the Lake District. I enjoyed visiting Scotland the most, even though I could not understand what some of the people were saying for the life of me. I was able to spot a capercaillie there—something of a rare find."

She smiled up at him with large brown eyes. "It would be wonderful to be able to travel a bit."

Andrew's eyes widened a touch in silent horror. Could she be encouraging his interest? There was one way to find out. He leaned in closer and suggestively said, "You ought to marry a man who likes to travel so he can take you places. Perhaps, once Napoleon can be reined in, the rest of Europe could be open to us again."

She forced an uncomfortable smile, and Andrew could smell victory. She clearly didn't like him after all—what a relief! They danced again, and Lady Virginia seemed positively miserable by the end of it. If he could discourage her interest thoroughly enough, perhaps he would not need to spend the rest of the season at her side in order to avoid the wrath of his mother.

After a last dance, they finally parted ways. He immediately searched for Miss Grenfeld as soon as he was free of Lady Virginia, but was informed by Lady Norbury that she had just left. He rushed after her, but was out the door just in time to see her carriage disappear around the corner.

Chapter Ten

October 27, 1813

Louisa had caught a glimpse of Mr. Brougham soon after entering the ball, but had studiously avoided meeting him, instead fluttering about the room like the social butterfly she was. She greeted perhaps a dozen acquaintances before settling into a short conversation with Mr. Brummell, whose friendship always lent her that edge of distinction so many young ladies lacked, and then readied herself to receive invitations to dance.

She did not wait long before Robert Dalton was cheerfully leading her onto the floor. She danced the first with him, and the next with Lord Derington, who was far too old for her, but who always treated her with respect and acted the perfect gentleman. After two more dances and a short rest to drink a glass of punch, she finally turned her attention to Mr. Brougham. It was actually his mother calling to him that caught her ear first. She would have recognized that voice anywhere. Mr. Brougham went to his mother's side and was introduced to a young lady that Louisa had to stare at for a moment before she recognized her.

"The Duchess of Dorset's daughter?" she thought to herself. "No! If they have the duchess's approval there's no telling how this might end. She's been wanting to marry off that shy little creature for two full seasons." Louisa unwillingly admitted to herself that the girl was looking remarkably beautiful, and had a more confident carriage than she'd had only the season before. She might just furnish Louisa with a bit of competition this year.

She watched, hastily flapping her fan, as Mr. Brougham spoke to Lady Virginia and smiled at her. She almost didn't notice when Thomas Harbottle asked her for a dance. She graciously accepted, and determined to rid her mind of Mr. Brougham and enjoy herself. She focused entirely on her partner during the dance, apart from the single glance it took to assure her that Mr. Brougham was thoroughly enjoying the company of Lady Virginia.

She steeled her heart and laughed the louder for it. As soon as the dance was over, she risked another glimpse, and saw that Mr. Brougham was still in the company of Lady Virginia, speaking to her in an animated fashion, a warm look in his eyes. Her heart deflated like a failed soufflé and her ears began to ring. Louisa glared at the couple for another instant before escaping, exhausted, into the comfort of a card room.

"He was dancing with Lady Virginia just before I left the ball," Louisa grumbled. "I suppose that's it, then."

Aunt Frances glanced up from her embroidery to raise an eyebrow. "That's what, dear?"

"I suppose he'll marry Lady Virginia now."

"What makes you say that?"

"She is a rather obvious choice. Pretty, titled, wealthy . . . but she has almost no conversation, poor thing, and little independence of thought."

Aunt Frances chuckled and shook her head.

"What is so diverting?" Louisa asked.

Aunt Frances just smiled at her. "You *like* him."

Louisa's cheeks flushed. "Brougham? Of course not! I was only irritated that after all my hard work the brilliant connection was one made by his mother and not by me."

Aunt Frances seemed skeptical. "And you're certain that is the only reason you are in such a mood right now?"

Louisa picked at the fabric of her gown on her lap. "Yes," she said stubbornly. "He is nothing so very special, after all." Her stomach shifted to inform her she was lying. She could not define precisely what it was that made him special, but he already mattered more to her than most of her other friends, and they'd barely known one another a month.

Aunt Frances tutted. "Last week you were telling me how proud you were of how far he has come. What an excellent pupil he was. Why are you not happier for your *protégé's* apparent success?"

She looked down. "His success was not because of me."

Aunt Frances shrugged. "That does not mean you cannot take the credit for it. Many take credit for far more after doing far less."

This was finally enough to draw a reluctant chuckle out of Louisa. "I *am* being petulant."

"Yes, but I don't like you any less for it."

Louisa smiled at her aunt's unconditional love. She was very fortunate to have had something very much like two mothers within her lifetime.

"Aunt Frances . . ." Louisa wondered how to broach the subject with her aunt. The conversations she had accidentally eavesdropped on were never far from her mind while she was with either her aunt or her father, and it made her heart pound whenever she thought of them. "I overheard you and Father talking a few weeks ago."

"Louisa!"

Aunt Frances's color rose, but it would have been impossible to discern if Louisa had not been carefully watching for it.

"Father asked you to call him Arthur."

Her aunt made another stitch or two in silence. "He did," she said.

Aunt Frances glanced up suspiciously when Louisa remained too quiet.

"Do you not like him, Aunt? He's a perfectly amiable man."

Aunt Frances sighed and shook her head. "He is an amiable man, but I am an old maid! A long-forgotten spinster."

Louisa raised an eyebrow and took in the shades of gray in her aunt's soft brown hair, the peaceful gray of her eyes, her elegant figure, and the soft curve of her cheek.

"Forgive me, Aunt, but that's all fustian nonsense. You are still very beautiful."

Her aunt's cheeks glowed with embarrassment. "That is enough, Louisa. Quit your outrageous flattery. I am a spinster, and your father is like a brother to me. Have done now!"

"*Like* a brother," Louisa pressed, "but he isn't really your brother. He could just as easily have married you instead of my mother. Then you would have been my mother!"

"Please, Louisa. No more."

"But why—"

"I said *no more*!"

Louisa sat back in her seat. It was rare that Aunt Frances raised her voice or scolded her, but her cheeks were burning and she looked uncommonly disconcerted.

"Louisa, I beg you. It can never be—it would cause a dreadful scandal."

Louisa pursed her lips. "I think I could manage a scandal," she insisted.

Aunt Frances shook her head. "No. Not of this sort. I'm not willing to risk your making a good match to pursue this foolish idea any further, Louisa. Go and get yourself married before you try to marry me off to anyone."

"But—"

"That's final."

Louisa stood and left the room. It was easy to think of others getting married—her aunt, her father, her friends. It was much harder to picture herself getting married. Marriage seemed so very . . . *final*. What if she did not like the arrangement? She was choosing her fate for the rest of her existence.

Would she be able to maintain her current level of freedom and autonomy, or would it be curtailed? Would she be able to admire and respect her partner in life upon closer acquaintance? And when the marriage eventually grew stale, as so many seemed to, would he begin frequenting bits of muslin on the side to entertain himself? Her reputation would be tied fully and completely to that of whomever she chose. It was a weighty responsibility, and one that gave her a headache and made her breathing shallow whenever she thought too much of it.

Why did it seem so easy for so many other young ladies to fantasize about their ideal companions? She smiled to herself—she already knew why. She'd read her fair share of novels and had sighed along with the happy heroine melting into the arms of her sweetheart. But when it came to envisioning *herself* in a similar situation, her mind became a tangle of anxiety.

She had no desire to be sequestered away in the country for the rest of her life and fade into obscurity. London was the place for her. And since this was the last season her father would furnish her with, she had to marry soon.

It wasn't only her fate on the line, either. Aunt Frances deserved to be happy and her final declaration had inadvertently provided Louisa with a ray of hope. She did not explicitly refuse to allow Louisa to marry her off to someone in the future—she only insisted that Louisa be married first. That meant her aunt could likely be persuaded to court her father in earnest if Louisa were already well settled.

Louisa wandered past her father's study and saw that the door was cracked open. She gave two soft knocks as she pushed open the door. "Father?"

He glanced up from the book he was reading on the sofa near the window. "Yes, my dear?"

Louisa smiled. Her father was a good man. He was kind, endlessly patient, independent, and she knew that he always kept her best interests at heart, even when he embarrassed her.

"I just wanted to see you, Papa."

He set down his book and sat up straighter. "Come in, come in."

Louisa took a seat in a chair not far from him and inspected the several bookcases about the room. She had pored over the same tomes in her quiet hours, and she and her father shared many of the same interests. Her carefully executed, detailed paintings of birds adorned the walls. It was not terribly often that she was able to depict a rare species, but the few times she had were all on display here.

Mr. Grenfeld followed her gaze to the walls. "They are my favorite pieces you have done, my dear. Your talents quite astonish me."

Louisa felt warm to her toes. Her father was not generally quick to compliment her, and each time he did she felt it deeply.

They sat in amicable silence for a long moment before Louisa finally got up the courage to ask him the question at the front of her mind.

"Do you care for Aunt Frances, Papa?"

His cheeks immediately flushed and he frowned. "I . . . what do you . . . she is a member of our household, Louisa. Of course I care for her."

Louisa looked away. "I meant in a more serious manner. Do you love her?"

Her father shook his head. "Louisa you ought not to be asking questions of this nature. It is really none of your concern."

Louisa inspected her nails, chagrined.

"But yes," he finally said with a sigh. "Of course I love her. How could anyone not love her?"

Louisa stared at him, pleased when he continued.

"She is my very dearest friend aside from you and your brother, Louisa, and I would be quite lost without her. But I think you must know this. Why do you ask?"

Louisa blinked back tears and stood abruptly, hurrying toward her father to wrap him in an embrace and kiss his cheek. She left the room in a rush, wiping her cheek with the back of her hand.

Yes, she finally had a reason strong enough to wade through the discomfort the courtship process would inevitably cause—seeing her father and aunt happy together. It was time for her to begin seeking a husband in earnest.

Chapter Eleven

November 3, 1813

Andrew was troubled. The conversation he'd had with his mother two days before made it perfectly clear that she and the duchess thought that a match was in the making. He did not know how, exactly, this match to Lady Virginia was ever to take place against his will, but he knew his mother's plans had to be nipped in the bud regardless.

"Mother," he practiced to himself, "I do not *wish* to marry Lady Virginia, genteel and pretty though she is."

No, that sounds like I am whining.

"Mother," he tried again, "you cannot simply decide who I am to marry. I am a grown man and this decision and its consequences lie in my hands alone!"

No, that speech did not even convince himself. He moaned softly. There was a gentle rap at the door, and then Henry bustled in. "I have your neckcloths, sir. Let us hope we go through no more than three or four before it is perfect!"

Andrew didn't respond, but sat down at his dressing table, still thinking to himself what he could say to his mother. He sighed and ran his fingers through his hair in frustration.

Henry squeaked in dismay and rushed over to repair the damage to Andrew's hairstyle, tutting all the while. His valet prided himself on helping Andrew perfectly arrange his loose curls.

There was nothing for it. Perhaps, if he could confess his feelings to Miss Grenfeld, she would understand his frustrations. She would likely know just what to do. She had been helping him before, after all. Why should helping him manage his mother be any different from helping him manage *ton* parties? But why had she left the ball so suddenly? She had not even greeted him. It could be that she was upset with him. But if she was . . . *why*?

He sighed again, and Henry finally said, "What is the matter, sir?"

"I worry Miss Grenfeld might be angry with me."

Henry frowned. "Isn't she that lady you were growing entirely too close to only a fortnight or so ago? Perhaps it is for the best. Plenty of other prospects on the mart, sir!"

Andrew shook his head. "Please do not say that, Henry. After all, you clearly haven't met this one."

Henry seemed unconvinced. "I heard gossip that you danced with a duke's daughter, sir! She's sure to have a fine fortune and very eligible connections. Isn't she also quite pretty?"

"Yes, she's pretty, but so dull I can hardly remain awake in her presence."

Henry frowned. "I am sorry to hear it, sir."

"I do not know how to go on. Mother has been insufferable lately. She's off on a mad spree trying to marry me off to the highest bidder. One would think I would get a say in it, but not even you seem inclined to allow me to choose."

Henry was quiet as he finished the last touches on Mr. Brougham's appearance.

Andrew had too many unanswered questions, and he was too conscious of his own ignorance about his exact offense to go directly to Miss Grenfeld. He would go and see if he could find one of his new friends at the club. Perhaps they would have some advice for him. He stood.

"Where are you going, sir?" Henry asked.

"White's," he grunted. He knew he was being sullen, but perhaps a light game of cards and a talk with a friend would help bring him out of it. He also could not help but think of Miss Grenfeld's urgent advice that he find other gentlemen to befriend as soon as possible.

"You managed to obtain admittance? Excellent," Henry said.

Andrew ignored him and walked out the door as soon as his coat was buttoned. He made his way nervously down St. James street toward the gentleman's club. He had already received notice of his admittance, but that did not mean he felt like he belonged there yet—he'd hardly even visited the place.

Louisa's voice replayed in his mind. *If you ask me, I would recommend you join White's and perhaps Brook's as well, if you are so inclined. Brummell is a member of Boodle's, but it is extremely exclusive. Unless you are particularly political you are likely to meet a wider circle of pleasant acquaintances at two clubs than at only one.*

He stood outside of the imposing gray structure, feeling dwarfed by the columns, but when a gentleman walked confidently through the doors ahead of him, he straightened his shoulders and followed.

He had been unsure of which club to join, if any, though he knew that Watier's was a place to avoid for those who wished their pockets to remain deep. With his name, fortune, and connections, Louisa informed him, he would likely be accepted into any of the four most prominent clubs in St. James Street, and he had followed Louisa's advice to join White's. There was almost certainly going to be someone of his acquaintance there at this time of day, even if his acquaintance was not yet extensive.

Shortly after he arrived at the club, he was pleased to see Philip Palmer and a number of his friends gathered around a table.

"Brougham!" Philip said cheerfully. "The man of the hour! Come here and tell us how it is done."

Andrew looked about him, as if someone else named Brougham were standing behind him, and then joined their table with a nervous laugh. "I do not know what makes you think me capable of dispensing advice, but if I did, you'd be a fool to take it!"

The five young men around the table laughed at his cheerful self-deprecation, and Philip nudged him again. "This is William Cox.

Don't believe you two've met yet. William, this is the fellow I told you about, who danced with Lady Virginia, and who's a personal friend of Louisa Grenfeld. He can help you out with your troubles, I'm sure."

"Troubles?" Andrew asked. Hearing that he was not the only one with troubles made him feel far less glum. "What exactly are your troubles? Let's hear it."

"He's hung up on Miss Mary Clavendish," Joseph Drayton inserted, to a light round of laughter at the table.

"Miss Clavendish?" Mr. Brougham asked, surprised. Miss Grenfeld had said the poor miss was nearly on the shelf. "Well, that's good news, isn't it?"

William Cox was sullen. "Not if she's setting her cap at *you*, it isn't!" he blurted.

Andrew worried that his expression betrayed the natural horror he felt at this pronouncement. The rest of the table laughed again.

"I'm terribly sorry," he finally said. "I'm not certain what I've done to deserve this . . . honor . . . but I am more than willing to help in any way I can."

Philip clapped him on the back. "Don't be so modest, Brougham. She isn't the first or the last, I can tell you that. Any young man who can capture as much of Miss Grenfeld's attention as you have is bound to become a subject of interest."

This was the first Mr. Brougham was hearing of this. "What is that supposed to mean?"

Philip shook his head and laughed, speaking to everyone but Andrew. "Look at him! He doesn't even know it!"

Andrew frowned as the table of young bucks burst into fresh peals of laughter. "*What* do I not know?"

Joseph finally said, "Brougham, you're all the rage! You are, perhaps, the biggest prize of the marriage mart this season, and it hasn't hardly begun yet!"

Andrew's eyes bulged. "I am?"

William nudged him. "There are already a few bets upstairs on which lucky lady, if any, you'll tie yourself down to this season."

"That's terrible!" Andrew said. "Who would bet on something like that?"

"Oh, I did," Michael Heron said.

"Me too," William added.

"I think we all did," Philip said cheerfully.

"You're welcome to put *my* name in the book if you'd like," chimed William.

"Wish someone would give me *his* face and fortune—I'd show you what I'd make of it!" Joseph muttered.

Mr. Brougham's head was whirling. "This is all Miss Grenfeld's doing," he murmured. "But . . . Miss Grenfeld doesn't even want to marry me."

"Perhaps not, but everyone else does!" Philip said.

When Andrew did not immediately join in the laughter, Philip paused before lowering his voice and leaning in closer. "You aren't hung up on Miss Grenfeld, are you?"

Andrew frowned. "How couldn't I be? She is incredible."

"Yes. Alas," Joseph said. "We've all taken our turn, but it's hopeless. Most of us are second sons, you know. But I would think you'd have a chance! You've already inherited a country seat, haven't you?"

Andrew sighed. "Yes, but I don't think she would want me. Especially not if she is as popular as you say. She left the ball early last night, before I even had the chance to ask her to dance."

"Left the ball early?" Philip frowned. "That's not like her."

"No, not at all," William agreed. "I wasn't there myself to see, but perhaps she was ill."

When the conversation continued without his joining it for a moment, Andrew finally turned to William with an idea of his. "I think I know what might help you with Miss Clavendish," he said abruptly.

William raised an eyebrow and set down his glass. "And what is that?"

"Will you be at the Duncans' soiree a week from Thursday?"

William frowned. "I can't think whether we've received that invitation or not," he said, put to a blush for admitting that, as a younger son, he was almost never the sole recipient of an invitation in his household.

"Miss Clavendish will almost certainly be there. In fact, I might drop by for a morning visit to be sure she is at *that* party that evening, and I will tell her I'll introduce her to a particular friend of mine. *You.*"

William folded his arms skeptically. "Thank you for the effort, but how do I know that will help my case?"

"Simple," Andrew said, gathering his courage, "because the four of us will make up a card table, and I will flirt outrageously with my partner." He wasn't entirely sure how he knew this would work, but something told him that it would.

Michael Heron chimed in then. "But who will you choose for your partner?" he asked. "You've enough caps set at you, to be sure, but which is the finest?"

"He ought to choose Lady Virginia," Joseph said. "He'd be rich as a nabob! And very well-respected, to boot. Isn't a soul in London who could get off snubbing Her Grace, I've heard."

Andrew inwardly paled at this ominous vision of a potential mother-in-law.

"No, no," Philip insisted, "It's Miss Grenfeld! Don't care who you are, or what your title is, it's *her* opinion that matters the most. If she wore a green hat to the park on Tuesday, the milliners would run out of green cloth by Thursday!"

"There are other ladies yet," Michael inserted.

"Are ladies all you ever talk about?" Andrew asked, feeling mildly overwhelmed.

William gave an ungentlemanly snort. "When you've as little female attention as we do, *yes*."

Chapter Twelve

November 10, 1813

Louisa tickled her nose with the end of her quill as she thought to herself. This was a very important list. She needed to be serious. But every time she caught a glimpse of the title at the top of the page her nerves would only allow her to laugh. She really had no choice but to marry, and perhaps it was because of this that she had no desire to. After all, who enjoys being compelled to do as they ought?

"Potential husbands," she read to herself. She sighed, shaking her head. The rest of Louisa's page was blank, after this title. She could not think of a single person she wanted to marry, because she did not wish to be married at all. She had never been one to set her cap at a gentleman. Though she'd been out more than three years she had yet to even develop a real *tendre* for anyone.

Aside from lacking the natural inclination, she had been too frightened to do so. As she'd told Aunt Frances, it was an enormous decision, entrusting your entire future and fate into the hands of a single person. The power a husband had over a wife was far too high for Louisa's taste. Ever since she had met the Baroness Fairbourne, who controlled her own fortune, Louisa's already meager interest in matrimony had all but evaporated. There was no end to her frustration on this subject. All she wanted was a tidy fortune completely under her control in order to live her own life and do as she pleased. Even as she considered this, she sighed. The women fortunate enough to match that description were rare indeed, and it was no good dwelling on what could never be.

But to be married to an admirable gentleman was vastly preferable to the uncertain future her Aunt Frances faced. She was dependent on joining the households of one or another of her family members to avoid necessary employment as a companion or governess—or worse. What would happen to her if Louisa failed to contract an eligible match?

She felt a fresh surge of determination. If it would help Aunt Frances if she chose a suitable, trustworthy, enjoyable companion, then that is precisely what she would do. The prospect still made her nervous. She had heard far too many frightening stories of husbands who mistreated the women in their lives, or grossly mismanaged their affairs, and although she knew she was perfectly capable of influencing those about her, she would never fool herself into thinking a husband would be entirely under her control.

Besides, that is not what she would wish, in any case. Such a husband would be little better than a puppet and could never be good company. What she really needed was a friend. One who thought differently from her, but whose thoughts were synchronous with hers, like the perfect dancing partner.

She pulled out a second, blank piece of paper, doubting the likelihood of ever finding such an ideal match.

She closed her eyes and thought. "Let's see . . . what do I *need*? He needs to inherit an estate—that goes without question," she said to herself, then shook her head, crossing out the last line she wrote. "No, even an estate is not essential. He needs to at least own a house of his own in the fashionable part of town, for I'll not settle in the country forever."

She wrote this down. "He must also possess social graces," she said. "I don't wish to be tied down to a perpetual embarrassment."

She dipped her pen in the inkwell for her next thought. "Kind and attractive," she wrote next. "I can find beauty in unusual places, so I don't think that's *too* immoderate a request, and I shall try to keep an open mind." Even as she wrote it, though, she frowned. She thought many men were pleasant to look at, but had never taken the time to imagine what it might be like to be held in the arms of one of them. Or kissed by one of them. She imagined one or two society gentleman of her acquaintance taking her into their arms and soon realized a horrified grimace was etched onto her face. She shook her head, wrinkling her nose. Perhaps friendship and familiarity would come before *that* sort of attraction ever did.

She continued her list, writing several more traits, and when she had written all she could think of, she sat back and looked at it. Now she needed to find gentlemen with these traits. However, when she read through her entire list, she could not think of a single man among her acquaintance who exemplified all of these attributes. She groaned quietly. She had been out in society for three full seasons already and had already met everyone who was anyone. Who else was there to consider?

She had always been discerning, but perhaps her aunt had been correct—she was simply too picky when it came to gentlemen. If she did not want to die an old maid in the countryside (and she did not), she would simply need to settle for less. She took a deep breath and decided to start with one attribute at a time.

She wrote down on another sheet of paper the names of all the gentlemen she knew of who stood to inherit or who already had their own house in town and who were younger than thirty-five. It took her quite some time to think of them all, but by the time she was certain she wasn't forgetting or missing anyone there were forty names.

"There. That looks like a better list," she murmured aloud to herself. It was only after she had the list made that she allowed herself to look through it more closely. There were four men whom she crossed out almost instantly. "Rakes," she murmured. Then another ten. "Reckless gamblers, all of them, likely haven't a sixpence to scratch with." Twenty-one names left. Two of them had not ever attended university. They were crossed off as well—how could they be expected to carry on a decent conversation? One of them spat whenever he spoke. Another's breath always smelled so awful she wondered if he even owned a toothbrush. Four more she happened to know were already courting young ladies of her acquaintance and would likely be soon engaged. She crossed these names off as well.

Thirteen names. She looked through the few names left. None of them would be *too* bad, she supposed, but none of them filled her with excitement, either. But perhaps excitement was too much to ask for in marriage. She read through the names until she had them all memorized. Then she ranked the top five gentlemen.

"Philip Palmer, Lucas Apperley, John Gisborne, Captain Miles Allen, and . . . Mr. Andrew Brougham."

November 12, 1813

The next morning, Louisa absently fiddled with the petals of a slightly wilted floral arrangement as she stared at nothing. The more she had thought of it the evening before, the more Mr. Brougham's suitability struck her. He was quite a perfect candidate for her to consider. He was kind and intelligent, handsome and comfortably wealthy. He was becoming quite confident in his address and she had heard several whispers that he was already becoming all the rage, which made her feel rather proud of what she had taught him.

Her pride withered when she remembered how very little of his transformation she was truly responsible for. She would explain a concept, they would practice it together for a few minutes, laughing all the while, and she would inevitably see him seamlessly employing the technique on his own at a social gathering later in the week. He was indeed a quick study. She was amazed that he remained as humble as he did when he had been blessed with so many positive characteristics. Wealth, position, education, good looks . . . it was a wonder he wasn't cock-sure enough to feel invincible.

The more she thought of him, the more she noticed a general warmth in her chest, and heat rising in her cheeks. Was this what a *tendre* felt like? Perhaps it really had been jealousy chasing her from the ball when she had seen Brougham with Lady Virginia. The more she took notice of his elegant figure and frame within her memories, the more she wondered what it would feel like to be held in his arms.

Her cheeks heated all over again and she certainly did not grimace this time, but she shook the thoughts from her mind. It did no good to count her chickens before they had hatched! She smiled to herself even as she thought this, however, for it *had* seemed rather clear, weeks ago, that Mr. Brougham had taken an eager interest in her, despite her discouragement.

"Good morning, Miss Grenfeld! Wonderful to see you, as always." Louisa nearly fell backwards in surprise, catching herself on the side table that held the vase of flowers she had been inspecting. Mr. Brougham rushed forward to catch the vase as it teetered precariously toward Louisa's pale pink morning gown. For a moment his face was mere inches from hers.

"Thank you," she said, as soon as he had stepped backward and regained enough composure.

Mr. Brougham smiled and swept a polite bow. Louisa smiled back at him, feeling suddenly conscious of the way her lips opened over her teeth for a smile. Were her teeth clean? Did she look strange or unnatural? Was she flushed? She shook the errant thoughts away.

"I am so pleased you have come for a visit," Louisa responded, holding out her hand for him to press. She was dismayed to realize that her heart was pounding. Why was she so flustered? Heaven forbid she become an object of ridicule. She needed to regain her usual equanimity. She closed her eyes and took a steadying breath.

He nodded over her hand, and she pulled it away from him as soon as she reasonably could, clearing her throat. "Well, now. Let's see. What have we left to learn?"

Mr. Brougham sat down in a chair across from her and obediently pulled a small notebook and a pencil from the inner pocket of his jacket. He flipped through this for a moment. "At our last visit we discussed additional polite topics for small talk. I wrote down the full list, and I have been staying up-to-date on current events so that I may discuss them in appropriate ways."

Louisa nodded and smiled. "Indeed. I have seen you thriving in this area at parties already. I do not know that I can help you any further! You are an excellent conversationalist, sir." It was true, and she spoke no flattery, but because she was careful to reserve her compliments for outstanding occasions, she noticed his ears turning red at this profession. If he could be so easily flattered by her, perhaps she still had a chance of earning his suit!

He glanced down through his notes again. "We've also practiced remaining polite in the face of rudeness, and methods for extricating oneself from a ridiculous circumstance without calling anyone out or being called out oneself."

Louisa giggled a bit louder and more quickly than normal, embarrassed by the nervous energy she released. "A very important one, that. Again—you needed precious little assistance in avoiding duels. I only helped you practice ignoring insults and soothing ruffled feathers."

He laughed. "I hardly know what to say. You were so convincing when you pretended to insult me."

She hesitated, eying him closely to ascertain that he was only teasing her. If she had actually hurt his feelings, she would've felt terrible.

"I've had precious few people ever be rude to me, you know," he said, "I hardly have an occasion to use these skills."

"There is precious little to gain by offending you, sir."

Mr. Brougham smiled at this and nodded. "*Touché*. On that note, we've also discussed examining others' motives to determine dangers before becoming ensnared in an ugly situation."

Louisa nodded approvingly. "Excellent. And what are the driving forces behind the majority of interactions in the *ton*?"

"Improving one's social connections and influence and increasing one's personal wealth. Both of these are most often sought through advantageous marriage alliances. You gave each of these several subcategories, and I must confess some of the lines from one category crossed into others and the resulting diagram is rather tangled."

Louisa shrugged and laughed at this. "That sounds accurate! Were you able to make sense of it?"

"Knowing the harmful categories is what has proven the most useful to me thus far. I've managed to avoid feeding potentially damaging information to malicious gossips, making business arrangements of questionable value, and forming imprudent matches."

Louisa nodded. Her heart was tripping, and she suddenly realized that she hadn't the first idea how to flirt. Nevertheless, she had to try. "So you aren't in any danger, then?" she asked, attempting to flutter her eyelashes at him.

He seemed confused for a moment, but then he smiled and shook his head. "No, I don't believe so!"

Louisa's smile stiffened. Had he noticed her behavior change? Perhaps she had taught him too well. Or perhaps she was losing her touch! She quickly returned to her old standby: flattery. "Blue is a very nice color on you, Mr. Brougham. It complements your lovely eyes so nicely."

He smiled. "Thank you very much, Miss Grenfeld! And may I say that your auburn hair is nicely complemented by that shade of pink?"

She smiled and looked down modestly at her lap, only to look up at him shyly a moment later, through her lashes. He was inspecting his little notebook again. Her smile disappeared. That maneuver had never failed to earn a dance from any man she had tried it on before. This was proving more difficult than she'd thought it would be.

"Mr. Brougham, would you care for some tea and cake?"

He hesitated a moment. "I . . . No, thank you. I've an appointment at White's after our visit and I imagine I will eat there."

Louisa's face fell. She had the sudden sensation of grasping and coming away empty, and a shiver of fear shook her. She could think of no response.

"But there is *one* thing I've been wanting to ask you, Miss Grenfeld."

Louisa held her breath and waited. Was he going to ask if he could court her?

"I've been wanting to see your artwork since the first day we met."

Louisa blinked a couple of times, disappointed. He really *had* asked several times about them. What, exactly, was her reason for refusing to show her work to him? Her stomach twisted with the usual nerves she felt when others asked to see her work. Most of her drawings and paintings were of birds, but they were not the soft, romantic, ladylike drawings that were fashionable for ladies to amuse themselves with. No, hers were better suited for a scientific treatise on wildlife. She smiled suddenly, and her nerves gave way to anticipatory butterflies. Mr. Brougham would almost certainly like her work, given his enthusiasm for ornithology. But would it be enough to spark his original interest in her anew? And what if they did not meet his high standards for scientific accuracy? If he did not like them, she did not know if she would be able to contain her embarrassment.

"But I do not wish to press you," Mr. Brougham said hastily. "Or make you feel uncomfortable."

She smiled. "I'm not uncomfortable, Mr. Brougham. You said so yourself—we are already friends. I am only thinking of which ones you may like the best. There are several framed and hanging in different places about the house. Would you like to take a turn with me and see a few of them?"

He smiled and followed her out of the drawing room. Her father was most fond of her bird paintings, and therefore many of them were hanging in his study, which they had no reason to visit. She had a landscape hanging in the east drawing room, however, and a small early morning scene in the breakfast room. Both of those were quite nice.

As she led Mr. Brougham to the first painting, her mind raced to think of appropriate topics of conversation. She wished she could look at the list he had made. She wanted to provide him ample opportunity to declare his feelings privately for her, so that she might be able to encourage them, but he had not said a single thing that could possibly be misconstrued as an "advance." She almost wished he would roughly grab her and passionately declare his feelings before kissing her into a frenzy like some reckless rake in a gothic novel.

No, she realized, shaking her head at the very thought. That wasn't really what she wanted. If she were being honest with herself, she would have to admit that she was not entirely sure what she wanted. But as she wondered what it might be like if—*when?*—Mr. Brougham kissed her, she smiled. He was a gentle man. She could not imagine him moving too quickly for her comfort. Her cheeks warmed as she thought of him gently taking her hand in his—no gloves. She would clearly need to wait longer for any of that. Still, though. Could he not tell how impatiently she waited for a declaration of his feelings? How much longer must she wait?

"Miss Grenfeld?"

She blinked a couple of times and turned to face him. Had he been speaking? She had been caught up in her own imagination. "I am terribly sorry," she said, flushed and a bit breathless. "What did you say?"

"I only said that . . . you look very pretty today," he said rather shyly as he continued walking beside her.

"Oh, thank you." She put a self-conscious hand up to her hair and hoped her blush she felt creeping to the tips of her ears was not unbecoming.

They arrived before her landscape painting. "There," Louisa said. "I hope it meets with your approval."

Mr. Brougham looked at the painting with a neutral expression for several seconds before finally nodding. "Very well executed, Miss Grenfeld. I quite like it."

She frowned. Was it just her imagination, or did he seem disappointed? Perhaps she had been right, and all he cared about was seeing her drawings of birds! She hurried to lead him to her next picture in the breakfast room, an early morning scene.

"Yes," Mr. Brougham said with an approving nod and a smile. "I like this one. The light is beautiful! You managed to capture the yellow sort of glow things take on early in the morning on sunny days. And I like the little bird on the branch . . . is that a blue tit?"

"Yes," Miss Grenfeld answered. "They are common near our estate in Kent."

He nodded. "Colorful little things."

They stood in awkward silence for another moment or two.

"Miss Grenfeld, I . . ."

"Yes?" she said, perhaps a trifle too eagerly.

Chapter Thirteen

November 12, 1813

The words got caught behind Andrew's lips. Miss Grenfeld seemed agitated. Was she in a hurry? Was she expecting another visitor? He looked away and cleared his throat to drive off a sudden twinge of jealousy. "What is our lesson today, Miss Grenfeld?" Andrew asked after a brief pause, a smile on his face.

Her face fell, and his spirits went with it. Had he misunderstood her? After a long moment of silence, she quietly replied, "Perhaps it is you who should be teaching me, Mr. Brougham."

He frowned. His heart was suddenly cutting a jagged rhythm that made it difficult to hear. "I beg your pardon?"

She met his gaze once more, her eyes hardening. "It does not appear I have any more to teach you, Mr. Brougham," she said stiffly as she turned and walked back toward the drawing room. "You have mastered it all."

He hurried to keep pace with her. "Do not say so, Miss Grenfeld! I would very much miss our daily lessons. Who else will teach me to escape the grasp of the dangerous fortune-hunters my mother is so worried about?"

He meant to draw out a chuckle by poking fun at his mother, but Louisa's mouth formed a grim line. "Of course. Your mother."

Louisa took a deep breath through flared nostrils. "She knows best, doesn't she? I think you will make her very happy, sir," her words were cold. "You seem to be doing well enough at pushing aside undesirable female attention without any help."

He only had a moment to look bewildered before they arrived at the front door.

She lifted her chin. "Thank you for honoring me with your presence here today, sir. Please do not hurry back again."

A knock sounded at the door and a bewildered Andrew stepped aside to allow Phelps to greet the newcomers. Mrs. and Miss Clavendish were announced and entered the room and Louisa greeted them far more warmly than usual. She ignored Mr. Brougham until he took the hint and accepted her dismissal, slipping out the open front door before the butler could close it again.

Andrew kicked at a pebble on the ground as he walked away from the house. His heart was in utter disarray. He had been cast off like an old shoe after doing absolutely everything Miss Grenfeld had recommended. It was true, then. That horrible little voice at the back of his mind that told him he'd never be enough for her was right. He clenched the notebook in his hand and was tempted for a moment to throw it into the dustbin.

He stopped himself and tucked it back into his pocket when a gentleman he'd been introduced to at White's passed by on the sidewalk. He tipped his hat and continued walking, willing his face to remain impassive and for the pain of Miss Grenfeld's snub to fade.

His mind raced backward past all of the lessons they'd had together. Normally their conversations happened easily. Naturally. What had felt so different about this one? She had not seemed like herself from the moment he'd first entered the room. Certainly not as calm and collected as she generally was. She did not seem . . . as *in control* of the situation as she normally did. And she seemed unusually displeased that he would not join her for tea—and he had indeed been tempted. He'd never tasted better teas than those he had been served in Miss Grenfeld's home. But her upset was especially odd to him given how much she encouraged him to seek out the company of other "pinks of the *ton*" and to not pass too much time in her home.

He stared at the cobblestones and continued walking, shaking his head sadly. He had clearly misjudged the situation somewhere and done something to offend her. He thought back to what she had said, replaying the conversation over and over in his mind until he was nearly nauseated by it. He was early for his appointment, but he went straight to the club anyway and, even though it was unlike him, immediately ordered a stiff drink.

November 12, 1813

Andrew was overjoyed to see his friends again when they arrived at last. He had already had two or three glasses of something tolerably strong by then, so he wasn't feeling quite like himself, but he was glad not to be alone anymore.

The topic of conversation, helping Mr. Cox claim the interest of Miss Clavendish, became a wonderfully distracting challenge to his mind. They were an eligible match, as far as Andrew could see. Miss Clavendish's fortune was respectable, and Mr. Cox was a second son with a good education, an excellent head on his shoulders, and a mind to succeed in parliament. He would do very well with the right young lady at his side.

As he readied himself for the party later that evening and as the courage from the afternoon's libations faded, he nervously realized that he wasn't at all certain how to 'flirt outrageously,' as he'd promised to do. He'd been too embarrassed to ask the other young gentlemen at the club how to do so—and had been frankly a little concerned by the sort of answer he thought he might receive—and he was certainly not brave enough to stop by Miss Grenfeld's house again after her cold dismissal that morning. But he had promised to flirt with a friend of Miss Clavendish that evening at the party, leaving her to turn to Mr. Cox for comfort. He had no choice.

"Henry?" he said tentatively, as his valet busied himself putting a shine on his Hessians.

"Yes, sir?"

"How, exactly, does one 'flirt outrageously' with a young lady?"

Henry raised an eyebrow, the corners of his lips lowering disapprovingly. "Why do you ask, sir?"

"I have promised to do so this evening."

Henry resumed shining Andrew's boots. "Bit of an odd promise to make, sir. Isn't it?"

Andrew sighed. "Yes, but it's made, and now I must do it. What does one *say*?"

Henry finished one boot and moved on to the next. "Begging your pardon, sir, but may I ask if you've taken a sudden interest in the petticoat line?"

Andrew frowned. "The petticoat line?" he asked. It sounded vaguely familiar—he was sure he'd heard young men speak of it at Oxford.

Henry closed his eyes in exasperation. "You know, sir . . . consorting with ladies of easy virtue."

Andrew grimaced. "Of course not, dash it! Whatever gave you that idea?"

Henry's cheeks were pink. "Nothing, sir! Just wanted to be sure. As for 'flirting outrageously,' I will remind you that *I* am no member of the *ton*, sir, and am ill-suited to offer advice."

Andrew sighed. "I know, I know! But when young ladies complain that a gentleman was *flirting*, what sorts of things does he do and say?"

"My experience is limited, sir." Henry thought for a moment. "But I suppose he . . . pays an excessive amount of attention to her, and offers many flattering compliments. He also likely acts as though everything she said were humorous or fascinating even when it isn't." He turned his attention back to the task at hand.

Andrew's mind flashed back to that morning's painful visit with Miss Grenfeld. She had complimented him more than usual, and laughed more, too. There had been an odd gleam in her eye, and she had blushed more frequently. Was it possible she had been flirting with him?

He frowned to himself. Why would Miss Grenfeld be flirting with him? His heart was beating more quickly than usual as he replayed their visit in his mind yet again.

But he often complimented her, as well. Did that amount to flirting? Is that why she had seemed so upset with him? Perhaps she did not want him to flirt with her. But then why would she be flirting with him? His brow knit heavily together at these questions. Perhaps he was so terrible at flirting that Miss Grenfeld thought that he did not like her.

What had he done wrong?

He had done all of those things Henry mentioned with Miss Grenfeld, he supposed, although was it truly flattery if all one said was absolutely true? Everything Miss Grenfeld ever said generally *was* either humorous or fascinating. And she deserved every compliment he had ever given, and more. He sighed. He was a hopeless case, and he still wasn't entirely certain how to flirt, but he would try to do what Henry described and hope that it worked.

The Duncans' party

Even Andrew was surprised at how quickly Miss Clavendish appeared at his side that evening, and he wasted no time. "Miss Clavendish! Wonderful to see you. Come, let me introduce you to my friend Mr. Cox!"

William preened as she came nearer and smiled broadly. He wasn't a bad-looking fellow, Andrew thought to himself, though he could stand to use less cologne and hang fewer fobs about his person.

"Miss Clavendish, this is Mr. William Cox! A fine gentleman, and an excellent card player. Mr. Cox, Miss Mary Clavendish."

"I believe we've been introduced at least once," Miss Clavendish said, hardly glancing at Mr. Cox before staring back up at Mr. Brougham, anxious to please.

Andrew carefully stepped to the side of William, so that he did not stand directly next to Miss Clavendish. "Shall we all have a game, then?" he asked. "We've almost enough to form a table for speculation!"

"Oh, do let's!" Miss Clavendish said eagerly, returning to Mr. Brougham's side as though attached to him by a string. He held in a sigh. This was going to be more difficult than he'd thought. He pulled out a chair for her and waited for her to sit down before hurrying away. He had to find a partner of his own.

His hopes that Miss Grenfeld might be there were in vain thus far—not that he would've dared involving her in this silly scheme to begin with. She had neither come to the party, nor informed the hostess whether she would be coming, a fact that Mrs. Duncan found quite upsetting.

He did, however, see another young lady he was reasonably well-acquainted with. "Miss Norris!" he said, hurrying to her side. "Please, won't you come and be my partner? We got it into our heads to play a game of speculation, and the evening will be desolate if you don't fill out our set!"

Miss Norris smiled at his flattery, and Andrew instantly felt guilty, but he barreled onward. At the very least, he was doing what he had set out to do.

His plan worked better than he had dared hope it would, although it had not seemed like it for the first several minutes. At first, Miss Clavendish seemed irritated and hurt by all the obsequious attentions Andrew showed to Miss Norris, but it did not take longer than half an hour for her to give up flirting with him entirely. She happily followed Mr. Cox's lead in the conversation from then on, and long after the game was finished, the pair of them were still laughing together.

Andrew drew Miss Norris off to the side of the room for a glass of refreshment after the card table broke up, but she was shyly folding her arms and avoiding his gaze. Once she had a cup in hand, she said, "Mr. Brougham? I . . . I am certainly f-flattered by your attentions, but I must tell you that I am likely to soon be engaged to Colonel—"

Mr. Brougham's brow knit with concern. "Miss Norris, I must truly beg your pardon. I really ought to have broached the subject with you before. I paid you special attention just now only because my friend Mr. Cox has had trouble catching Miss Clavendish's eye, and I wanted to help her see what a charming and interesting fellow he is."

Miss Norris's hand flew to her mouth to stifle a giggle. "Oh! I wondered. You see, Miss Clavendish told me last week that she thought you the finest gentleman in London and it's been fairly obvious she had set her cap at you, but after you snubbed her this evening I'll be surprised if she so much as mentions you again!"

Andrew smiled in triumph.

"Oh, look. Miss Grenfeld has arrived."

Andrew immediately swiveled about until his eyes rested on Miss Grenfeld walking through the door in a dark blue striped gown.

Miss Norris chuckled beside him. “I’m not such a slowtop as to miss seeing the way you feel about her, you know.”

Andrew could feel himself blushing, but he was so relieved that he hadn’t unintentionally engaged Miss Norris’s affections that he grinned. “Is it terribly obvious?” he asked ruefully.

Miss Norris laughed. “To me, it is! And I do wish you luck.”

Andrew saw Miss Grenfeld laughing across the room with another group of fashionable guests and he sighed. “I think I’ll need it.”

Miss Norris smiled sympathetically and shook her head. “Come now, Brougham. The two of you are already such good friends! It is a very smart match, if you can convince her of that—even my mama said so.”

A thought suddenly occurred to Mr. Brougham and he frowned. “Are you certain it would be a good match? Miss Grenfeld told me that young ladies in the marriage mart don’t . . . don’t usually like to help one another.”

Miss Norris waved a hand and answered his unasked question. “She isn’t wrong! If a young lady doesn’t make a good match, she can be left in quite dire straits. We can’t always afford to help one another with all this competition. But Miss Grenfeld is a friend of mine, and has always been kind to me. In fact . . . she is the one who introduced me to Colonel Cheyne.” She broke off shyly, smiling to herself.

Andrew smiled, and his heart seemed to swell in his chest as he thought of the kind, helpful things Miss Grenfeld had done to improve the lives of everyone around her. He saw her look up momentarily from a conversation she was in across the room and then look away just as quickly, but it was some time before he was able to take his eyes off her.

Chapter Fourteen

November 13, 1813

Louisa had left the Duncans' party early that evening by claiming a headache. She had never cried herself to sleep before, but that night she did, and she woke the next morning with puffy eyes, ruddy cheeks, and a splitting headache. She groaned as she sat up in bed. A knock at the door had awakened her.

"What is it?" she asked with a yawn.

"Still abed, Lou?" Aunt Frances said, peering into the room.

Louisa nodded. "I . . . had some trouble falling asleep last night," she admitted.

Aunt Frances's brow was knit with concern as she walked over to the bed with a small tea tray. "I know, darling. I heard you through the wall. But I could tell you wanted to be alone."

"Yes, I did. Thank you," Louisa said, gratefully accepting the proffered cup of tea. "But I wish I hadn't cried so! I must look an utter mess now, certainly in no state to accept visitors!"

"Yes," her aunt said, "that's why I brought you these." She gestured to a little dish on the tea tray with two soggy little sachets in it.

Louisa wrinkled her nose. "What are those?"

"Cold, damp packets of tea," her aunt replied. "Put them over your eyes, and be sure to drink plenty of tea and water. You'll be right as rain in no time."

Louisa chuckled as she held the cool little pouches against her eyes and almost immediately felt a little better. "Are there any problems tea *doesn't* solve?"

Aunt Frances laughed lightly. "Now," she said, "why did you come home early from the party last night instead of enjoying every ounce of the popularity you've worked so hard to earn? That isn't like you, Lou."

"I saw Mr. Brougham flirting with Miss Norris at the party and it made me so angry and embarrassed that I couldn't stand to be there one instant more."

Aunt Frances was quiet for a long moment. "You say Mr. Brougham was flirting with her?"

Louisa lowered the tea pouches and nodded, refusing to meet her aunt's eyes.

"But isn't Miss Norris courting Colonel Cheyne?"

Louisa seemed taken aback as memory flooded her. "Oh. You are right. But Brougham ought to know that, too. So why would he flirt with her?"

Aunt Frances smiled curiously. "And you are certain he was flirting? Could he not have merely been friendly with her?"

"It looked like flirting to me," Louisa said stubbornly.

"All right. Let's say he did. Why does it bother you so much?"

Louisa chewed thoughtfully on her lower lip. "Perhaps it's because . . . I tried my hand at flirting and I am terrible at it. I generally have wonderful social prowess, but I have never truly tried flirting in earnest before yesterday and now I am left feeling dejected and humiliated at my failure."

"Whom did you flirt with?" Aunt Frances asked.

"With Mr. Brougham, of course," Louisa mumbled.

Louisa was glad to obscure her eyes with the tea sachets so she wouldn't see her aunt laughing at her.

"What makes you so certain you have failed?" Aunt Frances asked after a long pause.

Louisa could feel her cheeks flushing again and tried to force herself to be calm. "Well, I dismissed him rather rudely after our conversation."

"Ah. Yes, that may not have been . . ." Aunt Frances took a deep breath. "But Louisa, he is your dear friend! I am certain if only you explained yourself to him—"

"And what would I say?" Louisa snapped, dropping the tea. "I apologize if I offended you the other day, but I am sincerely interested in becoming your wife and I hope you will consider courting me?"

Aunt Frances couldn't help but giggle at Louisa's despondent sarcasm. "Oh, you goose. I can try to smooth things over with him, if you'd like. It would be like nothing ever happened."

Louisa sighed. "It seems a hopeless business now in any case," she said. "Mr. Brougham has secured an introduction to the Duchess of Dorset's daughter, Virginia."

Aunt Frances seemed confused. "You've never envied her before, Louisa."

"But she has something I do not—something far more important," Louisa said with a sigh.

Aunt Frances raised an eyebrow. "An enormous fortune?"

"Besides that."

"A title?"

"*Besides* that!"

Aunt Frances shook her head. "What is it, Lou?"

"She has Lady Margaret's approval!" Louisa wailed, "and will almost certainly marry Mr. Brougham now."

Aunt Frances was quiet for a moment. "And you wanted to marry him yourself," she said.

Louisa couldn't look directly at her. She was so humiliated her voice shook. "Why shouldn't I? You and Father were certainly in raptures over him."

Her aunt smiled gently. "You've never taken a real interest in a gentleman before, Louisa. It is a frightening thing, isn't it? To have one's heart so vulnerable?"

Louisa could not look at her aunt, but her chin quivered and she nodded. "Yes. I am sorry I've been so rude, Aunt. I feel I hardly know myself anymore."

Aunt Frances put an arm about her. "Oh, Lou! I don't like seeing you so unhappy. And I'll tell you this in confidence—I think Lady Margaret is a perfectly wretched woman! But it is not so *very* bad, I'm sure. There are plenty of other nice young men in London you could consider."

"Yes, but he was the best one," Louisa whispered, and after heaving a sigh she tugged out the list of eligible bachelors that she'd hidden in her diary and handed it to Aunt Frances.

Aunt Frances looked over the names and nodded thoughtfully. "Hmm. Good choices. You have done your research, it seems."

"Yes, Brougham is head and shoulders above the others. I only wonder why I didn't see it before! He is the only one who already controls his own fortune, he's under thirty—under twenty-five, in fact—and has both a country estate *and* a house in town. That's a very promising combination of traits. He's also quite wonderful to talk to and I think we would suit. If only . . ." she sighed heavily.

"I still think you ought to speak with him openly about it," Aunt Frances said, shaking her head. "But I cannot make you do it if you do not wish to."

"I know that I ought to. But I am *frightened*, Aunt. Frightened of failure. Of success. Of being married, of remaining single . . ."

"Oh, my darling. It is good for you to be frightened."

Louisa glanced up, confused. "It is?"

Her aunt nodded. "Indeed. It demonstrates that you truly understand the importance of the decisions you are making. But you must not allow this fear to paralyze you."

Louisa nodded and placed the little sachets of tea back over her eyes while Aunt Frances continued surveying the list.

"What about this one?" Aunt Frances suddenly asked, "Captain Miles Allen. I do not know if I've met him."

"I met him only once last season," Louisa said, "but I heard that he was going to be selling out of the army and moving to London permanently very soon. He ought to be at either the Churchill ball or at Almack's by the twenty-fourth."

"What else do you know about him?"

Louisa smiled as she placed the sachets of tea back on the tray. "He's a good friend of Brummell's. And he's tolerably handsome."

"Oh, he is, is he? And does he have conversation?" Aunt Frances asked with a significant glance.

"From what I recall, he does!" Louisa said, and with a twinkle in her eye she added, "but fine eyes go a very long way toward forgiving a lack of conversation, you know."

Aunt Frances laughed. "Then I look forward to meeting him. Tell me about the other young men on your list and how they got there."

Louisa sighed and placed the little sachets of tea back on the tray. "I will! But later. I am feeling much better now, Aunt Frances. What do you think I ought to wear to the Churchill ball this evening?

"Your green gown?"

"Oh! Yes, I've got it now. The green gown, and my pearls. In my hair, a large white lily, and little else. It will be all the rage until well after Christmas, I'm quite sure of it. And I know just how it ought to be styled! I will talk to my maid directly and will ask a footman to stop by the florist this afternoon."

"I'm sure it will be lovely," Aunt Frances said with a smile.

November 16, 1813

Andrew grinned when William Cox entered White's a few days later looking as though he were walking on air. Philip crowed and Michael laughed when they saw him. William swaggered over to the group of them and requested a drink from a passing attendant. Then he sat at the table with a happy sigh.

"Brougham, you're a miracle worker."

"Go on, then. Tell us everything," Michael said.

William sat up straighter in his chair. "I had a capital time at the Duncans' party, and I asked if Miss Clavendish'd like me to come for a visit, and she said . . ."

The other gentlemen leaned forward in interest, and William grinned. "*Yes*. She said she'd like me to. So I didn't go Friday, like Philip said—I went this morning instead, and she seemed quite overjoyed to see me. I think she will encourage my suit!"

Michael clapped him on the back. "Happy for you, William! Glad she finally noticed you!"

"It's all Brougham," William said humbly, and took a swig of his drink. "If he hadn't paired us off at the Duncans' I'm sure she'd still look through me like a pane of glass."

"Well, then. To William's conquest! And Brougham's aid," Philip added, raising his glass.

"What did you *do*, Brougham?" Michael asked. "Maybe you really are a miracle worker."

Andrew laughed and shook his head. "Not at all! I only had a suspicion that flirting with another young lady in front of Miss Clavendish would have the desired effect of turning her attentions from me, and it seems to have done so!"

Philip nodded and let a full minute pass before asking. "It does make me wonder . . . could you do it again?"

Andrew looked up from his drink with a frown. "I am not sure. Why?"

"Michael here might benefit, as well."

Michael shot an irritated look at Philip. "I can manage my own affairs, thank you!"

Philip rolled his eyes heavenward. "Miss Gifford has never so much as spoken to you!"

"That's not true."

"Oh, really? And have you once been able to draw her into a conversation since you were formally introduced?"

Michael was silent.

"Then it is as I thought," Philip said. "If she's as enamored as half the girls in London are with Brougham here, it ought to work wonders."

Andrew smiled weakly when the two of them looked up at him for a response. It was true that he was still no nearer to puzzling out what he ought to do to soften his mother's mind toward Miss Grenfeld and stop her from pushing him at every titled young lady who walked by. He also wasn't certain how he could maintain his old friendship with Miss Grenfeld after her cold dismissal the other day.

"I can try if Michael wants me to," Andrew finally said. "But I don't make any promises it would actually work!"

Michael gave a little shrug and a begrudging smile. "I suppose I'd be bacon-brained if I turned down your help."

Andrew spent the next two hours with his friends, until they all left to promenade the park and ready themselves for the ball. He sat on his own in the club for a while longer, watching the other gentlemen about—some in groups, some alone—drink, play light games of cards, and read their papers. He picked up a nearby newspaper himself and began to flip through it.

Not long after, he saw two young men enter, one of whom he recognized. The two spoke to one another for a moment before hurrying over in his direction. He had never met the second gentleman but the first was Frank, an acquaintance from his time at Oxford. Frank had always seemed embarrassed to be seen with Andrew, but was kind enough when no one else was about.

In school, Frank had been perpetually short on blunt and was ever waiting for his next allowance. Being a spendthrift had gotten him into more than one scrape in the past, and if he were still the same man, letting him win a few pounds off Andrew at piquet was certain to get him into a good humor.

"Andrew!" Frank called.

Brougham stood. "Frank! It's been ages. How have you been? Might I interest you in a game of piquet?"

Frank's frown slowly melted into a smile. "Indeed! Let's have a game, shall we?"

Andrew began readying the cards. The man at Frank's side cleared his throat.

"Ah, and have you met my cousin Stephan?" Frank asked quickly.

Andrew shook his head as the other gentleman stepped forward.

"Stephan Grimsby of Somerset."

Andrew nodded politely. "Andrew Brougham, of Suffolk. Pleasure to meet any friend of Frank's."

Stephan smiled. "Shall we have a game of piquet, then? You two play, and I shall distract you both."

Andrew was happy to see Frank again. They had been friends, of a sort. Frank had teased him often, but had also relied heavily on Andrew for help with his schoolwork. Andrew never begrudged him the aid. He'd had few enough friends, and Frank had always been good company.

As they began to play, a pleasant, casual conversation ensued. Andrew rather liked this Stephan fellow. He seemed more quietly self-assured than many of the other young men he'd met about town. The unfashionable cut of his clothes made it clear he was from the country. Mr. Brummell certainly would've wrinkled his nose at Stephan, but he was not there, and his suit coat didn't bother Andrew in the slightest.

"Will you be at Lady Billings's ball tomorrow evening?" Stephan asked.

"I had planned to attend, yes. Why?"

"I am told you are acquainted with Lady Virginia, the daughter of the Duke of Dorset."

Andrew nodded, attempting a smile and finding himself momentarily incapable of one. "I am."

"And I was hoping . . . might you be able to secure me an introduction?"

Andrew's eyes lit with hope. Was this young man interested in the Lady Virginia? If so, more power to him! If she returned his affections, he would be liberated—surely his mother would stop foisting her upon him if she were courting another gentleman. "I would be overjoyed to introduce you." Then he hesitated. "Do you . . . if you need an introduction, I suppose you've never met her before?"

Stephan hesitated before responding. "I haven't. But there's something *familiar* about her, if I don't sound dicked in the nob for saying so."

Andrew smiled, thinking of the way he'd felt sometimes when he was talking with Miss Grenfeld—as though they'd been friends for thousands of years already and had simply forgotten it during their brief lifetime. The thought of it gave him a painful little pang. "I think I might understand," he said.

Chapter Fifteen

November 17, 1813

Andrew nervously tugged at his neckcloth, hoping against hope that he didn't ruin the knot that Henry had worked so hard on. His shirt points were starched more thoroughly than he normally liked, and he felt no inclination to begin the search for a dance partner.

He still hadn't seen Miss Grenfeld. She had disappeared shortly after he'd spoken with Miss Norris at the Duncans' party and when he had finally gotten up the courage to visit her again, the butler had said she was indisposed and could not receive him. Was she purposely avoiding meeting him? It seemed so.

"Mr. Brougham!" he was startled to be suddenly addressed by the Duchess of Dorset.

"Your Grace," he said with a bow.

"I do hope that you'll save a dance or two for my daughter this evening," she said.

"Of course." He tried to smile. "I would be delighted to."

To his dismay, Lady Virginia was not far away, and the duchess called her over immediately. Andrew barely held back a sigh. He would need to look for Miss Grenfeld later. As he led her toward the dance floor, he struggled to maintain the flow of conversation with Lady Virginia. She didn't seem terribly happy to be there, either. As he danced with her, however, a happy thought struck him.

What if that Stephan fellow really won Lady Virginia's heart? He was a country gentleman without a great deal of fashionable carriage, but at first blush he was quite pleasant, and, as far as Andrew could tell, good-looking. Andrew would be very happy to be rid of the forced connection to the duke's family, and Stephan may be just the man to help him do it.

He managed to carefully avoid Virginia and the duchess until her attention was claimed by other gentlemen and began looking for Miss Grenfeld. He had barely had the chance to circle the ballroom, however, before Michael Heron caught him, clapped him on the back, and cleared his throat meaningfully.

"Heron! There you are. How are you?" Andrew asked.

"Well enough, Brougham! I hope you haven't forgotten the little favor you promised me the other day?"

Andrew glanced up to see Miss Dorothy Gifford talking to another young lady he could recall meeting once before—Miss Ann Gardiner. He frowned. He did not see Miss Norris about—she would likely have been willing to help him again, so it seemed he would need to find another suitable lady to flirt with instead. He'd met Miss Gardiner before but had no way of warning her about his flirtation beforehand, and he hated to take her off guard as he had Miss Norris the previous evening. However, as he walked over to the giggling pair, Michael's nervous hand pressing into his back to guide him there, Andrew decided that, at least in this instance, forgiveness was better than permission.

"Ladies! How are you this evening?" Andrew asked with a cheerful bow.

"Very well indeed!" Miss Gifford said, waving her painted fan slowly as she smiled up at Andrew through her lashes.

Andrew quickly switched his attention to Miss Gardiner. "You are looking very well this evening, Miss Gardiner. If you are not engaged for the next dance, would you consider having me as a partner?"

He looked into her eyes and smiled. They were a lovely blue, and the blush that rose in her cheeks was most becoming. She was a very nice young lady, and another rush of guilt stung him at this thought. He hoped that she would not be harmed by his deception. He knew that young ladies frequently complained about the wickedness of flirtatious men, and yet they always seemed to welcome and encourage their advances, from what he could see. He did not quite understand it, but he could only hope that their apparent willingness to forgive rakes would extend to a hapless and occasionally insincere flirt such as he.

Miss Gardiner allowed him to lead her away for a more private conversation. Though the rudeness didn't come naturally to him, he snubbed Miss Gifford by turning away from her without so much as a backward glance, his full attention on Miss Gardiner. As soon as they were where Miss Gifford could no longer hear them, he said, "Miss Gardiner, may I tell you a small secret?"

She giggled nervously. "Of course."

"My friend Mr. Heron there is *quite* interested in Miss Gifford, and I think they would suit one another very well. What do you think?"

She looked over at the pair of them with a thoughtful expression. "He is a long way from commanding his own fortune, is he not?"

"Yes and no," Andrew said, "he will control a considerable portion of his inheritance upon his marriage to a suitable young lady, as per his grandfather's will. Miss Gifford's fortune is respectable, and her family is beyond reproach—as is his." Andrew wondered to himself when he began keeping track of this sort of information about the people he met. Miss Grenfeld seemed to do so as easily as breathing, as did all the rest of the *ton*. She had been right—one had to be prepared to hear others talk of one's fortune as if it were common property.

"I suppose you are right," she said. "Miss Gifford had not considered him, of course. Her sights are set on er . . . more eligible gentlemen, I suppose." She shot a sweet, shy glance at Mr. Brougham, and his stomach sank. They couldn't have *both* set their caps at him, could they?

He sighed, but before he could respond, the last set ended and the next began arranging itself. Andrew led Miss Gardiner into the set, regretful that it was a country dance, which would make it somewhat more difficult to talk to her. He may have to wait until after the dance to apologize.

"If only I were able to court every young lady who cast her eye my way—I've never met so many pretty girls and wonderful new friends than I have this season in London." It was difficult to make this pronouncement while bouncing up and down. He hoped she heard it all.

"I am certain you are very popular indeed," she replied humbly. "I cannot think why you've chosen *me* to dance with, sir!"

Andrew blanched, but it wasn't until the dance was over that he caught a quiet moment to speak frankly with her. "Miss Gardiner, I must be open with you. I apologize if I've given you the wrong impression," he said. "But my intentions toward you are merely friendly. I only wanted to give my friend Mr. Heron a chance to speak with Miss Gifford uninterrupted."

She looked down at her feet. "Oh, of c-course!" she said. "That is what I . . . naturally I didn't assume . . ." she bobbed a quick curtsy and fled.

Andrew's hand came to his forehead in frustration. That had been even worse than he had feared it might be. He certainly was making a mess of things, wasn't he?

November 17, 1813

Louisa stopped and stared. First, Miss Norris and now poor little Miss Gardiner? What was he thinking of? He made little Miss Gardiner the object of his gallantry, making Miss Gifford fume at the edge of the dance floor, and then after a single dance with her, excused himself. The poor child was red as a beet and trying not to cry. *What on earth did he say to her?*

Louisa straightened her long gloves and marched over to where Mr. Brougham stood.

"I doubt that went the way that you intended," she said.

He nearly jumped to hear her address him. "I . . . no, it didn't." Only a moment later, his look of consternation melted into a smile. "Miss Grenfeld, it's good to see you," he said.

She barely kept herself from smiling back. It *was* good to see him. She forced her mouth into a stern expression. She could not reward such an incorrigible flirt. "You certainly have become a man about town. I never would've thought it of you."

His face flushed. "I haven't . . . Miss Grenfeld, I'm not . . ."

She raised an eyebrow. "Who would have thought that teaching a few social skills to a green young man would turn him into one of the most shamelessly accomplished flirts in London?"

He didn't miss the bite to her tone, and he visibly winced. "I would not call myself a flirt, Louisa."

She folded her arms and raised her eyebrows, daring him to defy her.

He frowned. She could tell he was growing nervous. Louisa was uncomfortable too, but she was far too practiced to ever let it show. She recognized that she might seem a jealous harpy, but she could not stop herself, and Aunt Frances was not there to cool her temper.

"You have the daughters of duchesses dangling after you. Every young debutante in London seems to be setting her cap at you, sir!" she said. "It would appear that you have everything you could desire."

He frowned, seeming hurt. "Not everything," he said sadly.

She could feel her cheeks warming. "I am not a jewel to be added to your collection, sir," she said quietly, and she turned on her heel and walked away.

The nerve of him! She could barely contain her frustration and anger. To continue to flirt with her even after she called him out for it! She hurried to get herself something to drink.

"And there she is!" a familiar voice intercepted her. "Miss Louisa, my dear! You look as if you've swallowed a lemon. Tell me, what did Brougham say to you just now to set you off? Don't think I didn't notice."

She looked down at the cup in her hands and drank deeply from it before responding. It had only taken a few seconds for her anger to dissolve into the sadness waiting just behind it. "He is turning into a most accomplished flirt. I think perhaps I've lost him entirely."

"I have my doubts about *that*," Mr. Brummell said, guiding her along the edge of the ballroom as they spoke. "He seemed ready to make you an offer only a few weeks ago!"

She shook her head. "He stopped visiting me some days ago, Brummell. You haven't been by much lately, either, you know."

Brummell frowned, and his tone became sincere for a moment. "I had no idea you were so fond of him, Miss Grenfeld."

She blinked away tears in silence. "Never mind," she said with difficulty. "No sense in crying over it, in any case."

Mr. Brummell nodded. "I am sorry, my dear. But perhaps all he needs is a little reminder of how desirable you are."

She smiled curiously and quirked an eyebrow at him in question.

"You need another suitor, of course!" he said.

She laughed. "A suitor?"

He nodded knowingly. "Nothing makes a gentleman want something more than to be told he cannot have it."

She giggled. "And what are you proposing, sir? Are *you* offering to court me?"

His eyes widened. "*Heavens* no, child! Besides, it wouldn't work. Everyone knows I'd never make you an offer."

She laughed at that, for that was true. "You're also nearly twice my age, Brummell."

He waved her comment away. "What does that signify these days? But oh! I've hit upon it. I've a young friend who's a military captain. Miles Allen. He's just the man."

She smiled. "I met him once last season. I wasn't sure if he was going to be here this evening or not. Is he about town already?"

"Oh, certainly! He prefers the table to the ballroom, generally, but he's about, and fairly well set up. I wouldn't call him *full* of juice, but his pockets are always lined. His portion was generous and he has . . ." Mr. Brummell hesitated.

"Been more careful with his fortune than you have with yours?"

"What cheek!" Mr. Brummell sniffed. "But I won't deny it. In any case, he's just the fellow to help you."

Louisa pursed her lips in suspicion. "Why *him*, specifically?"

"My dear, anyone with half a wit would know that you'd never court a man that did not dress as well as Allen does!"

She blinked twice and gave a little sigh. "And does anything lead you to believe he really *does* wish to court me?"

"'Course he does—who wouldn't? He is here this evening. I will furnish the reintroduction myself. He's a famous sport, a capital Corinthian, and a jolly fine flirt. I think he could suit you very well indeed. And if you do decide to abandon Brougham entirely, he *is* looking to settle down before too long, you know."

Louisa giggled. "Really? Well, I am not otherwise engaged this evening, I suppose."

Only a few minutes later, Mr. Brummell made good on his word and escorted Louisa to Mr. Allen's side, and Louisa was anything but disappointed. Mr. Allen was meticulously well-groomed but affected an air of carelessness about his person that called attention to his sporting endeavors. He was well-known among the Corinthian set as a regular at Jackson's, an exceptional fighter, and an excellent horseman.

He commanded a respectable place in society, but Louisa knew her father would not have been impressed by his more rakish tendencies. However, he stayed firmly in the company of bachelor fare, for the most part, and did not make a habit of toying with innocent young hearts of respectable birth.

From the moment they met, they were laughing, and it only took a sidelong glance and a couple of whispered words from Mr. Brummell for Mr. Allen to smile at Louisa and gallantly take her hand. "Brummell tells me your cavalier has failed to come up to scratch!" he said. "Shall I see if I can make you forget him entirely, Miss Grenfeld?" His tone was playful and his velvet voice seemed a bare inch from laughter.

She played along, her hand flying to her heart. "Oh, dear. I hope I'm not setting myself up for disappointment."

Mr. Allen laughed. His laugh was marvelous—full-voiced, loud, and infectious. "Let us say no more then. I shall not make you take me at my word. I remain, as ever, your humble servant." He swept a comically deep bow and held out an arm to lead her onto the dance floor. She accepted with a smile. This was going to be most diverting.

Chapter Sixteen

November 18, 1813

"That Allen is a real dasher, an out-and-outer!" Philip crowed. "No woman looks twice at a man who stands next to him! It's no wonder you were so cowed at the ball last evening, Brougham."

Mr. Brougham sighed and swished his drink about in his glass. That was not the answer he'd hoped for when asking for information about Miles Allen. "There. You see? I am not nearly so brave as you seemed to think I was," he said.

Philip nodded and leaned forward. "You know, I heard that Frank Compton knew you at Oxford. He was telling me you were a real bore, forever going on about birds, your nose always in a book."

Andrew's cheeks colored. "I *am* quite fond of birds," he said, "but Miss Grenfeld told me they do not make an appropriate subject for small talk, and so I don't speak of them much anymore."

Philip laughed. "Indeed they do not," he said. "I never would've believed it of you, though. You're such a proper pink of the *ton* I'd never think you a bore."

Andrew smiled at this and drank deeply from his glass. "Not as much of an out-and-outer as Captain Miles Allen though, eh?"

Mr. Palmer shook his head. "Different camp entirely! He's thirty if he's a day, and is chock-full of military exploits, sporting stories, and he's . . . well, he's all the crack, Andrew! But he's not going to have nearly as many ladies setting caps at him as you, simply because he won't look twice at any of 'em and because he hasn't got an estate. Granted, though, Miss Grenfeld is a special exception. If one woman in London could catch his eye and bring him up to scratch, she probably could!"

Andrew grimaced at the thought that the captain would 'come up to scratch.' The only proposal he wanted Miss Grenfeld to receive was the one he would offer. Just as soon as he could bring his mother around to the idea. And Miss Grenfeld around to the idea. And find the courage to do it.

"Why didn't you court her when you had the chance?" Philip asked curiously.

A familiar uneasy feeling settled in Andrew's stomach. "I wanted to," he admitted. "But Miss Grenfeld made it clear early on that she saw me as only a friend, and I have no idea whether that can change or not. And my mother is still against it. I may be legally free to do as I will, but a disapproving mother is a heavy ball and chain to carry about while courting. Mothers can be that way. I am fairly certain Lady Virginia only spends time with me because her mother requests it of her, you know. Not that I understand a thing about women."

Philip leaned forward on his elbows. "My sister told me something that completely changed the way I think about women, Andrew. She said that the reason it's hard to know what a girl thinks or feels is that half the time she doesn't know, herself."

Andrew thought about this, finishing the last of his drink. "She certainly doesn't seem to want me to court her anymore," he murmured.

"We don't know that. Why doesn't your mother like Miss Grenfeld, anyway? She's a real diamond of the first water. If Miss Grenfeld would look at any of us twice, none of us would be able to resist her."

"I already told you. My mother wishes me to marry a title of some sort."

Philip wrinkled his nose. "And she thinks the quiet, mousy daughter of the Duke of Dorset is going to increase her consequence more than the most fashionable young lady in London?"

"Oh, Miss Grenfeld probably hates me now," Andrew groaned.

"I wouldn't be too quick to say so," Philip said. "You are, after all, still one of the best prospects on the marriage mart at the moment, and you've spent hours in her company, which sets you above the rest. You said you two had a capital time together, didn't you?"

Andrew smiled, remembering some of their conversations. It had felt like no one else existed in the world in those moments. He couldn't remember ever feeling happier. He nodded but did not remain buoyant for long. "Yes, but now . . . now she seems to despise me."

"How did things leave off between you, if you don't mind my asking?"

"Last night, or at my last morning visit?"

"Your last . . . wait just a moment. Just how long has it been since you visited her?"

Andrew mentally counted the days. "About two weeks?"

"You mean that you no longer so much as drop in for a morning visit anymore? Not visit Miss Grenfeld? *Everyone* visits Miss Grenfeld! I don't normally stay longer than about three or four minutes when I do, but it's usually crowded. Why on earth did you stop visiting her?"

Andrew colored. "I . . . she asked me to leave in no uncertain terms. I was clearly outstaying my welcome."

"Well, don't stay all day, I suppose, but to stop visiting entirely? Silly idea. Even your mother ought to see that. In fact, if she knows what's good for her, she ought to visit Miss Grenfeld a bit more, too. She's full of useful information, and not only gossip. She always manages to help one improve one's influence in society without being so dismissive and abrupt as Brummell tends to be. Miss Grenfeld's a remarkable lady, by all counts."

Andrew sighed. "You needn't remind me. So you think I still ought to visit her, even though it seems she has a new beau dangling after her?"

Philip looked thoughtful. "You said she spoke to you at the ball last evening. What did she say?"

Andrew grimaced as her words came back to his mind. "She accused me of becoming the most accomplished flirt in London, and told me she was not a jewel to be added to my collection."

Philip paused, his eyes widening, and put a hand on Andrew's arm. "Brougham, that might be a good sign."

Andrew's gaze jerked up. "What? Do you mean it? How could it be?"

Philip nodded slowly, withdrawing his hand. "I would need to ask my sister to be certain—it seems to me she knows everything there is to know about young ladies—but it might be a good thing."

"How could something like that be good?"

"If she didn't care two straws for you it wouldn't be so hard for her to be polite. She's endlessly civil—everyone knows that. If she snapped at you that way, it means you've upset her somehow. That's the only reason a lady as lovely as Miss Grenfeld might snap at someone."

"I upset her?" he asked. "But how? What did I do?"

"Dash it, you slow-top!" Philip cried. "You hurt her pride! Embarrassed her! You gave up far too easily! She likely wanted you to pursue her."

Andrew's mind boggled. "But . . . she told me I ought to leave."

Philip looked heavenward. "You could have put up a bit of a fight, you know."

Andrew tossed back the last of his drink. "You have some fascinating insights about women, Palmer."

Philip looked only slightly embarrassed, but he smiled. "I have sisters," he said, almost apologetically.

Andrew nodded. "Lucky man. But tell me something. Supposing you're right. If the reason she's angry at me is that I didn't offer to court her soon enough . . . what am I supposed to do to repair the damage?"

Philip took a deep breath, as if ready to launch into a discourse, but then the air flapped through his lips. "I haven't the foggiest," he said. "Everyone's different, you know. But I know you ought to begin by at least visiting her again."

Andrew frowned. It seemed as though he was going to need to choose whether to try to please Miss Grenfeld or his mother, and he wasn't certain which task was more daunting to him at present.

November 20, 1813

When Andrew finally gathered the courage to visit Miss Grenfeld again, he came with what he hoped was a suitable peace offering. The florist had listened to his story and recommended that a bouquet composed of zinnias and roses would exactly convey the sort of emotion he wished to, and Mr. Brougham had complied, even though he wondered if the suggestion arose only from the florist's seeming abundance of these two flowers.

As he knocked at the door, he faced the sudden ludicrous temptation to hide in the bushes, but he stood his ground.

As the butler led him into the drawing room, Mr. Brougham's hands were shaking lightly. He tried to calm himself by closing his eyes and remembering the pleasant feeling he'd had conversing with Miss Grenfeld weeks ago, when they were friends and things still seemed simple. Before he had adequately prepared, however, he stood before the elegant Miss Grenfeld, less sure of himself than he had felt in quite some time.

"Miss Grenfeld," he said, bowing and handing her the bouquet.

She smiled placidly and took the flowers, handing them to a footman to put into some water. When Andrew looked up about the room, he noticed his flowers weren't the only ones resting on the center table. She sat and indicated for him to do likewise.

"Miss Grenfeld, I hope you have been keeping well."

"Indeed," she said. "I have been very well." Her voice remained cool, and her countenance was reserved.

The only other person present for a visit was Mrs. Abbott, holding a large fur muff in her lap and looking at Mr. Brougham with more curiosity than irritation. Mr. Brougham ducked a nod in her direction and cleared his throat.

Miss Grenfeld softened a little. "What brings you by today, sir?"

"I . . . wished to visit with you," he said awkwardly. "It has been some time. And . . . I had wondered if you would do me the honor of walking in the park with me today."

She frowned and inspected her fingernails for a moment before looking back at Mr. Brougham. "I'm afraid I have a previous engagement," she said. "I am very sorry. Another time, perhaps?"

Andrew stared at her curiously. Something was different. She was avoiding his gaze, and she did not seem quite as comfortable as she normally did. It finally hit him when Miss Grenfeld turned to Mrs. Abbott and asked her a question, pulling the lady back into the conversation. Miss Grenfeld was wearing a mask. He had never noticed it during their other meetings, but it was the same mask she normally wore in social settings. It was a perfectly polite, more formal, less *real* version of the Miss Grenfeld he had come to know during their many visits together. Would she never again allow him to peer behind that mask and hear a burst of her honest laughter? He narrowed his eyes in thought.

What was he doing wrong? If he could only learn what was putting her on her guard, he could perhaps fix it, and all would be well once more. While he was still racking his brain for an answer, the door opened, and Captain Allen entered, holding a single small posy. He handed the graceful little flower to Miss Grenfeld with a flourish, and she giggled.

"How do you do, sir?" she asked him, taking the flower.

Mr. Brougham felt the bottom of his stomach drop. It would appear things with Captain Allen were progressing even more quickly than he'd worried they might. Andrew sat on the sofa, spectating. He nodded and smiled when there was a break in Miss Grenfeld's and the captain's conversation. When one of them asked for his response, he gave it. To say he felt awkward was putting it mildly.

He forced himself to look through a lens of calm disinterest as Miss Grenfeld had taught him to and had to admit to himself that they would make an excellent pair. They conversed easily and naturally with one another, and they were both strikingly good-looking and well dressed. He came to himself as he watched them and was dismayed to realize that Louisa used to speak to him with that same openness. Perhaps there was a time she had liked him as much as she now seemed to like the captain. He could not decide if this thought brought him comfort or merely discouragement, but either way he felt he had outstayed his welcome and wanted to continue his meditations in private.

"I had best be off," he said, standing during a lull in the conversation. "I will see myself out. Good day to you, Miss Grenfeld. Mrs. Abbott . . . Captain Allen." He was very careful to say the captain's name in a neutral tone of voice. It would never do for him to give in to jealousy and lose his composure after all the lessons Miss Grenfeld had taught him in self-control.

"It was very good to see you, Mr. Brougham. I hope you will visit again." The sincerity of Louisa's tone gave Andrew pause. It did not seem to match the visit they'd just had.

His exit from the room was briefly barred by the entrance of Miss Grenfeld's aunt. Miss Bickham took one glance at Mr. Brougham's downcast countenance and at Louisa and Captain Allen's smiling faces before narrowing her eyes at Louisa.

"Mr. Brougham," she said, quickly addressing him before he could leave. "It is good to see you again, sir. We have missed your morning visits."

Andrew could not help but doubt that this 'we' included Miss Grenfeld, given her smiling attentions to Mr. Allen. "I am sorry to have disappointed you, Miss Bickham. I remain as ever in your service." He dropped a quick bow and left the house without a backward glance.

Chapter Seventeen

November 20, 1813

Louisa was first exhilarated then embarrassed by the way she had acted with Captain Allen during Mr. Brougham's visit. Captain Allen was charming and handsome and easy to talk with, but holding Mr. Brougham at such a distance felt so unnatural to her as to be painful. At first it had felt wonderful—she had felt utterly vindicated for her awkward failed flirtations of the past week. But it was not long into the conversation that she began to feel an almost unbearable itch to drop the pretenses and speak with Mr. Brougham as openly and comfortably as they used to.

What had ruined everything? How had it come to this?

Louisa poked her needle into the screen she was covering with a vengeance. She had developed a *tendre* for Mr. Brougham. *That* is what had done it. It was endlessly frustrating. Before she had decided within herself that she wanted to marry him they had been easy friends and companions. Why could she not speak with him normally anymore?

"Did you want to tell me what happened today, Lou?" Aunt Frances asked somewhat severely.

Louisa avoided her gaze until Aunt Frances heaved a sigh and quietly began working next to her. Then she said, "It's no use. I still prefer Mr. Brougham, I think."

Aunt Frances made a frustrated sound. "Then why didn't you . . ."

"I know. I'm sorry," Louisa said in a small voice.

Frances let her breath out all at once, shaking her head. "Truth be told, I prefer Brougham too," Aunt Frances said. "Just don't tell the captain, since I also like him a great deal."

Louisa chuckled.

Aunt Frances sat next to Louisa. "I do wish you would tell me more about that conversation with Mr. Brougham that so embarrassed and frustrated you."

Louisa pursed her lips and did not look up, but eventually she did speak. "I attempted to flirt with him. I told you."

"And he did not respond the way you hoped he would?"

Louisa shook her head. She could feel her cheeks flaming. "He acted as though I had said nothing out of the common way at all. He showed no extraordinary interest, no significant glances were shared . . ."

When Louisa finally looked back up at Frances, her aunt was smiling sympathetically. "Oh, Lou. I wanted to warn you something like this might happen."

Louisa stared at her aunt through narrowed eyes. "What do you mean? Something like *what*?"

Aunt Frances chuckled. "Darling, any half-wit could've told you that fool was madly in love with you from the very beginning. Didn't you sense it?"

Louisa's cheeks flushed anew. "Of course I did! At least I thought I did. And I did not want him to embarrass himself, so I . . . I . . ."

"You carefully established the relationship as a friendship and nothing more."

"Yes."

"And when you finally turned around and learned that he was not pursuing you nearly as closely as you had hoped he would be, you were disappointed."

Louisa stared at the work in her hands, her fingers unmoving. "It does sound awful when you put it that way."

"I have started to notice him flirting more with other young ladies," Aunt Frances said hesitantly. "It is possible that he has moved on, dearest."

Louisa sighed and shook her head. "I know. I know! It is too late. I should have been more honest with myself about my feelings, but really, until I overheard you and Father talking that night about this being my last season in town, I had not begun to think seriously about matrimony. I think I liked to imagine myself being an eventual Baroness Fairbourne."

Aunt Frances laughed. "Wouldn't we all like to be like the baroness! But we, like most women, do not control our own fortunes."

"Yes, we remain at the mercy of the men," Louisa grumbled, poking her needle back into the screen.

"Indeed. But at the very least, we have some say in deciding our prison and choosing the masters of our fates."

Louisa blinked. "Now that is a cheerful thought," she said sarcastically.

Aunt Frances sighed and chuckled. "Perhaps. However, the only thing more horrible than being married in our society is *not* being married."

Louisa laughed. "Nay! The only thing worse than not being married is being married to Sir Alfred Stanley. I'd rather take my chances remaining single than chained to that excuse for a man!"

"*Touché*!"

They both surrendered to their pent-up giggles at last, clutching at their sides until tears streamed from the corners of their eyes. When Louisa's father popped his head into the drawing room to investigate, he pronounced them both very silly indeed.

December 14, 1813

Louisa hoped and waited for another visit from Mr. Brougham, but in the meantime, there was Captain Allen. The captain came almost daily, a grin spanning his handsome face, and he always said the most charming and flattering things without fail. Then he and Louisa would talk and laugh and flirt for a time before he left. It was just so *easy* that Louisa could not help but enjoy his visits.

It was only after he would leave that her mind would leap straight back to Mr. Brougham. When Brougham finally came again for a visit a few days later, Captain Allen was already there, and it was clear Mr. Brougham felt uncomfortable talking openly with Louisa around the other gentleman, who shared few of his interests and who seemed to be teasing him half the time. Mr. Brougham did not return for weeks after that awkward encounter, and she found that she missed him more than ever.

Despite her persistent thoughts of Mr. Brougham, with the help of Captain Allen's charmingly distracting visits and a gradual surrender to disappointment, time slowly started to resume its usual pace, and the emptiness caused by Brougham's absence began to ache less as the weeks passed.

On a comfortable Tuesday in December, Louisa smiled at the captain while stirring sugar into her tea as Aunt Frances calmly embroidered in the corner.

"Does it still hurt?" Louisa asked of the captain's wounded arm.

"Not a whit, unless I strain it. It's not nearly so strong as it once was, but it's nearly all the way recovered."

"Tell me again what happened!" Louisa said. "Which battle was it in?"

Captain Allen laughed. "I wish that I could say that there was a wonderfully brave exploit associated with it, but it was just after the Zuazo Ridge was captured at the Battle of Vitoria and things were winding down, the men triumphant but exhausted, and I was ready to fall asleep on the back of my horse. My guard was down after standing at ease for hours, and my horse was spooked by a sudden accidental musket discharge on the field and bucked me off. I caught myself with my left arm in just such a way that I broke it and was taken out of commission. The lucky dogs went to battle without me just a few days later while I recovered at camp. As soon as I was well enough, I decided to sell out and return home. I need to settle down someday, and I daresay I had adventures enough."

"Wealth enough, too, if the rumors are true."

Captain Allen grinned. "They are. Now, Miss Grenfeld, I believe *you* were about to tell me why on earth a young lady as captivating as you are remains unmarried in her fourth season."

Louisa laughed, but she responded fairly seriously. "Was I? I don't believe I promised to do any such thing."

"Are you determined to remain unattached?" His blue eyes sparkled at her in a way that made her heart beat faster.

"Not so determined as I once was, I suppose," she said quietly, matching his gaze with one of her own.

A maid came in just then with the tea things and they both sat back in their seats, suddenly aware that they had been leaning toward one another.

"Captain Allen, tell me more of your family," Aunt Frances said. "I am told your elder brother has inherited your family's estate in Warwickshire."

"Indeed he has, ma'am, and I am to join him and his family there for a fortnight over Christmas."

"That is coming up so soon!" Louisa said. "I had not taken note of how quickly the season has been passing, but December is nearly half-finished."

"Have you plans for the holiday season, Miss Grenfeld?" Captain Allen asked. Her heart skipped a beat. Was she to be included in his family invitation? That would represent a far more serious commitment from Captain Allen than she had prepared herself for so far, but it was an exciting prospect.

"We likely will return to our country estate," Louisa said evasively, "but do not have any firmly settled plans."

Captain Allen smiled. "Well, I shall certainly try to have a fur or a muff made for you if we manage to catch a fox."

Louisa carefully concealed her disappointment and moved the conversation forward. It wasn't until Captain Allen had bade her a warm farewell and left that she allowed herself to ruminate in her own darker thoughts. Why did he not wish to invite her? She had already turned down two invitations to Christmas house parties in the countryside in the hopes that Captain Allen would invite her to his family home. She sighed. If not Captain Allen, then whom? Did she need to look to the next young fellow on her list?

Captain Allen entered the club with a grin and a swagger, his hat jauntily askew in the most fashionable way, his jacket and breeches molded to his perfect physical form, and a row of straight white teeth all taunting Andrew.

Miss Grenfeld had told him about the different sorts of gentlemen there were to be found in the *ton*: rakes, Corinthians, gamesters, and dandies. The captain was decidedly a Corinthian, and a fashionable leader among that set.

If Miss Grenfeld were still dispensing him advice, she probably would've told him to try to befriend members of the Corinthian set, especially those older than he was so that he might learn from them. These more established men about town were easy enough to spot about the club. They moved with an almost lazy grace, careless of the opinions of those about them. They drank brandy, smoked their pipes, made intelligent bets on horses they seemed to know intimately, and laughed together over the more humorous of the latest *on-dits*—or they kept to themselves.

Yes, Captain Allen would likely be an ideal man to learn from, according to Miss Grenfeld. Andrew glared at the captain but forced his face into a pleasant expression when the man himself looked over. Allen smiled at him and walked toward his table.

"Captain." Andrew nodded genially.

Captain Allen stopped and bowed politely to Mr. Brougham. "Brougham, isn't it? If I may take the liberty?"

Andrew gestured toward an empty seat at his table and Captain Allen made himself comfortable.

"I've heard a great deal about you, sir, but we've hardly been acquainted," the captain said pleasantly.

Andrew smiled, wondering why he hated how polite and pleasant the captain was. "I am not sure what you could have heard of me, aside from my being rather green. I've just joined the season fresh from a home tour."

"A home tour! Fascinating. If I hadn't been off on the continent for quite another reason, I would have loved some leisure travel. Did you enjoy yourself?"

Andrew could not tell if the captain was trying to be patronizing or not, but he steeled himself to remain as outwardly pleasant and amicable as the captain was being. "Indeed, I did, sir. I must confess that while at Oxford my studies and interests were primarily focused on wildlife, so taking the time to identify and study our local fauna and that of Scotland, particularly the avian varieties, was quite enjoyable."

Captain Allen's expression grew warmer and he smiled humbly. "I can see that I could have much to learn from you, sir, and I hope I will have the opportunity to do so in the future."

Andrew nodded politely. *Can he possibly mean it?* "And I you, sir."

Captain Allen requested a drink from a footman and leaned back in his seat. "And what is it you would like to learn of me?" he asked. "How to ride?"

Andrew could not help but laugh. "That would certainly not harm anything. I enjoy riding but I tend to disgrace myself during hunts. I'm always distracted by the birds I identify, you see."

Captain Allen laughed warmly.

"No, I suppose I'd prefer advice from you about . . . well, about charming the young ladies," Andrew confessed, his cheeks flushing.

Captain Allen did not laugh, but he smiled and looked thoughtful. "I had thought to ask you the same," he said.

Andrew choked on the mouthful of tea he had just swallowed. "What?" he asked.

"Do not laugh at me, sir," Captain Allen said. "I'll confess I have a fair bit of experience taming lightskirts, but I have far less experience with respectable young ladies than I might like, and it's high time I looked at settling down now that I've sold my commission. I mean to aim for a career in parliament now that I've put the war behind me."

"That is an excellent plan," Andrew said honestly. "I think you'd do very well in parliament."

"Thank you. But I remain rather terrified about how to act around respectable young ladies, you see. I may look like I know what I am doing, but I am told it is *you* that most of the eligible young ladies are setting their caps at this season."

Andrew shook his head humbly. He had already heard this sort of gossip, of course, but it was still difficult for him to believe, feeling as green as he did.

"To be honest," Andrew finally said, "anything truly useful I've learned has been from Miss Louisa Grenfeld."

This really seemed to spark the captain's curiosity. "Indeed? She is quite the fine lady."

"Yes. She has given me lessons, more or less, on how to behave properly in society and following her advice has, in her words, made me 'all the rage.'"

The captain laughed. "I do not doubt it! I would wager we're the envy of the surrounding tables at this moment. Me, the war hero and you the most eligible bachelor in London! I'm told your fortune and estate is quite a tidy sum as well, sir."

"It is quite comfortable," Andrew confessed.

"This you also have to your advantage," Captain Allen said with a sigh. "I do have a fine house in town of my own, but I don't stand to inherit a country estate."

Andrew shrugged and took another sip of his tea. "You remain well-known as a favorite among the ladies."

"Do I? See? *This* is what I might need your help with. How is it you have your ear tuned to pick up all the latest *on-dit*? Brummell helps me a great deal with style, but he can only tell me so much gossip before even he tires of it."

Andrew chuckled. "I do all I can to avoid it, sir, and yet it seems to find me anyway, so I do not know if I'd be much help to you."

"Well, what sort of help did you want of me regarding ladies?"

Brougham sighed. He could feel himself letting his guard down. "How do you make your interest known so confidently?"

Captain Allen smiled curiously. "What do you mean?"

Andrew pressed forward. "Interest in a young lady, I mean. Some call it flirting."

Allen looked down for a moment, smiling to himself. "My method of learning was traditional—to start in the petticoat line fairly young. An Oxford man yourself, I'm sure you're familiar with the idea. You would be amazed at the confidence it can give you."

Andrew frowned. He wasn't sure what answer he had expected but passing time with ladies of questionable virtue was not it. Perhaps he ought not to have been surprised. "I see," he finally said. "No, I'm afraid that doesn't help me much."

"I know a place or two in London you might like to visit, and I could recommend a couple of ladies particularly skilled at helping the, erm . . . inexperienced gentleman."

Andrew shook his head resolutely, his ears hot. "No, I don't believe that is the answer. Not for me."

"Suit yourself. It is a good way to pass the time over the Christmas holiday—if you remain in London, that is."

"Where else would I be but London?"

"At your country estate, of course! If only I were lucky enough to have one, I'd host a party in the country myself. Nothing like a country house party."

"Is that so?" Andrew's curiosity was piqued. Life in the country had always seemed dull and placid. Their country estate was generally an escape from social gatherings, not an active excuse to have even more of them.

"Oh, indeed. I'm off to my brother's seat this Christmas. I've been told his wife has several young ladies she'd like me to meet, and I've already promised that I would."

Andrew frowned. He could not help but think of Miss Grenfeld and how disappointed she might be by this news.

Before Andrew could respond, Captain Allen saw an acquaintance he knew. "Ah, Lovell! Wonderful to see you, my friend. How have you been keeping?"

Andrew was all too happy for an excuse to bow out of the conversation. He had much to think about, and a long overdue visit to Miss Grenfeld he intended to make, especially now that he could be certain of who *wouldn't* be there.

Chapter Eighteen

December 14, 1813

When Andrew's carriage arrived at the Grenfeld abode in Park Street there were no other visitors present, and he sent up a small prayer of gratitude. He jogged up the steps two at a time and knocked. As soon as he was granted entrance to the drawing room and saw Miss Grenfeld seated in her usual place near the fire, her needlework in hand, he smiled. She looked surprised by his sudden appearance but very pleased, and at the look on her face, he quickened his step and broadened his smile.

"Miss Grenfeld," he said breathlessly, dropping a bow.

She and her aunt stood and greeted him with curtsies. "Mr. Brougham! What brings you by in such a hurry?" Miss Bickham asked.

Andrew laughed at the sight he must have presented. He had not even allowed the footman to remove his coat. He felt ridiculous, but he simply had to see her. It had been far too long, and an opportunity to speak with her without Captain Allen silently laughing at him was invaluable. Once they were all seated, he said, "I . . . only wanted to know what your plans were for the Christmas holiday, Miss Grenfeld."

Louisa stared at him for a moment before bursting into surprised laughter. Andrew's face turned red, but he silently waited for her to respond.

"I am sorry," she said, blinking, "I simply did not expect . . . I do not yet have plans for Christmas, no. I imagine that I will be at home with my father and aunt if nothing else presents itself. Perhaps we will go home to Kent. Father would like that."

"That sounds fine to me," Mr. Brougham said, then hastily backtracked. "What I mean is, that seems quite a fine thing. Your family is wonderful. I do not know what I had hoped to do, but a . . . friend of mine," he stumbled over the word. Perhaps that wasn't an entirely accurate way to describe his relationship to Captain Allen, but he couldn't exactly say *rival,* ". . . suggested that a house party is by far the best way to enjoy the season, and I had to come and see you immediately because I am not entirely certain I know what a house party is. Is it simply as it sounds?"

Louisa shared a glance with her aunt. "Of course," she said, "if one has an estate large enough to comfortably house several guests, they may make up a jolly private party for several days and have some great fun. I myself have only taken part in a few, but they remain happy memories."

"Would you like to have a house party with me for Christmas?" Andrew asked eagerly. "And your father and aunt, of course, if they wish. I confess I have no idea what the conventions are, but I had hoped you might guide me."

Louisa blinked a couple of times in surprise, but she and her aunt were both smiling. "I would be delighted," she said quickly, before pausing. Her face fell and she looked down at her lap. "However, I would hate to make the lady of the house uncomfortable."

Andrew frowned in confusion until he registered the fact that she was talking about his mother. "Oh, my mother is . . ." He pursed his lips and remembered his conversations with Henry about standing up for his own interests. "Well, it isn't her decision, is it? It's mine."

Louisa bit her lower lip and did not speak.

"Miss Grenfeld," Andrew said after long pause, "you know how I rely on you to guide me. I have never hosted an event of this nature, and I had hoped to make it a rather jolly party. I will *need* your help and guidance to make it a success."

The doubts in Louisa's eyes slowly faded and finally, she nodded. "I can help you make a guest list that even Lady Margaret will not find unexceptionable. You'll have to send out invitations right away if you are to get a response, however. This is shockingly late notice, you know."

Andrew grinned. "You're a capital friend, Miss Grenfeld. I've no idea what I would ever do without you."

Louisa was unable to hide her smile.

December 21, 1813

Less than a fortnight later, Louisa, Aunt Frances, and her father, who had not wanted to be left behind alone while Charlie spent Christmas with some of his Oxford friends, were on their way to Mr. Brougham's country estate for the Christmas holiday. They'd been blessed with a lack of snow, but the traveling temperatures were far from pleasant, and Louisa's own nerves kept her shivering even beneath the warm furs in their carriage.

It had been a whirlwind of work and planning to organize this little party, but in the end, it appeared they would have quite a fine turnout, in part because it was less than a week-long engagement. Louisa had been careful to invite two additional eligible bachelors whose company did them credit and six young ladies that even Lady Margaret would consider acceptable daughters-in-law. Planning the party had been a great deal of fun—more fun than Louisa had had in quite some time.

The Lady Virginia had been invited but was, unfortunately, unable to attend. Mr. Brougham had been careful to pass as much time with her as possible before leaving, which kept him in his mother's good graces. They had also submitted the entire guest list to that formidable lady for approval before sending out their invitations, despite Mr. Brougham's quiet grumblings that her approval shouldn't be necessary.

Louisa's concerns that Captain Allen had lost interest in her proved to be unfounded. He continued to visit her nearly every day before he left, and they even went for a drive in the park together in his high-perched sporting phaeton. Her impeccable reputation, breeding, and behavior on all other occasions rendered this little bit of adventurous behavior acceptable. Captain Allen had remained a great friend and companion, and after all of the parties and events he had accompanied her to, she was well aware of the nature of the rumors circulated about them.

She thought of these rumors as she watched the skeletal branches blow in the chilly wind outside the carriage window. They bothered her far more than she liked to admit. She was accustomed to being talked of but had hitherto been so resolutely unattached that she'd largely managed to avoid being the subject of matrimonial gossip until now. Her friends had informed her that there were already bets in place at White's for her to become engaged to either Mr. Brougham or Captain Allen before the end of the season. Apparently, a great deal of money had already been staked on this decision, and if she hadn't been so rattled by the speculative nature of the attention, she might have laughed at the absurd amount of money that followed her seemingly insignificant public decisions.

Perhaps if she had any idea how her story would end, or even quite how she *wanted* it to end, she might feel less rattled by the speculation, but she was as eager to see how events would unfold as anyone was. She fiddled with the slender gold chain about her neck while she busied her legs to remain warm beneath the furs. Which gentleman she most preferred still depended on the day.

Mr. Brougham had already been crossed off her list, but now that her disastrous flirting had been buried by several weeks and a recent rekindling of the friendship, she was considering adding it back again, despite the protective sentries around her heart and pride.

Captain Allen was naturally still a top contender for her affections. No man who dressed as well as he did, danced and laughed as charmingly as he did, and was such a delight to speak with could possibly *not* be a top contender. He was genial, kind, friendly, fashionable, and everything charming. Everywhere he went he was a perennial favorite, and even if a formidable matron was inclined to disapprove him after hearing tell of his many sporting exploits, a few minutes in his company always seemed to be enough to melt even the stoniest heart.

Captain Allen sent shivers of delight and excitement down her spine. He made her laugh. He made her feel beautiful, elegant, popular, and her position as the center of attention felt even more sure. They were a nearly perfect match, for what they each lacked in fortune they made up for in handsomeness, fashion, and respectability. And yet, whenever she was in Mr. Brougham's company, she did not think of Captain Allen at all.

Mr. Brougham's presence no longer made her feel overly nervous or excited, now that she had managed to categorize him neatly as a mere friend once more. The time they spent together was always pleasant. Their conversations were enjoyable and perfectly easy, and there was as much comfortable silence as there was chatter. Louisa never felt the slightest pressure to come up with something witty to say, and she knew she would be accepted by him regardless of what she wore or what her hair looked like. Mr. Brougham was a tranquil bastion from the minor barbs and dangers presented by public life.

She had initially been disappointed to be excluded from Captain Allen's Christmas holidays, but the more planning she and Mr. Brougham had done together, the more grateful she was that things had turned out exactly as they had. It was sure to be an interesting few days, even if his mother remained a thorn in her side. When Mr. Brougham's smiling gray-green eyes were trained on hers, it was difficult to fear something so far-removed and seemingly inconsequential as a disapproving mother.

But perhaps she ought not underestimate the woman.

Chapter Nineteen

December 21, 1813

Mr. Brougham glanced out the window of Hillside Manor for what seemed the thousandth time that morning. The house was ready, he had seen to every detail suggested to him by both Miss Grenfeld and his mother, and now there was nothing to do but eagerly await the arrival of his guests. He had been too agitated to work effectively on straightening the estate ledgers but had buried himself in one of his favorite tomes about birds and was in the act of adding a messy scrawl of marginalia when he saw the Grenfelds' carriage approach.

He hurried down the stairs and into the entry hall the instant he saw it, straightening his jacket nervously and recounting to himself all the various preparations that had already been made. The suite Louisa and her aunt would share had been prepared for days, as had those reserved for the other guests. All that was left for them to do was enjoy themselves.

As soon as Miss Grenfeld's carriage pulled up to the front of the house, he hurried down the portentous front steps with a smile, personally welcoming them to his home.

"Wonderful to see you again, sir!" her father said enthusiastically, pumping Andrew's arm up and down. Andrew smiled and returned the sentiment.

"You have some very impressive hunting grounds, Mr. Brougham, and I hope that our shooting party meets with some success!"

Andrew nodded, hoping that Mr. Grenfeld would not revise his glowing opinion of him after seeing what a poor hunting companion he made. He handed Miss Grenfeld and her aunt out of the carriage and shepherded his guests indoors where hot chocolate had been prepared for them and was waiting in the eastern sitting room.

His mother would not arrive from town until later that evening, so he had a brief respite to enjoy Miss Grenfeld's company while they awaited the arrival of the lady of the house and the other guests. He had carefully planned it this way, and he could only hope that she did not mind and could be persuaded to enjoy his company as much as he enjoyed hers.

December 22, 1813

Louisa sat up in bed and stretched. She had overestimated herself yesterday. They had, as planned, arrived at Hillside Manor in plenty of time to dress for a dinner, which was held promptly at the country hour of six o'clock. However, after a hearty meal, instead of organizing a game of cards as she had intended, she promptly fell asleep on a chaise lounge while waiting for the gentlemen to join them in the drawing room after their glasses of port. Aunt Frances had needed to wake her and usher her back to her chamber to be readied for bed before the gentlemen had even arrived.

She'd also slept for far longer than she was accustomed to in town, and yet she still woke at the unfashionably early hour of seven thirty. She was not sure what to do with herself and wondered what on earth had made her fall asleep so horribly early. It hadn't even been nine o'clock when her eyes had closed! She felt she was back in the nursery. What on earth was she to do until breakfast was served?

Her maid came in momentarily, humming cheerfully to herself. "Good morning, miss! Thought you might wake early. Did you sleep well?"

"Yes," she said, rather embarrassed. "Too well. I do not know how I could have slept so long!"

"You certainly seem to feel at home at Hillside Manor, miss."

Louisa's cheeks felt warm at this insinuation, but before she could respond, her maid continued, clucking her tongue. "But it's likely you were just exhausted from those town hours you keep."

"But *everyone* stays up late in town," Louisa insisted with a yawn.

"They sleep late, too, and I know *you* could never help rising before nine despite it all. Perhaps you were made for country hours!"

Louisa thought of how at ease she had felt in Brougham's cozy drawing room last evening, and how comfortable everything had been, from the meal to the general scent of the furniture to the cloudy gray hills visible from her bedroom window.

"Perhaps I was," she said wistfully.

"Breakfast is downstairs, miss, unless you'd prefer a tray."

Louisa smiled. She wasn't completely impervious to her maid's irrepressible cheer.

"Would you please dress me for the morning, then, Abby? Surely our host is not yet awake."

"Mr. Brougham? Why he's been down to the breakfast room this half-hour, miss!"

Louisa nearly choked in embarrassment. "He must think me the laziest woman on earth! Quickly, Abby! My blue morning dress!"

A record-breaking fifteen minutes later Louisa was descending the staircase, impeccably dressed and groomed, last evening's curls miraculously having largely survived the night. Mr. Brougham stood as soon as she entered the breakfast room. He set down the book he had been reading and gave a short bow.

"Miss Grenfeld. I hope you slept well?"

Louisa ignored the heat rising in her cheeks. "Very well, thank you," she said calmly, still embarrassed by her long night's sleep. She walked to the buffet and went to claim her usual breakfast of a scone with tea and milk, but in place of scones, there was an empty platter covered in scone crumbs and currants. She stared at the empty platter but collected herself after barely a moment had passed. "Well, Mr. Brougham, it would appear that we share a fondness for black currant scones!"

Mr. Brougham glanced up and leapt apologetically from his chair when he saw the empty tray, nearly dropping the book he was reading. "I am terribly sorry not to have saved one for you! I was reading and not keeping track of what I was eating, you see."

"It is no matter!" she said cheerfully, filling her plate with toast and jam, "for I am also quite fond of toast. However, I must admit I am impressed at your size, given what appears to be a hearty appetite."

Mr. Brougham laughed ruefully as he sat back down. "Yes! My mother curses my slenderness. She says it is all my father's fault that I will never have a fashionable figure."

Louisa shook her head as she sat down in the chair he offered. "But to be slender *is* quite fashionable now, sir!"

Mr. Brougham's face had gradually darkened to a reddish hue as they'd discussed his form. "I'm certain there are more interesting things we could speak of," he said, seating himself beside her. "How are you?"

Louisa took a large bite of toast and chewed thoughtfully to avoid his question. When she had swallowed, she said, "You must have been reading something very interesting as you breakfasted. Something from your library?"

"Yes I was, Miss Grenfeld. And I trust your room and accommodations were all agreeable? Please do not hesitate to discuss any suggested improvements with my housekeeper. Ask any of the maids or footmen to speak with her and she will attend to you right away—I have already asked her to do so."

Louisa's cheeks flushed. "Everything has been quite comfortable, thank you. I was very flattered to be included in the invitation."

She smiled and turned to continue eating as Mr. Brougham returned his attention to his reading. He became so absorbed that he did not even appear to notice when she stood, walked behind him, and leaned over his shoulder to examine the page he was looking at.

"I've seen a few of these," she said, pointing to an illustration of a bird on the page. "Mostly in the woods but once or twice on shrubs in the gardens. I think them quite pretty."

"Yes. The redpoll. Acanthis flammea. They are rather common, but I never tire of seeing them. Perhaps it's the cheerful red color on their heads."

She nodded. "Yes, and they chirp and squawk so sweetly. Even when snow rests on the ground, they are still fluttering about, adding life to the scenery."

He smiled and craned his neck to look up at her. "You seem to know rather more about birds than other young ladies do."

Louisa shrugged. "I do not think the natural world belongs only to men. Do you?"

He chuckled. "Of course not! I only meant that I've been teased for my interests before."

Louisa clucked her tongue. "I'm no bluestocking, but I applied myself in the schoolroom and am perfectly capable of discussing subjects other than weather, gossip, and the latest fashions."

Louisa's stomach twisted guiltily at the embarrassment on Mr. Brougham's face. He had made it clear from their first encounter that he was an enthusiastic scholar of avian wildlife, but were *her* enthusiasm for the same subject to be generally known, it may well ruin her carefully earned reputation as an arbiter of taste.

"Miss Grenfeld, would you like a brief tour of some of the grounds close to the house? I would be happy to show you some of my favorite places. The weather may be brisk, but we will not go far."

She perked up at the invitation. "I would like that very much, Mr. Brougham."

Andrew had been pleased to find himself on a hunt with only Mr. Grenfeld and his other male guests later that day. The ladies had been invited to join them but had all thankfully demurred due to the icy weather.

It was therefore easy to draw Mr. Grenfeld into a conversation as they rode through the woods, and Andrew was filled with relief that the man still seemed fond of him.

"Yes, indeed! Charlie is a capital young fellow—just what a young man ought to be. His older sister and his aunt make up for a great deal of what his mother's loss robbed him of. His address is good, and he applies himself as much to his studies as he does to his sporting endeavors."

Mr. Brougham nodded. "He sounds an excellent fellow. With an excellent elder sister to watch over him."

"Yes, and I've seen to it he doesn't er . . . *game away* his inheritance, the way so many rackety young men do."

Andrew smiled again. That had to have been the third or fourth time Mr. Grenfeld had used the word *rackety* in the conversation.

"And he's avoided the petticoat line, too," Mr. Grenfeld said. "I've high hopes he'll switch straight from his studies to making calf-eyes at eligible young ladies once he has his own seasons in town. To have both of my children married to fine individuals within the next few years would make me a very proud father indeed."

"What sort of individuals would you think fine companions to your children?" Mr. Brougham asked, struggling to remain casual.

Mr. Grenfeld shot him a brief look before glancing ahead down the road. "Well, if you recall what I told you before, *you* would be, sir!"

Andrew straightened in his saddle and held in the grin that threatened to spread across his cheeks. He struggled to think of an appropriate response. "I hope very much that Miss Grenfeld agrees with you."

"Are you saying you're interested in courting my daughter?"

Andrew took in a sharp breath. "I . . . yes. Yes, I am."

Mr. Grenfeld nodded, pleased at this revelation. "You would do very well for her. She's a good girl," he said, his bushy eyebrows resting low over his eyes. "But she's quite the, er . . . I don't know if you noticed, but she's quite a *social* creature, sir. She'd as lief attend even a dull party as stay at home with nothing to do. I'm sure she'd love nothing more than a house in town with her own ballroom."

Mr. Brougham frowned. He was well aware that Miss Grenfeld was fashionable, respected, and well-liked, but had not stopped to consider what effect that would have on a potential relationship. Were they ever to marry, would she be forever going off to social events, displeased to spend time with him alone? That certainly would not be the life he had imagined and hoped for.

His mind leapt back to his conversation with her on the frigid grounds earlier that morning. The way her brown eyes sparkled when she spoke of something that interested her, the way she hung on his every word even when he was speaking of birds. She had seemed fascinated and utterly delighted by his dovecote, and she had so sweetly cooed at and befriended one of his doves that he had nearly proposed marriage on the spot.

When Mr. Grenfeld glanced over at him, Andrew came to himself and quickly forged the response the older man likely hoped to hear. "I don't pretend to be an excellent host myself, sir, but if Miss Grenfeld were to become mistress of my household, she would have the resources to host plenty of balls and parties."

Even saying the words gave him a shiver of pleasure that made him feel guilty. What would Miss Grenfeld think about this conversation? Despite the curiosity that burned within him, Andrew carefully maneuvered the conversation toward different topics. He would never want to plan her life without her—he already knew what that felt like.

Chapter Twenty

December 22, 1813

Louisa stared into the mirror in her bedchamber, unseeing, her brush aimlessly passing through her thick auburn hair.

"What is the matter, Lou?" Aunt Frances asked, looking up from her novel.

Louisa sighed. "Nothing, Aunt. I am well." She forced a brief smile and crawled into her bed, shivering under her covers from the cold she'd earned by being still so long.

"It isn't nothing. You've been in an odd humor all day, sweet. What is bothering you?"

Louisa couldn't meet Aunt Frances's gaze but knew there was no sense in hiding her feelings from her. She would discover them sooner or later anyway. "I've just been . . . disappointed, I suppose."

"In what? Do you not like Hillside Manor? I think it's quite charming!"

"Yes, it is! Everything is perfection, from the way the house is so charmingly nestled in the ancient trees to the comfort of the furniture. It even smells nice! Yes, I like it very much, and it is far more tastefully decorated than I had dared hope it would be."

"Indeed. Did you see the chaise in the east sitting room?"

"The red one? Yes! I loved it too. I wonder where they found it. It's quite striking, and the blue tones of the room are very soothing."

"I did not think you cared about having a seat in the country."

Louisa smiled despite herself. "That was before I came here, Aunt Frances. I have no idea how else to describe what I feel aside from . . . *home.* It feels like home here. It is all so comfortable and delightfully well-appointed. And the dovecote! Simply beautiful."

Aunt Frances nodded, but then put away her book and came to sit expectantly on the bed near Louisa. When Louisa saw that Aunt Frances had returned to probing for her feelings, she laughed lightly. "I'm not unhappy. I am just not accustomed to . . . to reaching and failing to grasp my target," she admitted. "And I was embarrassed and disappointed when Mr. Brougham seemed immune to my clumsy charms all those weeks ago. I am not certain what I ought to do now. I wonder if it's too late, as you said it may be."

"I thought you had set your cap at the captain instead," Aunt Frances confessed.

Louisa could feel her cheeks color. "I do like the captain, I just . . . I think I prefer Mr. Brougham."

Aunt Frances's face grew stern. "You ought to choose between them sooner rather than later, Louisa."

"I know. But I hadn't dared think that I still had a chance with Mr. Brougham after my failed attempts at flirting. And his mother was just so . . ." She grimaced and gave a little sigh. "But planning this retreat, passing time with him, seeing his lovely home . . ." She shrugged. "If the two men are running a race for my affections, Mr. Brougham remains ahead."

Aunt Frances was thoughtful for a moment. "If I'm not mistaken, you've had your sights set on Brougham since the beginning of the season. Long before you were even aware that you did."

Louisa picked at the coverlet. "What makes you think so?"

"You offered him those silly tutoring lessons instead of politely informing him of your lack of interest in him, for one thing."

Louisa smiled to herself. "Those were quite diverting."

"And for all the talk that you were preparing him for another young lady, it seemed that you were molding him into your own perfect match."

Louisa chewed on her lower lip. "You may be right. There has always been something about him that makes me feel quite comfortable and safe, as if I am at home wherever he is. I would not like Hillside Manor half so much if he were not here. I am forever changing little things about myself to please various members of society—I am very good at it. But he has never made me feel the need to change myself. However, I am not sure why he would ever choose *me* when Lady Virginia is an option."

Aunt Frances's answering smile was warm. "Perhaps he feels the same way about you and the captain, Lou."

Louisa smiled at this, her spirits swelling with hope.

"Besides, I have seen the two of them together and saw no real affection on his part. And Lady Virginia has lately been entertaining the interest of Mr. Desford, from what I recall."

"Hmm. Terrible rake," Louisa said, wrinkling her nose and shaking her head.

Aunt Frances's gaze was cautious, however. "But it's as I suspected, Louisa. If it's true that you prefer Mr. Brougham to any other man, you will need to fight for him. Just like your mother fought for your father."

"*Fight* for him?" Louisa said.

"Of course!" Aunt Frances said. "This is no time to be preening and congratulating yourself on your social success, Louisa. It is a time for *action*. If what you have tried so far has not worked, you must try something new! Your mother certainly needed to fight for what *she* wanted."

"But she was fighting her own parents' disapproval. I will need to fight someone else's! I feel I have a decided disadvantage."

Aunt Frances tried to conceal a growing smile. "I am certain that you'll find a way to manage it. You always do somehow."

Louisa hid underneath her blankets with a moan. "But it would never work."

"You've hardly tried a thing!" Aunt Frances was exasperated. "What wouldn't work?"

Louisa threw her hands up. "I have nothing more to offer than I already have!" she said. "I have already shared my connections, my experience, and my influence with him. What else do I have to bargain with? I have nothing left to reveal. Besides, he appears to be getting by in society *quite* well without my assistance."

"You have *yourself*, Louisa. And he cares for you, if I am not mistaken. You had much better tell him how you feel."

Louisa thought back to Andrew's clumsy attempts to flirt with her early in the season. She had been embarrassed by them at the time, but after they had ceased, she realized that she ached for those same attentions now. *When had everything changed?*

"What if he does not still feel the same way?" Louisa voiced her fear.

Her aunt reached out and squeezed her hand. "Then you will find a way to heal and move forward. Either way, you haven't anything to lose but your pride, and you have more than enough of that, my dear."

Louisa nodded, feeling properly ashamed. "You are right."

She fiddled with her fingernails for a moment before looking back at her aunt. Frances was staring at the candle, her gray-tinged chestnut hair beneath a little lace cap, the skin about her mouth just barely beginning to soften with age. Even in her plain white nightgown she was lovely. Louisa could not help herself.

"Why do you not take your own advice, Aunt? Why do you not tell Father how you feel?"

Frances's mouth formed a grim line. "Louisa . . ." Her voice was a gentle warning.

"I am serious. If I am going to be married by the end of the season to one eligible bachelor or another, that will leave a path open for the two of you to—"

"Louisa!"

Louisa put up her hands. "All right. No more talk of you and Father. I think I know what I need to do. And even though it sounds like the worst thing in the world, I know I'd never forgive myself if I didn't try it."

"If you didn't try *what*?"

"I need to get on his mother's good side, no matter how frustrating or humiliating the process. Like you said, I'm far too proud. Then, once she no longer violently disapproves of me, I will speak to Brougham of my feelings."

Aunt Frances chuckled in surprise before reaching forward to hug Louisa. "That will be no small feat! Good luck, my darling. I am proud of you."

Louisa reveled in her aunt's embrace until her aunt said, "Take care not to wait *too* long before talking to Brougham about your feelings for him."

"I shan't."

"And let me know if you need my help."

"I certainly shall. Now let us go to sleep—I'm fagged!"

December 23, 1813

After a morning filled to bursting with pleasant conversation among the young ladies and a delicious luncheon with the entire party of young people gathered together and talking energetically, Louisa craved a short rest on her own. She and her aunt found their respite in the library, where a plushy window seat welcomed her, and she caught a glimpse of a little starling enjoying the last of the afternoon sunshine.

Louisa opened her notebook to a fresh page, took a sharpened pencil from her case, and set to drawing the little creature in perfect contentment. She worked on her drawing in silence until the bird flew away. Afterward, she continued adding remembered detail onto the feathers about the little bird's neck for some time.

They were interrupted by a knock at the door only a few minutes later, and Mr. Brougham peeked his head through the door. "Good afternoon, Miss Grenfeld. Miss Bickham. May I join you?"

Aunt Frances nodded a greeting. "How are you today, Mr. Brougham? Lovely to see you, as always."

He nodded and entered the room, taking a seat after a moment of hesitation, as he usually did. When his eye flitted to the sketchbook Louisa held, his eyes lit up.

"Do let me see what you are drawing, Miss Louisa. I would love to look at your work."

She hid the notebook behind her back, caught off guard. Her face felt hot. "I . . ." She was not sure why she felt suddenly vulnerable but could not think of a suitable reason not to show him. Hesitantly, she handed him the notebook.

He took it from her hands and examined the little bird. "Remarkable," he whispered. "A starling?"

She nodded, suddenly finding herself unable to meet his eyes. Her mind raced, trying to recall the initial reasons she hadn't wanted him to see her pictures of birds. She knew that, of all people, he would never tease her for them. But she'd kept them hidden from others since the first time one of her brother's friends had told her that her drawings were fit only to bore one from the pages of a scientific manual.

Mr. Brougham tore his eyes away from the picture. "The detail is incredible," he said almost reverently. "Where did you learn to draw like this?"

Aunt Frances's eyes twinkled. "She learned the basic principles of art from me, but that is all. The rest is from personal study, practice, and an extraordinary talent all her own."

It was so infrequent for Aunt Frances to glowingly praise Louisa in front of others that her face was flaming. "Aunt!" she said, shaking her head. "Really. Extraordinary talent, indeed."

"But it truly is!" Mr. Brougham declared. "Do you have any other pictures here?"

Louisa smiled, feeling gratified by his obvious admiration. She reached over to turn the pages of the notebook and show him a dove she had drawn the week before. He had at least as much effusive praise for that one, and immediately recognized the species and told her a detail or two about it. He turned the next page himself, without waiting for permission, and the next and the next.

Louisa could not stop smiling at the delight he seemed to take in her meaningless little sketches. It made her want to show him some of the oil paintings she had made specifically of birds—he had seen only her landscapes thus far.

When Mr. Brougham turned another page and, instead of finding a kitten or a bird or a pile of fruit, found a self-portrait of Louisa, she felt her face grow hot. He stared at the image. She had drawn it in her chamber a few weeks before while looking at the mirror by candlelight, her hair flowing about her shoulders.

"Is this you?" he asked quietly, looking up at her.

She quickly reached out to take the notebook from him. "Portraits never were my strong suit," she said.

"I disagree with you," he said. "I think it a very fine likeness. I would cherish that portrait if I were fortunate enough to own it."

She was too flattered and embarrassed to do more than smile and clutch the notebook to her chest for a moment. *He wanted a portrait of her!*

"Perhaps I can make a portrait for you," she finally said. "Would you like one of your mother?"

His smile instantly vanished, and he shook his head. "No, I would only want one of you, Miss Grenfeld."

Louisa's eyes widened and she bit her lip. Her heart was fluttering so quickly she wondered if he noticed.

His face flushed as he watched her reaction and he corrected himself. "Have I said something wrong, Miss Grenfeld? That's too forward, isn't it? I am not certain if that is something I am allowed to ask for or not."

Aunt Frances cleared her throat and they both glanced over. "Portraits are usually a privilege reserved for couples who are formally courting."

Mr. Brougham's blush intensified.

"Perhaps I could draw one of you instead?" Louisa asked hesitantly.

He frowned. "But I am nothing special to look at!"

"Nonsense! You are very handsome, sir."

"I'd sooner have that picture of the starling," he said stubbornly.

Louisa laughed. "Very well, then. I am not particularly good at drawing portraits in any case." She opened her notebook and pulled out the picture of the starling she had just drawn, handing it to Mr. Brougham without hesitation.

He took the paper reverently and gave her a bow of gratitude. "I don't know what to say, Miss Grenfeld! Thank you."

They soon fell into a comfortable conversation about pictures and birds, artwork and wildlife, until the sunlight faded and a servant came to ask Mr. Brougham about supper that evening. He hurried to attend to his other guests, leaving Louisa to flop back onto the window seat and sigh.

That evening had been reserved for music. It had been Miss Grenfeld's idea, so Andrew had high hopes that she would be participating, but thus far every single number had been performed by Miss Wrenn, a wealthy young heiress whom his mother seemed to like very much and who had been trained by a master in London. Her voice was rather heavy, with a vibrato that made his ears ring. She was clearly well-practiced, but if he was honest with himself, he vastly preferred Miss Grenfeld's lighter, less formal tone.

He didn't even have the pleasure of sitting next to Miss Grenfeld—that honor belonged to his mother. He frowned as he watched the pair of them. His mother was murmuring something to Miss Grenfeld and Miss Grenfeld's placid smile was beginning to look strained around the edges. He had to come to her rescue. *If only Miss Wrenn would stop singing . . .*

The song finally wound to a close and Mr. Brougham leapt to his feet and hurried to the pianoforte. "Miss Wrenn, I am so honored by the way you have generously favored us with your abundant talent! I would not have you injure your voice by having you sing too long, however. May I have a refreshment fetched for you?" He gestured to a footman, who immediately offered a cup of chamomile tea.

"Mr. Brougham, you really are too kind," Miss Wrenn simpered, batting her eyelashes at him. She couldn't have been older than perhaps seventeen or eighteen, and still had a few spots here and there. Andrew smiled uneasily as Miss Wrenn drank her tea and he excused himself as soon as he possibly could to attend to his other guests.

Miss Chapman and Miss Rowden appeared to be arguing politely about which of them should perform next, and he swiftly recognized that Miss Rowden was the younger and more petulant of the two, so he turned to Miss Chapman and asked her to favor them all with a song next. Miss Chapman seemed instantly gratified, and Miss Rowden capitulated quickly, turning to Andrew with a humble smile likely meant to ingratiate herself to him. He nodded and returned her smile.

But the next song was about to begin and still he had not been able to come to Miss Grenfeld's aid. His mother looked far less self-satisfied during Miss Chapman's number, however, and Miss Grenfeld's smile did not look so strained as it had before, so he allowed himself to relax.

It wasn't until all of the guests had left the music room and were milling about the sitting room after the performances were all finished that Andrew was finally able to approach Miss Grenfeld and make sure she was comfortable.

As soon as he walked toward her, however, his mother murmured something to Miss Grenfeld and Miss Grenfeld immediately hurried out of the room. Andrew tried to stop her, but she did not see him. *Is she upset?*

"Mother," he said with a frown.

"Andrew, darling! You have such delightfully talented friends and young ladies here! A very accomplished set of young ladies indeed."

Andrew nodded at her to both accept and dismiss her comment before asking in a low voice, "Did you say something to upset Miss Grenfeld, Mother?"

Annoyance—or was it embarrassment? —flashed in his mother's eyes before being quickly masked. "Of course not," she insisted. "She was merely being obliging and fetching my wrap that I left in the music room only a moment ago."

"You have her running errands for you?" Andrew asked, his temper flaring.

His mother sighed. "Not *errands*. I merely said I was rather chilled and said I wished I had my wrap from the music room. She was good enough to go and fetch it for me."

At that moment, Miss Grenfeld returned with the wrap, holding it out in just the right way for his mother to drape it artfully about her shoulders. "There," Miss Grenfeld said with a smile. "Is that better?"

"Indeed," his mother said.

Andrew stared at his mother and cleared his throat meaningfully.

"Thank you, Miss Grenfeld," Lady Margaret added begrudgingly, her cheeks pink.

His mother then turned to Miss Wrenn to obsequiously compliment her stunning performance. Andrew was relieved to finally find himself at liberty to speak with Miss Grenfeld for a moment. "Miss

Grenfeld," he said, "I do hope my mother was not treating you too badly." He spoke quietly enough that his words were for her alone.

She took a step closer to him and smiled back, making his heart pound a pleasantly jagged rhythm in his chest. "It is nice to speak with you again," was all she said.

Andrew frowned in his mother's direction before gently taking Miss Grenfeld's elbow to lead her to a quieter part of the room where they would not be overheard. "Indeed, Miss Grenfeld, you seemed mildly distressed at something my mother said. If she has said anything at all to offend you, I will speak with her about it directly."

Miss Grenfeld grimaced. "No! I . . . I would not have you do so. You cannot be unaware of how little your mother thinks of me. Any intervention on your part could potentially make it worse. I think you know that."

The truthfulness of this statement sent a jab of pain to Andrew's heart.

"Please do not worry on my account, though, Mr. Brougham," she said, collecting herself quickly. "I am perfectly comfortable, and you are an excellent host."

He frowned. "It has felt as though I have hardly been able to speak with you today. My other guests have occupied so much of my time and attention."

Even as he said this, he glanced up to see Miss Wrenn making her way toward him with a familiar predatory gleam in her eye. He sighed and was surprised to hear Miss Grenfeld let out a small giggle.

"I have been having a very pleasant time," she said. "And I am certain we will be able to steal a few moments to ourselves tomorrow."

He allowed himself only an instant to admire the smooth curve of Miss Grenfeld's cheek and the way her deep brown eyes caught the candlelight. He could feel his heart beating in his ears, and he swallowed. Before Miss Wrenn descended upon him, he had time only to lean forward and murmur into Miss Grenfeld's ear the words, "I cannot wait."

Chapter Twenty-One

December 24, 1813

The next day was Christmas Eve, and while feasting would follow in the evening and the following day, along with the singing of carols and perhaps some dancing and stories, the morning was clear for a winter's walk.

The entire party, with the exception of Louisa's father and Lady Margaret, expressed delight at the prospect of a sleigh ride through the snow, but there was little enough snow that it could not be done. The lane was also rather muddy, which caused Miss Wrenn, Miss Rowden, and others to cry off and remain in the house to avoid soiling their gowns. This left Miss Chapman, Mr. Brougham, Philip Palmer, Aunt Frances, and Louisa to set out in their warmest clothes to hunt for mistletoe in Mr. Brougham's woods.

Louisa was careful, at least while still within view of the house, to walk next to Mr. Palmer instead of Mr. Brougham, whom she silently encouraged to escort Miss Chapman instead. She was gratified that a subtle wrinkle of Brougham's forehead demonstrated his mild displeasure with the arrangement.

If her plan was to work, Lady Margaret could not think that she had any designs whatsoever on her son. Her insistence that he marry a young lady of superior birth or fortune had been made abundantly clear during Miss Wrenn's eternal serenade the evening before.

"Miss Wrenn is a very fine young lady," she had said, "and *so* accomplished! She would make a fine wife for any young man. Unlike . . . well, never mind."

The pointed exclusion of Louisa's virtues was not lost on her, and she saw she had far to go to ingratiate herself to the exacting woman. But Miss Grenfeld had not gotten as far as she had without learning to please others around her, including those who resisted being pleased. It would take time, but she was confident that eventually Lady Margaret could be made to see her in a positive light.

The fact that Philip Palmer was also on her list of potential suitors was not lost on her either. She was eager to get to know him better.

"Mr. Palmer! We have been introduced, of course, but I've never felt properly acquainted." She smiled in what she hoped was a flirtatious manner. "Tell me all about yourself."

His answering smile did not quite match hers, but he seemed cheerful enough. "I am at your command, Miss Grenfeld! I am not terribly interesting, though. Not like Brougham."

Louisa frowned. "Do not say so, Mr. Palmer! I am certain you are filled to bursting with admirable qualities I only wish I knew about. I feel that way about most people, don't you?"

He finally seemed to relax a little and he let out a chuckle. "That is what I love best about you, Miss Grenfeld—your determination to always see and bring out the best in others! If I may be frank, I've known some young ladies who have wanted to dislike you purely out of jealousy for your overwhelming popularity and even they were unable to do so. You are a friend to everyone, and I do hope I can always be a friend to you, as well."

Louisa was touched by this little ode, and she smiled warmly. "That is entirely too kind of you. Perhaps my bad qualities are simply harder for others to see, but I can assure you they are still there." She thought back with shame about her abominable pride and how it had spoiled things early on with Lady Margaret and Mr. Brougham, and she sighed.

"I do not think we always see things very clearly," he said, waxing philosophical. "Sometimes we see others as perfect and our own selves as grossly lacking, when the opposite is just as easily true. Sometimes we fail to see our own faults when we easily can see the faults of others. But I think your method is generally the best one."

"I have a method?" Louisa said, laughing. "I wasn't aware. Do tell me what my method is."

His answering laugh was infectious. "Your method is to see the very best in others around you *and* in yourself. Your confidence in yourself and in the goodness of others makes everything better. I know I, for one, appreciate it."

Warmth started in her chest and washed through her to her toes. His words were so kind and so well thought-out. Perhaps he ought to be higher on her list! They were hidden from the house by this point, walking through the gently dripping trees, avoiding puddles as they went. She turned to Mr. Palmer to say something she hoped would be witty and charming, but was interrupted.

"Miss Grenfeld, I . . ." He looked about them to see if the others could overhear, and he lowered his voice. "I would love to, as you say, become better acquainted with one another. However, I must tell you what it is that weighs most on my mind."

The conversation's suddenly serious turn was alarming. "Of course," she said.

"I have been very curious to know if you have any preference for my friend Brougham. You two would certainly make a fine match."

Louisa's heart skipped a beat. She had forgotten that Mr. Palmer and Mr. Brougham were already good friends, and was touched by Mr. Palmer's consideration of his friend's feelings. Looking about to be sure they would not be overheard, she decided that honesty was the best policy, especially when asked a direct question. "If he pursued me, I would receive his attentions very favorably," she said carefully.

Mr. Palmer's eyes lit. "I am certain those are his intentions," he said.

Louisa's heart began pounding. "Really?" she said. "I . . . that is, has he told you so?"

Mr. Palmer nodded, staring straight down the path ahead. "So, you see, although I am flattered to be so singled out, I must tell you that I could never pursue you if it would hurt a friend like Brougham."

Louisa was taken aback by his frankness, but was still riding the mild euphoria of learning from a friend that Brougham liked her.

"Thank you for telling me," she said quietly.

They walked on in silence for a while until Mr. Palmer said, "I do quite like going for walks, but winter is not my favorite season."

"Oh? Which season do you prefer?"

"All of the others!" he said genially, and they continued conversing and laughing easily for the next several minutes.

When Mr. Palmer spotted a cluster of mistletoe, he exclaimed. "Up there! I see some!"

Louisa hurried over and stared up at it. "It is quite high up there," she said, "I do not think we'll be able to reach it without a branch or a cane."

Mr. Palmer sized up the tree as though he were thinking of climbing it. "It's rather wet," he added. "So I think you're right." They began looking about for a branch they could use to extricate the mistletoe, giggling all the while like a pair of children.

Andrew was finding it difficult to keep up with what Miss Chapman was saying. When he failed to hear her yet again, after trying and failing to listen in on Miss Grenfeld's conversation with Philip Palmer, she grew visibly frustrated.

"I'm terribly sorry," he said, turning to her at once. "I was not listening, and you deserve a much better conversation partner!"

She seemed somewhat gratified by his apology, but she shook her head with a smile. "I think it fairly clear to see, sir, that there is another young lady here you would much prefer to walk with."

Andrew could feel himself blush, and he chastised himself for not concealing his true feelings better. "I am quite happy to walk with you, and I am honored you were able to join us for our celebrations. I meant to tell you last evening how very much I enjoyed your performance."

She smiled gratefully, but her gaze flickered up toward Miss Grenfeld. "Thank you. But I still think you would rather be walking with Miss Grenfeld."

Andrew considered lying to spare her feelings, but he did not have it in him. "Is it really so obvious?" he asked shamefacedly.

She laughed, and Andrew could recognize that she was indeed very pretty—perhaps the prettiest young lady in their party, by society's standards, but he had eyes only for Miss Grenfeld. "Indeed it is! How long have you liked her?" she asked.

"Since the moment we met," he confessed. "At a party. That was a few months ago now, and we've become good friends since then."

"You sound sad about this," Miss Chapman said.

"Not *sad*, exactly," he hedged.

"What is standing in your way, then?" she asked, gesturing toward Miss Grenfeld. "There has to be *something*."

Andrew grimaced. "This and that," he said, "Miss Grenfeld has another admirer at the moment. But it's mostly been my mother. She has determined Miss Grenfeld is not wealthy or titled enough for me."

Miss Chapman sighed and nodded understandingly. "I see. So if my father weren't a lord and I weren't set to inherit twenty thousand pounds, I might not have been invited."

Andrew's eyes widened at her frank surmisal of the situation, but he was determined to avoid giving offense. "My mother thinks you're a very accomplished, admirable young lady."

Miss Chapman looked ahead down the pathway and her eyes suddenly lit. "They've found some!" she said. "Up ahead. Look!" She started to run toward the others.

Andrew almost immediately spotted the telltale white berries of the mistletoe when they were pointed out, and saw that Miss Grenfeld was standing directly beneath it with a stick, trying to knock the berries down. He wasn't sure what came over him next, but he broke into a run, sprinting past Miss Chapman to arrive breathless at Miss Grenfeld's side. Before he could talk himself out of it, he wrapped an arm around her waist, pulled her close, and pressed a kiss to her surprised little mouth.

Her nose was ice-cold, but her lips were warm and soft against his, and she fit so perfectly into his arms that he never wanted to let go. He had never kissed anyone before, although he had wondered what it might be like to kiss Miss Grenfeld several times. It was even nicer than he'd thought it might be. He wished the kiss could last forever, but he pulled away almost as soon as it began, leaving Miss

Chapman laughing in surprise, Aunt Frances clearing her throat in stern disapproval, and Miss Grenfeld blushing furiously.

He reached up on tiptoe to pluck a single white berry from the bunch of mistletoe and tossed it away before grinning at Miss Grenfeld. "I am very sorry to take you by surprise, Miss Grenfeld, but you *were* standing beneath the mistletoe."

She tried very hard to scowl at him but failed miserably. She finally surrendered to a smile, laughed, and brought her hand up to brush self-consciously against her freshly kissed lips. "Mr. Brougham, *really*. That was quite shocking!"

He chuckled, his heart throbbing pleasantly against his ribs, and proceeded to help a laughing Philip Palmer gently remove the bunch of mistletoe from the tree and take it into the house.

The time passed too quickly. At their wonderful Christmas party Louisa ate and drank far too much and stayed up far too late. The next day she woke exhausted and was looking forward to a respite. She'd had a great deal of fun at the party the evening before, playing blind man's bluff, singing carols, and telling stories together around the fire. It had felt almost like being a child again, if it weren't for the pleasantly warm sensation in her heart every time she and Mr. Brougham looked at one another from across the room in the warm evening firelight.

She could not stop thinking of their kiss, though she knew that mistletoe kisses were granted an exception from the usual rules of society. It seemed that he still cared for her, despite all of his recent attentions to Lady Virginia, and Lady Margaret's obvious efforts to pair him off with various other eligible young ladies.

The end of the evening had come all too soon, and the morning even sooner. Louisa yawned again and began to droop in her chair while her maid styled her hair. She would much rather still be in bed, but she had promised to make herself useful to Lady Margaret, who was an early riser. She hurried down the steps to the breakfast room to meet the formidable lady.

"Good morning, madam," Louisa said.

"Good morning, my dear!" Lady Margaret said enthusiastically before she saw who had walked through the door. "Oh." Her face fell. "I had thought you were Miss Chapman. Good morning, Miss Grenfeld." Lady Margaret turned back to her breakfast and Louisa covered her grimace with a smile.

Louisa helped herself to a scone (the platter had overflowed with black currant scones every morning since the day Mr. Brougham had eaten them all) and sat beside her ladyship.

"What do you have planned for today, Lady Margaret?" Miss Grenfeld asked politely between bites.

"Not much at all," the lady said brusquely. "I had hoped to ask Miss Wrenn her advice on some fabrics for the breakfast room curtains. I am considering having them remade."

Louisa nodded. "You have very discerning taste, Lady Margaret. The house is exquisitely furnished."

Lady Margaret flushed, quite clearly very pleased by the compliment. Then she seemed to remember herself. "Thank you, Miss Grenfeld. I come from a long line of ladies with very discerning taste, and I flatter myself to have learned a great deal from them."

Louisa nodded politely. Since she had resigned herself to being pleasant to the lady no matter what, it had grown easier to maintain her composure when the lady said something mildly ridiculous. She probably would not have batted an eye even if the lady insulted her directly and called her out for a duel. Bolstering the lady's confidence would only help things in the long run.

"What colors are you considering?" Miss Grenfeld asked curiously.

Lady Margaret paused for a long while before answering. "Gold," she said. "With a floral pattern."

Louisa looked at the curtains as they presently stood, deep red brocade framing the iron gray morning sky outside. She nodded. "I think that could work very well in this room," she said. "It would certainly lend some cheer in here on dreary winter days."

"I think so too!" The lady cleared her throat, apparently chagrined to be caught treating Miss Grenfeld amicably. "That is . . . I thought it out carefully and it makes sense." She sipped resolutely from her tea while Miss Grenfeld smiled into her cup. Sometimes the smallest victories felt the most triumphant.

Chapter Twenty-Two

December 27, 1813

The entire party had committed to attending the same upcoming ball on Harley Street, so everyone left by ten o'clock in the morning to sleep in their own beds the evening before the ball. Miss Grenfeld had been the first to leave, and Andrew felt so much of his own energy leave with her that it was difficult to play the congenial host until the last guests were out the door. He collapsed onto his favorite chair as soon as they left, still having much to prepare before his own journey. He and his mother would have to stay the night at a posting house in order to arrive in London in time for the ball.

Andrew wouldn't have bothered hurrying back with his mother, but she desired an escort and he knew Miss Grenfeld would be there at the end of the long journey. He felt as though he hadn't managed to spend anywhere near enough time with her while she was visiting his home. Had it all been a waste of time?

When he sat up and looked at the end table nearest him, he was surprised to see a single folded and sealed piece of paper addressed to him. He picked it up with a curious frown. "Brougham," it said simply, in very elegant handwriting. A hopeful premonition hinted at what it was as he opened it, but he was still stunned by its contents.

It was a simple piece of paper, but the drawing on it surprised him with its complexity. It was himself, and although it was a fair likeness and could have been no other, it was far more flattering than any looking glass he'd seen. He stared at it for a long while, amazed at not only the attractiveness of the person in the image, but the expressiveness in the eyes, the emotion written on his face. It was of his profile, a slight smile playing at his lips, a glint in his eye as if he were laughing silently at something. He could not believe that much expression was possible to convey with merely a pencil and a piece of paper, and knew that only Miss Grenfeld could have done it.

When he noticed that there was a second piece of paper tucked behind the first, hope throbbed in his chest as he unfolded it.

It was her. But it was not the image of Miss Grenfeld he had seen in her notebook, with her hair cascading about her shoulders. In this image, her hair was decorously piled atop her head in the latest style and she was looking directly at the beholder of the image with a brave, amused, determined expression that once again amazed him.

"Such talent," he whispered. When he heard his mother outside the door, he swiftly folded the papers together and tucked them into the breast pocket of his jacket. He had never felt more in love with Miss Grenfeld than he did at that moment.

December 28, 1813

Louisa and her family had to drive late into the night to avoid staying at a posting house, but her little brother, Charlie, was coming for a short visit before returning to school and they wanted to see him first thing in the morning when they all awoke. Louisa had slept much of the carriage ride home, but when she had been awake, she had been gazing out the window at the low-slung moon peering through the clouds and wondering what Mr. Brougham had thought of her little note. She had worked hard on the drawing of him, trying two or three times before she was able to achieve a result she was pleased with. She had spent so long staring at his face she had memorized it and could picture him perfectly whenever she closed her eyes. She had considered leaving the self-portrait that he had so admired, but his mother would be angry enough were she to discover the more decorous picture she ultimately gave him.

She *did* prefer Mr. Brougham. She thought back to their brief, surprising kiss in the woods. She had been shocked to suddenly feel his lips against hers, but although it was unplanned, it was not at all unpleasant. His lips were so much softer than she would have guessed. His cheek and nose pressed against hers had felt wonderfully warm, solid, and *his*. She had felt, as she always did, utterly safe in his presence, and briefly wondered what she would have felt if Captain Allen had done the same thing. She had no way of truly knowing, but she suspected she would feel far more angry at the captain than she did at Mr. Brougham. Perhaps Brougham was so easy to forgive because it was difficult to imagine him ever sharing that sort of intimacy with another young lady. With Captain Allen it was regrettably easy to imagine—his reputation preceded him.

When she dreamed that night in her bed, it was of running through a sunny wood and a tangled maze of a mansion, Mr. Brougham hot on her heels and both of them laughing all the while until he caught her up in an embrace.

The next morning, she was awakened by an exuberant knock on her door.

"Wake up, Lou! I've been waiting and waiting!"

"Charlie! She's likely exhausted from the journey," she heard her aunt scold him outside the door.

"Well, you're awake enough, aren't you?" he told their aunt.

Louisa smiled as she yawned. "Charlie!" she said.

He knocked twice and popped his head through the door. "Lou!" he said. "It's good to see you!"

She huddled beneath her covers, trying and failing to scowl at him. "I am awake! I shall be out directly."

"Charlie, really!" Aunt Frances shooed him out of the room and he left after winking at Louisa and laughing.

Louisa hurried to dress herself for the day before running out of the room and into Charlie's arms. "It's so good to see you, Charlie!" she said.

He picked her up and twirled her once, as he had done ever since he had grown taller and stronger than she. She laughed. "How have you been?"

"Quite well! I've been enjoying my studies and having plenty of fun out of the nest and on my own. I have some fantastic friends, and it's all been a jolly good time."

"You will tell me *all* about it! Come, what would you like to do today? I am at your disposal."

"I would like to finally defeat you at chess! I've learned quite a few new tricks from my fellows and I even had a schoolmaster willing to sit down with me and teach me a move or two."

"I am certain I will lose in six moves, then," she teased, recalling the time she had done just that to him as children.

He laughed and they went down to the library to play together as soon as she had eaten breakfast. It was only about fifteen minutes into their game that he grew rather serious and stopped making jokes, his hand taking firm residence on his chin as he carefully thought through potential moves he could make.

"I've been told you have a few different suitors you're considering," he said, moving his knight to threaten her queen.

She moved the queen to capture the bishop he'd left unprotected, and he muttered a curse under his breath.

"There are a couple of gentlemen I've been considering more seriously than others."

"Captain Allen and Brougham, yes?"

"How did you know?"

"Aunt Frances," he said with a grin, and he triumphantly moved in to check her king. "Check."

Louisa shook her head and let out a long breath. "Are you acquainted with either of them?"

"I only know both of them by reputation."

"Indeed? And what have you heard?"

Louisa safely castled her king and Charlie scowled at the board for a long while before making another move. When he didn't respond immediately, she cleared her throat.

"Oh. Er . . . Captain Allen is a great gun—capital sportsman, war hero, all the crack! But he's also notorious for taking up with the petticoat line—you know, consorting with Paphians. It's been said he'd never let himself become a tenant for life, but I'd bet you could change his mind on that."

Louisa frowned. "Oh?"

"But I've heard less about Brougham. Quiet fellow. Perfectly respectable. Excellent academic record."

Louisa smiled at this. She was surprised by neither description, and was trying to decipher which gentleman her brother preferred without asking directly. She silently pondered her next three moves, and once she had several scenarios taken into account, moved her knight to check Charlie's king.

He gave a sharp intake of breath and stared at the board. His lips were in a thin line as he moved his king—his only option, and when her rook put him into checkmate just three moves later, he threw up his hands. "Not again!"

Louisa laughed. "You really have gotten much better, Charlie! But remember without you to play against I've been playing more against Father."

Charlie grumblingly acknowledged their father's ability and surveyed Louisa thoughtfully. "I like Brougham better for you, in case you couldn't tell."

Louisa smiled. "You always were a bit protective."

"Only as much as you were of me!"

"I appreciate it! Truly, I do. What is it that makes you think Brougham better?" she asked curiously. It had sounded like he had far more admiration for Captain Allen.

"He's not necessarily better, but I think he'd make a better husband from the sounds of things. Sturdy, respectable, *safe* . . ."

Louisa raised an eyebrow. "Yes, I suppose so. And Captain Allen is too rackety to make a good husband?"

Charlie chuckled at her use of their father's favorite word. "He just doesn't seem the marrying type to me. It's difficult to imagine a man like that slowing down enough to treat just one woman well for life."

Louisa sighed. "I've wondered about that myself."

"You like Brougham better, then, too?"

She nodded. "Yes, although not precisely for the reasons you mentioned. I like him because he's interesting to talk with, and we've become good friends. He's also taken my advice to heart and become quite the man about town himself. You might be surprised."

"I have heard that all the young ladies seem to be setting their caps at him this season, but you always were a bit competitive, Lou."

She laughed. "In some ways, I suppose."

"What of the captain?" he asked. "Does he treat you well?"

"Oh, very well, yes! He's charming, pleasant to spend time with, dashing, handsome, gallant, and he always makes me laugh."

Charlie frowned but raised his eyebrows, nodding thoughtfully. "It sounds as though it's going to be a difficult decision for you."

"It may not be a decision at all," she said, suddenly deflating. "After all, neither one of them has made an offer yet. Either of courtship or marriage."

"*Neither* has made a formal offer?" Charlie said incredulously.

Louisa could feel her cheeks warm. "I am doing what I can." She could not help feeling defensive. "I am not certain why they are dragging their feet."

He frowned. "Perhaps you can do better than either of them."

Louisa shook her head with a smile. "You do wonders for my self-confidence."

"And you tear mine to pieces," he said, gesturing hopelessly at the chess board. "But perhaps someday I will win against you."

They were interrupted then by a maid knocking at the library door. "You've a visitor, miss," she said.

Louisa stood. "Mr. Brougham?" she said hopefully.

"No, Captain Allen."

She frowned. Of course Mr. Brougham would not yet be back in London. He was still at his home in Suffolk for luncheon yesterday. But she had not expected the captain to return to town for another three or four days, either.

When she walked into the drawing room to meet him, he was standing at the window, staring out into the street with his hands clasped behind his back, tapping his foot.

"Captain Allen," she said softly. "How have you been?"

"Miss Grenfeld," he said, hastening over to take her hand and bow over it. "I hope you passed a pleasant holiday?" His face was surprisingly anxious.

"I did," she said, bemused by the way he was acting. "Did not you? What on earth is the matter?" she asked. "I had not expected to see you so soon."

He chuckled, coming to himself, and waited for her to be seated before sitting across from her. "I came back early," he said, "because I missed you. I had to see you again."

Louisa blinked in surprise. He was being unusually serious and unusually earnest. She had never seen him act in quite this way before.

"Oh," she said. "I had thought you would have a tolerable time at your brother's estate."

"So did I," he said. He scratched the back of his neck and looked away from her. "But I must be honest with you. My brother's primary motivation in inviting me was to allow me to meet several young women he thought well suited to me."

Louisa was not certain how to react. It sounded as though she were losing a suitor. She felt mild deflation at the thought of defeat, combined with relief at being able to focus more fully on winning over Mr. Brougham and his mother.

"And?" she finally asked.

He met her gaze head on. "And none of them compared to you, Louisa."

A shiver ran down her spine at his burning gaze and his use of her Christian name. "Oh?" she breathed.

He moved to sit next to her on the sofa and, after a moment of hesitation, took her hand in his. His hand was warm, clean, strong. Her heart was pounding in her ears and it was difficult to hear. She had no idea what to think.

His serious blue eyes met hers, and he smiled hesitantly. "Louisa, I think I have fallen in love with you."

Louisa took a deep breath and looked away. "I do not know what to say."

Captain Allen remained quiet for a long moment. "You needn't say anything now," he said. "I have no cause to hope for your immediate interest or acceptance, but I hope you will allow me to remain by your side while you think on it."

She looked up at him. He was indeed in earnest. There was no laughter, no joking in his eyes. He looked crestfallen at her response, but hopeful, humble, and determined. Her admiration of him was growing every second.

She hesitated. "I do like spending time with you, Captain Allen, but I cannot make any promises to you now."

He shook his head. "No, do not tell me so. Only tell me if there is *any* hope for me at all."

She surveyed him carefully. "What manner of hope?"

"Hope that one day I could make you mine."

She smiled despite herself at his frank confidence. He *was* a very attractive man. "There is hope," she finally said. "Although I cannot say how much."

He smiled back at her. "I will not smother you with my affections, Miss Grenfeld. I only ask for a fair opportunity to win your heart."

Louisa smiled and nodded. "That I can grant you," she said quietly, and he pressed a swift kiss to the back of her hand.

Chapter Twenty-Three

December 28, 1813

Despite being exhausted from a full day's travel, Andrew arrived at the ball on Harley Street early, eager to see Miss Grenfeld again. His jacket was not nearly so crisp as it perhaps ought to have been, and he was not entirely certain what his hair was doing. The face his valet had made when he was leaving the house had not inspired much confidence, but he could not be still and could not wait longer. He had to see her.

"Hello there!" Philip Palmer said. "It has been a *very* long time since I have seen you, old friend." There was a sarcastic twinkle in his eye, and Andrew could not help but laugh.

"Indeed. It appears you've arrived safely back in London. I trust your journey went well?"

"As well as twelve hours of road can be traversed," Philip said with a grimace. "How was yours?"

"I've only just returned," Andrew said, suddenly worried he would not be able to keep from yawning by the end of the night.

Philip chuckled. "Eager to see her again, then?"

Andrew turned to his friend. "It's that obvious?"

"Perhaps only to me."

"I do not know what to do," Andrew said, his throat feeling dry. "I had hoped you might be able to advise me."

"*Me*? What could I possibly know that you wouldn't?"

"What should I say to her? What if she . . . could I be misreading things? Seeing signs of hope that are not there? She established us firmly as mere friends only a few months ago. Should I continue to try for her, or do you think she'll reject me?"

"She'd be foolish to," Philip said. "Besides, I have a suspicion that she'd receive your attentions favorably if you offered them."

"You do? Why?"

"Because she told me so," Philip said with a smirk, clapping Andrew on the back. "Do not worry! The worst she can say is 'no,' and that at least leaves you free to mourn her and move on."

Andrew pondered this, wondering if it could possibly be as easy to 'mourn and move on' as Philip suggested. He shook his head. "You are right. I need to at least try," he said resolutely. "I am not certain what I have been waiting for."

Miss Grenfeld appeared a mere half hour later and was immediately pulled into first one conversation, then another. The moment the dancing began, she was whisked onto the floor by her first partner. Andrew frowned as he watched. Immediately after that dance her conversation was interrupted by Captain Allen, who remained close to her for the remainder of the evening. Each time the captain made her laugh felt like a knife in Andrew's ear. He felt powerless to change anything—like an invisible observer looking in on a party through a window from the cold street below.

When Lady Virginia arrived and his mother began urging him to go and speak with her, tired and gruff after a long day of travel, he had no strength to resist her, and spent most of the rest of the evening in Lady Virginia's company. He could not forever remain stiff and unpleasant, and he did think her a very nice, pretty sort of girl. However, there was something about her that made him feel distinctly uncomfortable, and he could not for the life of him decipher what it was.

The evening's enjoyment quickly faded, without his having the opportunity to speak with Miss Grenfeld even once. He would need to visit her soon—the very next morning could not be soon enough.

December 29, 1813

He did not take the time to stop for flowers. As soon as he awoke the next morning and Henry had attended to his appearance, he rushed out the door, the memories of her beautiful pencil drawings and of her dancing the evening away with Captain Allen taunting him every step of the way.

In record time, he was at her doorstep, knocking in what he hoped was not an impatient manner. He had to see her. When he was admitted into the drawing room, he was dismayed to see he was not her only visitor.

Captain Miles Allen was already there, looking resplendent in gray morning attire, his hair perfectly coiffed.

"Brougham! How are you doing, sir?" he asked. "Wonderful to see you." He looked directly at Andrew with a confident challenge in his eyes.

When Andrew looked at Miss Grenfeld, her eyes were on her shoes, but when she looked up, she smiled at him. "How do you do, Mr. Brougham?" She sounded almost shy.

A lump appeared in his throat. Was she reserved because she was embarrassed by his attentions? He shook this errant thought from his mind. If that were the case, why would she have drawn his portrait? Besides, Phillip had said that she *did* like him. He glanced at the captain. Apparently she liked him, too.

"I am well enough, thank you," he said pleasantly, taking a seat when invited to do so. He had no desire to directly challenge Captain Allen—he would almost certainly lose any competition if pitted against him. This was not a cheerful thought, and it was a struggle to keep a pleasant smile on his face.

He had to find a way to speak with her alone. But how?

"You are up quite early, sir," he said to Captain Allen.

The captain's smirk was subtle but undeniable. "We military men can never sleep when our quarry is near for the taking."

Louisa laughed at this. "Quarry? Do you take me for a pheasant, sir?"

Andrew smiled at her wit.

Captain Allen shook his head. "Never! You are far more handsome than a pheasant. Perhaps you are a fox."

Louisa rolled her eyes at this and shook her head, but the smile remained on her face as she turned to Andrew. "I hope your return journey was pleasant, sir. I had hoped to see you at last evening's ball but did not have the pleasure."

Andrew nodded. He was so nervous with the captain there that he thought he could hear his own heart beating. "I left rather early," he said. "It was indeed a long journey back to London, but it was well worth it to see you for even a few minutes."

He regretted his words almost as soon as they were out of his mouth, for an unmistakably competitive glint immediately appeared in Captain Allen's bright blue eyes.

"If it is such a pleasure to see Miss Grenfeld, I wonder that you did not take the trouble of greeting her yesterevening," he said.

Andrew frowned, but he ignored Captain Allen and spoke directly to Miss Grenfeld. "Miss Grenfeld knows I am not always swift to put myself forward and I never like to force my company on anyone who does not want it."

Her brow wrinkled in concern, but the captain replied almost immediately. "Very wise," he said, "not to assume your presence is desired."

Miss Grenfeld turned and stared at Captain Allen. "Captain, *really*! What a terrible thing to say."

The captain had the grace to look chastised and bowed briefly at Miss Grenfeld. "I apologize, Miss Grenfeld. Mr. Brougham. My attempts at humor are not always welcome."

Humor, Andrew thought. *Is that what gentlemen like him call it*?

"It would seem I am not welcome here, Miss Grenfeld," Andrew said, standing. "I would hate for my presence to cause any distress to you or to your guest."

"No," she said quickly. "Do not leave, Mr. Brougham. You've only just arrived!"

"Yes, stay," Captain Allen agreed. "I will behave. I promise."

Andrew did not quite believe this, but lowered himself slowly back into his seat. "I wanted to thank you, Miss Grenfeld," he said, "for the wonderful Christmas gift you gave me."

Her cheeks flushed prettily and she smiled. "I am glad you liked it."

"It was by far the best gift I've received this year. Perhaps the best gift I've ever been given. I shall treasure it always."

She said nothing, but glowed with pleasure, and it made Andrew feel warm to his toes to see her so happy. Captain Allen looked from one to the other and seemed at a loss of what to say. Andrew had learned more than enough from Miss Grenfeld about reading situations to see that Captain Allen was uncomfortable. This small moment was triumph enough for him. He had already enjoyed himself at the man's expense and had no desire to earn any real ire from him.

He turned to Captain Allen. "Well, Captain. It appears, sir, that you have no need for my advice on courtship, after all." It took every last effort to keep his face appropriately bland as he said this.

Captain Allen did not respond immediately, and Andrew dared only offer another minute or two of banal conversation before politely excusing himself. There was no sense in falling over himself with Allen there. A competitive footrace for a lady's affections seemed like a waste of time. Even if that were the way to Miss Grenfeld's heart (he doubted this), he would never win any race in which Captain Allen set the terms.

December 30, 1813

Louisa had had no idea what to think when the captain had shown up at her door at an unfashionably early hour the day before, and when Mr. Brougham had followed him not fifteen minutes later, she had been flummoxed. What could the pair of them have meant by it?

She understood Brougham well enough, she thought—he hadn't spoken with her at the ball, although he'd been in attendance. She had been quite busily engaged, so perhaps he had wanted to see her but had been unable to. But the captain . . . she could think of only one explanation for the captain's behavior.

He really was determined to win her, to have her for himself. It would seem he really was in love with her. She was flattered, but this realization also made her stomach twist with discomfort. She was still not entirely sure how she felt about the captain and was not at all certain she wanted to be hunted like a fox.

Louisa normally received so many morning visitors that she hardly had a chance to make any visits herself, but she needed to make one today. As soon as she was prepared for the day and the socially acceptable hour of ten-thirty had come about, she stepped into the waiting carriage and drove with her Aunt Frances to visit Lady Margaret.

She was not certain if Mr. Brougham would be home or not, and that was as she wanted it. If it appeared that she was seeking after him, it would make his mother uncomfortable. If the lady of the house was not in, she would simply leave. Even if Mr. Brougham begged them to stay for a visit and she had a socially acceptable chaperone . . . no. She would not stay. What was enjoyable in the short term would not benefit her larger designs.

She smiled nervously when she thought about her "designs." Louisa had narrowed her list of acceptable gentlemen from five to only three. The only man besides Mr. Brougham and Captain Allen that she still meant to become better acquainted with was Mr. Lucas Apperley. He had not yet come into his estate but he controlled a tolerable fortune already and was set to inherit upon his father's death. He was not bad looking, dressed fairly well, and spent most of his time with members of the Corinthian set. He was as tolerable an option as she was likely to find. She would almost certainly see him at Mrs. Whitmore's ball in mid-January.

January already? She shook her head. She still had plenty of time. The season wouldn't end until the London weather became almost unbearably hot, and then everyone would flee to Brighton. Those with a house there would, at any rate. She sighed. What she wouldn't give to spend a summer in Brighton by the seaside!

When they finally knocked on her esteemed ladyship's door and were led into the sitting room, Louisa's heart was pounding. She hoped she had the grace in reserve she would require to ingratiate herself to the lady. The door finally opened to admit none other than Mr. Brougham.

"Miss Grenfeld," he said in mild surprise. "How lovely to see you."

"I am here to visit your mother, if she is in," Louisa said quickly.

He frowned. "I believe she has gone out to conduct a few visits of her own."

"I see," Louisa said, disappointed. "Well, in that case I suppose I can leave one of my cards for her. Perhaps I can repeat the visit on another occasion."

Mr. Brougham paused and pursed his lips, one eyebrow twitching upward. "You came here only to visit . . . my mother?"

Louisa was not certain what Mr. Brougham was thinking or feeling but something about this question embarrassed her. She felt her cheeks grow hot. "Yes," she said. "I wanted her advice on . . . indoor wraps for formal affairs."

"I see," Mr. Brougham said slowly. "Yes, you are welcome to leave a card for her, but will you not stay and sit down a moment?"

Louisa shook her head. "You are too kind. We would not trespass on your hospitality."

Mr. Brougham opened his mouth, then closed it. He looked from Louisa to her aunt and back again. "I am always glad to see you and would be happy to have your company. I expect my mother to return home at any moment. However, if you must be going already, I will not stand in your way."

"I do not see anything amiss in remaining until your mother returns," Aunt Frances said, making herself comfortable on a sofa.

Louisa hesitated for a moment before sitting down next to her aunt. "I hope you've been well, sir."

"Indeed, I am quite well. And again, *thank you*. You really are very talented, Miss Grenfeld. If I could commission a whole gallery of artwork from you, I would do so in a heartbeat and it would never be enough."

"You gave Mr. Brougham one of your drawings, Louisa?" Aunt Frances asked curiously.

Louisa nodded shyly. "Yes, I drew a new one of Mr. Brougham's profile."

Mr. Brougham seemed to realize Louisa wanted to speak of the drawings no more, although he looked as though he were bursting with questions.

They spoke of mundane subjects in a pleasant manner until a few minutes later when someone entered the front door and began imperiously ordering the household staff about.

"Lady Margaret," Louisa murmured nervously.

This was all the warning there was before Lady Margaret charged into the room. When she saw Miss Grenfeld, her expression immediately soured. "What are you doing here?" she asked.

Louisa was taken aback by the woman's rudeness, but hardly missed a step. "I came to visit you, my lady. I sincerely hope that you have been well."

Lady Margaret digested this for a moment before settling onto a chair. "I am well," she finally said. "Thank you for the visit."

The conversation stumbled forward, lingering only briefly on each of the usual topics in turn—the weather (dull, gray, and rainy), upcoming social events (a bit of a dry spell, isn't it?), and some light gossip (I have it on good authority Mr. John Gisborne is likely to be very soon engaged!).

"Can I assist you in any way before I take my leave, my lady?" Louisa asked politely.

The lady dissented and the visit concluded nearly as awkwardly as it had begun.

"Well," Louisa said miserably, descending the steps toward the carriage. "That went about as well as I expected."

Chapter Twenty-Four

January 1, 1814

Andrew knew that talking to his mother about his intentions toward Miss Grenfeld was long overdue. Courtship was the only social subject that Miss Grenfeld had not taught Andrew much about, and because his own father wasn't alive to guide him, he had no one to advise him aside from his mother and his equally inexperienced friends. He was on his own.

Before standing up from his desk to seek out his mother, he opened the drawer where he kept Miss Grenfeld's portrait to sneak a quick glance at it for courage. It was not there. He frowned and looked carefully through the entire contents of the drawer. Then the next drawer. Then beneath each paper on his desk. Then he combed through the contents of each drawer, one by one, growing gradually more frantic as he searched fruitlessly for the drawings she'd given him.

His heart was throbbing in his chest and he felt mildly sick. He could not think of where else he could have put it, or where it could have disappeared to. The idea that his mother might have taken it occurred to him but was so repulsive that he dismissed it at first.

When no other ideas presented themselves, he frowned, and immediately stood and went to speak with his mother.

He was nervous, as he always was before a serious discussion with his mother. And it was for a good reason—he had nearly always been verbally strongarmed into capitulating to her will. She could stomach more tension than he could and was willing to allow discord to reign in their household until he submitted to her requests. But this time would be different. It *had* to be different.

His resolve grew with each step, as he remembered the various times his mother had manipulated him or concealed something from him. It had taken him four years to discover that his favorite old hunting dog when he was a child had not, in fact, run away. He rounded the corner and came face to face with her in her private sitting room.

"Oh!" she said. "Andrew, you frightened me, my dear. Is everything all right?" she asked innocently.

He knew he looked angry. He *felt* angry. "Mother, where is my drawing of Miss Grenfeld?"

His mother stared at him for a moment. "You had a drawing of Miss Grenfeld?" she finally asked. "Is that proper?"

Andrew narrowed his eyes. "Yes, I did. Where is it?"

"How should I know?" she asked. "But really, perhaps it is good that you mention it to me now, because that is not appropriate behavior for a young lady! Bestowing favors on a gentleman to whom she is not betrothed? Shameful."

"Mother, you're doing it much too brown," he said. "But now that *you* mention it, I had meant to inform you that I intend to propose marriage to Miss Grenfeld as soon as possible."

"B-b-but *why*?" she cried.

"Because I am in love with her!" he shouted.

They both stared at one another in silence while Andrew caught his breath again and tried to calm himself.

"Mother," he said, after regaining some composure, "This is . . . not precisely how I had imagined this conversation going."

She looked almost frightened at his sudden transformation, but he knew from the hard, stubborn look in her eyes that she would not give up easily. He was likely in for a week or more of monosyllabic conversations and frosty glares. But it was too late now. He had to soldier on.

"I need your advice," he finally said. "That is, I need advice from someone, and since you are my mother, I had hoped you might help me. But it appears I was wrong."

He turned around to leave, but she stopped him. "Wait," she said. "I am your mother and I love you! What advice are you seeking, Andrew?"

Andrew turned back toward her, but hesitated before saying, "I have already told you my intentions. I would like to court Miss Grenfeld."

"You're *certain* there are no other ladies who have caught your eye? Miss Wrenn, perhaps? Or Lady Virginia?"

He took a deep, calming breath. "No. I want to marry Miss Grenfeld."

His mother's wheedle faded, leaving behind a brisk tone. "I do not think that is a good idea," she said. "She is a tolerable sort of person, I suppose, but you can do far better."

Andrew did not speak for a moment. He was too irritated. At last he said, "You will not advise me in this, then?" He stood once more to leave.

"Wait." His mother hesitated, seemingly recognizing for the first time that her son had too much power and autonomy for her to control him anymore. Andrew might have cheered if he weren't still so apprehensive about what she may be planning.

He paused, raising an eyebrow and waiting for her to speak.

"I . . . am your mother," she said, "but you are of age. I cannot order you about, but I do hope you will consider my guidance."

This sounded reasonable enough. Andrew nodded, cautiously taking a seat in the chair opposite hers. She visibly relaxed.

"I do not think Miss Grenfeld is bad *ton*," she admitted, "although her giving you a portrait is a most scandalous thing to—"

Andrew cleared his throat.

"I was saying," his mother said quickly, "that although Miss Grenfeld is a tolerable choice, there are other young ladies you may do well to consider before making an offer to Miss Grenfeld."

Andrew thought about this. He knew his own mind well enough to know he did not want another young lady—especially not any of the young ladies his mother had seemed to like thus far. But his mother held a valuable bargaining chip in the form of her approval. He wasn't so foolish that he couldn't recognize the very great irritation an angry mother could be both to himself and his future bride, if he should be successful in his suit.

"Very well, Mother," he said.

She smiled disbelievingly. Before she could grow too hopeful, he spoke again.

"What must I do before you will give your full support to Miss Grenfeld's becoming the lady of my house?"

His mother's hopeful expression crumpled, and she scowled at Andrew. She pursed her lips thoughtfully for some time. "I think you ought to court another young lady," she said.

"And if I court another young lady before becoming engaged to Miss Grenfeld, will you be satisfied? Will you be kind to Miss Grenfeld and welcome her as my wife, should she accept my suit?"

"I . . . I think that if you court another young lady, you will quickly see that you can do better than Miss Grenfeld."

"Mother?" his voice held a warning.

"Yes, yes. I will. If I must."

"Excellent." Andrew chuckled. "I assume you would like to choose the lady that I court."

His mother nodded. "Lady Virginia," she said quickly.

Andrew frowned. There was no way a courtship with Lady Virginia could go unnoticed by the general *ton*, and especially not by Miss Grenfeld. But if it meant that his mother would drop her constant battle against his choice of a bride, it was worth a try. He could not very well remove his mother from his household without drawing the ire of polite society, and he naturally did not wish her ill—he knew her bullying nature was rooted in a place of great love. It was simply mistaken, and he had to make her see that.

"Very well," he said.

His mother's eyes widened, and a smile began to sprout.

"I will court Lady Virginia."

"Wonderful! At least two or three months would be more than sufficient. But you must not be forever visiting Miss Grenfeld if you are to do this. I expect an honest effort!"

Andrew closed his eyes and took a deep breath. The season would be nearly over by then. Spring might have arrived. He sighed. He could only hope he wouldn't be too late. "Very well. On one condition."

"Anything!" his mother said cheerfully.

"Give me back the portrait of Miss Grenfeld that you took."

Lady Margaret pursed her lips with displeasure but turned around and pulled the picture out of her dressing table's drawer, handing it to him without another word.

As Andrew turned and walked away from this conversation, he wondered who had come away the stronger from their argument. Only time would tell.

January 6, 1814

When Louisa noticed Brougham had been avoiding her, she was devastated. He had been spending more and more time with Lady Virginia. She had caught him staring at her longingly from across more than one crowded ballroom, but he had not asked her to dance. Something was definitely smoky about this sudden transformation, and the one most likely to know anything was Lady Margaret, so Louisa took the precaution of sending a note with the day and time of her intended visit to the lady, lest they should happen upon Brougham at home and invoke her ire.

When Louisa and Aunt Frances arrived, Lady Margaret was expecting them, and was wearing her finest morning gown. She nodded politely but coldly to Louisa and responded in monosyllables to each question she was asked.

Louisa carefully checked her inclination to panic by reminding herself that she kept a finger on the pulse of all the latest gossip, and there wasn't a shred of negative gossip about her. The lady's coldness had to reflect a personal disapproval, and Louisa simply couldn't allow the lady to continue to think that way of her.

So during their visit she smiled cheerfully, complimented Lady Margaret, let drop an innocent but tasty morsel of gossip, and by the time they left for home she could already see Lady Margaret beginning to thaw despite herself.

Not a single word was spoken about her son, except for Louisa and Aunt Frances complimenting the eligibility of Lady Virginia Sackville, whom he was currently courting. The words felt like a knife in her heart, but Louisa was nothing if not stubbornly hopeful. If Brougham did not come to her, he had to have a good reason why. Didn't he? The alternative was that he had actually begun to develop a *tendre* for Lady Virginia, but that thought was depressing enough that she refused to dwell upon it.

The visit ended before too long and Louisa promised to come and visit again the following week. The lady was clearly pleased by this and nodded genially.

As soon as the door closed behind her and she stepped into the carriage, Louisa sighed. "It's only a question of time now . . . Unless he truly cares for Virginia and she him. Then there's not much I can do, is there?"

Aunt Frances gave her a sympathetic look and patted her hand.

January 12, 1814

Andrew stood up straight, smiled, passed time at the club with his friends, and, above all, spent time with Lady Virginia. The longer he spent with her, the more determined he became that the two of them would never suit one another. Nevertheless, he did care for her and her welfare, and there were a couple of mysterious tidbits that made him want to unravel her secret, since he knew she had to have one.

He was careful to remain as dull and uninteresting as possible whenever he was with her, lest she change her mind and fall in love with him. Having the handsome, rakish Mr. Desford constantly hanging about her did not make this scenario seem likely, but Andrew did not like the man one jot.

He knew Captain Allen to be a good enough fellow, despite having had his share of dalliances. But he had no such faith in Mr. Desford. The man commanded little to no respect even among the more rakish circles and had been embroiled in enough scandal that Andrew did not feel comfortable leaving a young lady alone in his presence for one instant. Desford also had this way of looking down his nose at him and making Andrew feel about three feet tall, despite his being the taller of the two. He was glad to step away from Lady Virginia for a few minutes in a crowded ballroom when Desford was near her, but he did not like to see the man continually hanging about.

He had been thrilled when Frank's cousin Stephan had resurfaced after the Christmas and new year holidays, eager to make Lady Virginia's acquaintance. Stephan was determined to see her at the very next ball they were both invited to, and Andrew was eager to be of assistance, only he needed to be sure his mother was looking elsewhere when he introduced Lady Virginia to another gentleman. He did not want her to think he was doing anything whatsoever to sabotage his suit with that lady.

That evening, Desford had already claimed Lady Virginia's attention and Andrew was loathe to confront him. He was more than happy to speak with his other acquaintances while Desford amused himself for a few minutes, although he kept an eye on Lady Virginia to be sure she was not made to feel uncomfortable.

When Stephan arrived, however, Andrew found the courage to walk directly up to Desford and Lady Virginia and clear his throat. He made the introduction, and was both stunned and overjoyed to see the way Lady Virginia reacted to this country gentleman she'd supposedly just met. Her eyes lit from within and she had difficulty looking away from him. Andrew raised his eyebrows and smiled at Stephan, but he was heedlessly staring back at his lady.

There's clearly something happening here already, he thought gleefully to himself. For an instant, he let his imagination run away with him and smiled as he thought of Mr. Desford's humiliation at losing his quarry and the sweet freedom that an engagement between Lady Virginia and Stephan would offer to him.

Chapter Twenty-Five

January 16, 1814

It wasn't long after this ball that Andrew overheard the rumor that Lady Virginia had been seen walking in the park with that Desford rake, with hardly a chaperone to be seen. That likely did not make the duchess happy, and Andrew knew what it was to deal with an offended society matron as a mother. One had to tread lightly. He was determined to keep a more watchful eye on Lady Virginia that evening and not leave Mr. Desford to entertain her. He hoped that Stephan would be there to help with that instead.

He wondered if he would see Miss Grenfeld at the ball that evening. It had already been weeks since he'd spoken with her, and he was determined to choose his words carefully and keep the visit brief, so that he could reassure Miss Grenfeld of his affections for her while appeasing his mother by keeping his distance. She had been keeping a close eye on him.

It felt as though hardly any time had passed that evening before he lost track of Lady Virginia. He frowned. He had already seen her dancing with Desford that evening but would not put it past the man to whisk the lady away to ensnare her in a scandal. He walked as quickly as he could without raising suspicion, casting an eye down each hallway he saw until he caught a glimpse of Lady Virginia's coral and cream gown disappearing through a private doorway. His breath caught and he hurried to catch up with her, but before he could he heard Mr. Desford's telltale raucous laughter coming from the ballroom behind him.

He frowned down the hallway. If Lady Virginia was not with Desford, then whom was she with? He hurried to the door and listened carefully at it for a moment. He heard voices, and as he focused, he caught snatches of a conversation. If he wasn't mistaken, the voice sounded like it belonged to Stephan Grimsby.

"Harriet . . . dangerous! How did you . . . Apparently so! . . . but how could you!?"

He frowned. Was she in danger? He could not resist ducking down to listen to the conversation more clearly through the keyhole.

"The daughter of the duchess—the real Lady Virginia—is in confinement right now. My role is to prevent others from discovering the truth of her condition."

Andrew's mouth dropped open and his eyes bulged. He had suspected there was something odd and secretive about Lady Virginia, but he never would have guessed it was the lady herself! He'd never heard of such a scheme before, but there was no mistaking the voices behind the door.

If the real Lady Virginia were in confinement and this other lady—Harriet, he'd called her—was some sort of double, that explained a great deal. Naturally she would be submissive to the duchess, who more than likely had orchestrated the deception herself. Lady Virginia was likely well enough, and as long as his new friend Stephan Grimsby could be relied upon to care for Miss Harriet, he need not be terribly concerned with her wellbeing, either. But, it was more important than ever for her double to avoid exactly the sort of scandal that Desford tended to threaten those around him with. An untitled woman taking the place of one of London's most eligible young ladies was a vulnerable target indeed.

". . . She and I have become friends and companions, and I care very much about her. I cannot leave her now."

"What of the . . . father?" Stephan asked.

"No one is certain where he is," she said after a pause, "but she and I hope very much that he will return for her."

Someone passed by the hallway then and shot Andrew an odd look. He made a show of picking something up off the floor and straightened himself. He had to head back to the ballroom if he did not wish to arouse suspicion, but he had already heard more than enough to both puzzle him and lift his spirits.

The Lady Virginia he knew was apparently *not* the real Lady Virginia. And this Miss Harriet had said that the real Lady Virginia was with child and hoped the father would return for her! No marriage agreement forced upon him with either Harriet or the real Lady Virginia could possibly be valid, knowing what he knew now. This was a great relief to him, but he was stung with sympathy at the difficult situation both young ladies had found themselves in.

It was with this knowledge buoying his countenance that he caught a sudden glimpse of Miss Grenfeld across the dance floor with Captain Allen. He had no idea what gave him the courage, but he walked directly up to her, bowed, and asked her for the next dance, ignoring the captain completely. She blinked at him in surprise, but he did not miss the involuntary roses that bloomed in her cheeks, and he smiled at her.

She nodded, and when he whisked her onto the floor she said, "Should you not be dancing with Lady Virginia?"

He shrugged as best he could while completing the demanding steps of the dance. "I suppose so. But I would much rather be dancing with you."

She looked pleased despite herself but also flustered and confused. "Then, pray, if this is the case, why have you been avoiding me?"

He frowned. "I am sorry. It has to do with my mother and if you are patient and give me a bit more time I hope that—"

"*Time*? You haven't spoken to me in over two weeks!"

He did not answer immediately. She had every right to be angry with him. "I am sorry," he repeated, holding her eyes with his. "But I am doing all I can to make my way to your side. Please believe me."

She stared at him for a long moment. "Is it your mother?"

He nodded, relieved that she seemed to understand him so quickly. No one else understood and accepted him so completely as

Miss Grenfeld did. His stomach twisted nervously, remembering that he had no real reason, aside from Philip's word and her gift of those beautiful portraits, to believe that she would welcome his advances, let alone patiently wait for them to come. For now, he could only hope she would, with every fiber of his being. The dance wound to a close and he led her off the floor. When he was about to depart, he lifted her hand to his lips and pressed a swift kiss onto the back of it.

He then turned and walked away, hoping his mother had been engaged elsewhere and had not seen that exchange.

February 8, 1814

Louisa had never felt this way before. She normally felt as bubbly as champagne at a good party, but these days she was constantly looking about for Mr. Brougham, to see if he was with Lady Virginia. He almost always was. It had been weeks since she'd danced with him at the ball and he'd made his mysterious declaration.

He had said he was trying to make his way to her side, but now and then she wondered if he had succumbed to Lady Virginia's charms. The fire in his gaze that evening was enough to reassure her that the man who loved her artwork and wanted to spend every moment at her side was still there somewhere, and now and then he would catch her eye from across the room and she would suddenly feel they were the only two people present.

If he was staying away from her to appease his mother . . . she sighed. Given how hard she had been working at earning the respect and good opinion of the lady lately, she could easily believe poor Mr. Brougham had to work at least as hard. Lady Margaret was proving herself a truly formidable obstacle.

He may have full control over his future and fortunes, but he could not exactly cast off his mother. Like it or not, both of them had to find a gentle way to change the lady's mind, because forcing change upon her was unlikely to work. That was exactly what Louisa was doing by frequently visiting the lady while keeping her distance from Brougham. The more she sensed Lady Margaret relying on her opinions and guidance, the more confident she felt that her efforts to ingratiate herself to the woman could ultimately result in her approval.

Brougham's avoidance of her in some ways helped this plan, but it was still painful to her. Even with her legendary confidence it was difficult for her not to constantly wonder if he had changed his mind and heart toward her and if all was lost. She stared out the window and sighed. The sun had burst through the clouds, offering a bright yellow light in place of the usual diffused gray-white. She was seizing the opportunity to sketch the interesting shadows cast by the empty streetlamps. No birds adorned the bare, empty streets, and despite the bright sunshine, she felt drab inside. Drab all over.

The only bright spots were the frequent visits of Captain Allen, who would stay away for days on end only to eagerly return again with stories to tell of his exploits. He made her laugh, and he was handsome and thoughtful. When he was there it was easier to stop thinking of Brougham long enough to feel contented.

She also still entertained frequent visits from the elite ladies of the *ton*, but they failed to entertain her as they once had. Louisa caught a glimpse of Lady Bridlington hurrying up the road with her goddaughter in tow, and when she saw her go up the front steps, Louisa sat up straighter and set her drawing aside.

"Miss Grenfeld!" the lady said as soon as she entered, nearly beside herself, "have you heard that Mr. Brougham is courting Lady Virginia?"

Louisa was not sure how she managed to maintain a calm, politely interested expression at this bit of ancient gossip. "Oh?"

Lady Bridlington proceeded to tell her all about how they had been seen together at all the last few balls and parties, and how Lady Virginia hardly ever seemed to dance with anyone else! Louisa tried to react with enthusiasm, as she normally would for any juicy bit of gossip, but she already knew this particular *on-dit* all too well, and it did nothing to lift her spirits.

Aunt Frances looked up from her needlework long enough to attempt to steer the conversation onto other frivolous, pleasant subjects at which her ladyship excelled, and thankfully the lady did not stay long, but Louisa still sighed as soon as they were once more alone in the room.

"What is the matter, dear?" Aunt Frances asked.

Louisa looked up morosely. "I miss him."

"Captain Allen? He was just here yester—"

"No. Mr. Brougham."

"Ah." Aunt Frances sighed. "Well, Mrs. Allen seems to *love* you, darling. Perhaps it's best you consider her son more. He is, after all, very fashionable and handsome. And his house in town is lovely."

"It is. I was happy to see it last week at his mother's soiree. But he does not have a house in the country."

"Country houses are meaningless sources of expense and income if left unused! You've often said yourself you wish you could remain in London year-round."

"I have said that," she admitted. However, the more she thought of how lovely their quiet Christmas in the countryside with Mr. Brougham had been, the less attractive the thought of remaining forever in London became.

"Let yourself be happy, my dear. You are doing all you can as far as Brougham and his mother are concerned."

"Am I?" Louisa asked.

"*Yes*. Now, have you read Charlie's latest letter? It was so incredibly diverting!"

Louisa smiled, pleased to cast her mind onto a less troubling subject.

March 16, 1814

The weeks passed by like cartwheels caught in a muddy track, sucking and pulling with each turn, but they did pass. Andrew's courtship of Lady Virginia was painless, steady, and dull, and even his mother's enthusiasm for the subject was gradually beginning to wane.

"Yes, Lady Virginia is a very pleasant young woman." He cut into his meat and took a bite.

His mother proceeded to talk about what Lady Virginia's portion was likely to be, and how fine it would be for Andrew to take a seat in parliament with the influence of her esteemed father, the duke, until Andrew could take no more.

"Mother, has it been long enough yet?" he asked.

She looked confused. "Whatever do you mean?" she asked.

He assessed her with narrowed eyes until he realized it was possible she had genuinely forgotten the entire purpose of this experiment. "Have I courted Lady Virginia long enough to satisfy you?"

Her smile fled. "But you said yourself she's a very nice young woman."

"That does not mean I wish to marry her."

His mother pouted, and looked a bit overcome. "Perhaps if you only gave it a little longer . . ."

Andrew laughed in disbelief. "I cannot believe this," he said. "No, unfortunately I can," he corrected himself.

"Andrew!" his mother said. "Lady Virginia is a beautiful young lady with an exalted position in society! Her mother is eager to see her wed, and you are very fortunate that she considers you an excellent candidate."

The truth behind this statement hit him suddenly. Of *course* the duchess would want to see her daughter wed as soon as possible if she were with child! And he was a perfectly respectable, untitled gentleman who commanded relatively little attention in society. He was a perfect candidate to have an unwilling, indisposed bride of high status foisted upon him. But he saw no reason to expose the deception—provided he was able to escape the connection without doing so—her secret was safe with him. He frowned at his mother. "You promised me that if I seriously considered Lady Virginia and courted her at least two months—and I have—that you would lend your support to my proposed match with Miss Grenfeld."

His mother's mouth straightened with displeasure, and the lines about it became more pronounced than usual. "I truly think," she finally said, "that if you gave Lady Virginia more serious consideration, you would see that—"

Andrew stood abruptly. "I would see what?" he asked. "That she and I are perfect for one another? That I cannot possibly be happy with anyone but she?"

His mother frowned at him, and her cheeks were flushed. "Do not mock me, Andrew."

He shook his head. "Forgive me if it seemed that way, Mother." He took a moment to calm himself and walked around the table, bending down to meet her gaze with his. "But you promised. Have I not done enough to please you?"

His mother looked back down at her plate and said nothing.

After a moment, Andrew straightened and walked out of the room. He felt an overwhelming surge of disappointment. He had hoped that perhaps his mother could be reasoned with. Bargained with. But now that he saw there was no avoiding her disappointment no matter what he did, he had no intention of trying to do so any longer.

"What a pointless attempt. At least now I can visit Miss Grenfeld again and beg her to accept me in spite of my mother," he murmured to himself.

Chapter Twenty-Six

March 16, 1814

Louisa was adroitly entertaining several visitors when the captain arrived. He glanced into the room, grimaced at the assembled collection of guests, and, after sharing a brief glance with Louisa, left the room without saying anything.

She blinked a few times in confusion, and the din of chatter quieted until an awkward silence reigned. Louisa smiled and glanced about.

"Terribly sorry," she said. "Of what were we talking?"

The conversation started back up again, but one by one her current guests excused themselves. Barely fifteen minutes later, she was sitting alone in the drawing room once more, wondering why on earth the captain had not come in to greet her that morning. He had passed enough time with her at parties and balls for her to know he had no desire to keep his admiration of her a secret.

The door opened, and when she looked up she was surprised to see the captain again. She smiled at him, but there was something altogether different about his expression that day that made her a little nervous. He walked to Aunt Frances, murmured something to her, and Aunt Frances immediately stood and walked out the room, leaving Louisa with a smile and a wink.

Louisa's heart began to pound. There was only one explanation—the captain had requested a private audience with her.

Captain Allen remained standing, but he was fidgeting nervously, which was thoroughly unlike him. Louisa waited for him to address her, though it was difficult to sit still.

"Miss Grenfeld, I would like very much to call you Louisa."

She could hear her heartbeat in her ears, and her mouth was suddenly dry. She swallowed. "Very well," she said quietly.

He smiled, and walked over to sit next to her on the sofa. "My given name is Miles."

She took a deep breath. "I know . . . Miles."

He moistened his lips, seeming to find some confidence, and reached for one of her hands.

"Louisa, I have never made an attempt or confession of this nature, so forgive me if I do not know quite what to say." He paused briefly. "You are a remarkable young woman, and you are all I could desire in a wife. Will you make me the happiest man in London and consent to marry me?"

Louisa's eyes widened, and time suddenly seemed to be moving far too quickly. She only realized it was passing at all when she noticed his face begin to fall as he anxiously awaited her response.

"I . . . what an honor, Captain," she finally sputtered. "I . . . I had not expected such a declaration, and I must confess it has taken me by some surprise."

He frowned. "A surprise?"

It should not have been a surprise—he had been regularly visiting her for weeks and had openly admired her and remained by her side at parties. But still Louisa found herself completely overcome. To her dismay, her only urge in that moment was to run away. It was difficult for her to form a better response.

"Captain," she said haltingly, "I know that this is likely unusual, and disappointing to you, but may I have a few days to consider your proposal? It is indeed an honor! And I *am* very fond of you, but I am surprised by how frightening this decision is now that I am faced with it."

He squeezed her hand and forced a smile. He spoke after a long pause and a deep sigh. "Louisa, if you are half as terrified to answer as I have been to ask, I cannot begrudge you a bit more time."

She gave him a warm smile. "Thank you, Captain."

March 16, 1814

Andrew took care not to arrive empty-handed when he went to Park Street the next morning, bringing a bouquet of daffodils. He knew it was unlikely he would be her only visitor, as she seemed frequently bombarded with them, but he was disappointed to be treated to a view through the front window of Captain Allen clasping one of her hands in his and speaking earnestly to her. As soon as he entered, the captain grew silent and looked up at Mr. Brougham with a frown, then back to Miss Grenfeld, who slowly withdrew her hand from his.

"Very well, Miss Grenfeld. I will see you Tuesday next, when I return." He gave a slight bow to the both of them and whisked out of the room, leaving Miss Grenfeld flushed and uncomfortable.

"Mr. Brougham," she said, accepting the proffered flowers. "I had not expected . . . to see you today. Let me fetch my aunt. Do be seated!" She hurried away.

Andrew sat heavily on the nearest chair and dropped his face in his hands. Was he too late, then? Had the captain already made an offer and been accepted? He tried to keep his breath calm and steady. It would do no good for him to raise a fuss.

When Louisa and her aunt came back into the room, Andrew sat upright and smiled in what he hoped was a pleasant, tranquil manner.

"It is good to see you, Miss Grenfeld."

She smiled at him but said nothing.

He decided to get right to the point. "I saw you were having a private audience with Captain Allen. Am I to wish you happy?"

She hesitated before responding. "He did make me an offer, but I have told him I need a few days to supply a response. I would appreciate if this rumor did not spread."

Andrew was hurt that she felt the need to tell him this. "I would never share your secrets, Miss Grenfeld."

She smiled gratefully. "Thank you for the flowers."

He nodded, but felt foolish. Making pleasantly distracting conversation felt impossible right now. "Of course. What are . . . have you decided your answer to the captain?"

She bit her lip and glanced at her aunt as if in question. "I have not," she said.

Andrew's mind and heart raced. Was there a chance she was still open to an offer from him? Before he could stop himself, he blurted, "Would you consider marrying me instead, Miss Grenfeld?" He regretted the clumsy words almost as soon as they left his mouth.

Aunt France's eyes became wide and she froze with her needle just above her embroidery.

Louisa looked directly at him, her eyes shining, and her pink lips curved in a smile. "Certainly," she said quietly.

Euphoria blinded his vision as he stared at her in disbelief. "What?" he asked.

She nodded, smiling. "I would be a simpleton not to."

His daydreams abruptly stopped. "What do you mean?" he asked. A thousand thoughts were racing through his mind and not a single one of them made sense. Had he misunderstood what she'd said?

"You are the most eligible bachelor in London, after all," she said, smiling and speaking very quickly, "And who wouldn't want to be mistress of Hillside Manor? I had such a lovely time there with you."

He felt an apprehensive weight settle on his chest as his frenzied thoughts coalesced into a single terrifying idea—could his mother possibly have been right about Miss Grenfeld? Was she a calculating fortune hunter just like half the other young ladies in London? He did not want to believe it. He had thought there was something between them. Some real feelings. But the portraits!

"You . . . gave me your portrait," he said. "I had thought that indicated some affection on your part. Was I mistaken?"

Louisa sat up straighter. "Of course it was not without affection," she said.

"All right, affection. But not love?"

"I believe love is the product of many years."

"My niece has very tender feelings toward you, Mr. Brougham," Miss Bickham said quickly.

Andrew ignored her aunt. The sick feeling in the pit of his stomach was only growing. Were all his feelings for her only graciously received, then? Did she hold no true admiration for him? No preference for him over other gentlemen? He frowned. He had not expected to feel this way after having a proposal accepted.

"Will you reject the captain's proposal?" he asked.

"I . . ." She did not speak for a moment, but her moment of hesitation was long enough for him to lose his patience.

He stood abruptly. "Forgive me, Miss Grenfeld. You know that the last thing I want is to force my presence on those who do not wish it."

"But I do desire your company!" she exclaimed.

This was not at all how he had imagined a proposal to Miss Grenfeld would be. He felt humiliated, dejected, clumsy in everything he said. Raw, exposed . . .

His mind was spinning, and he felt sick. He had thought he might be able to take her in his arms and be able to steal an enthusiastically reciprocated kiss. He had dared to hope she would be happy. He had thought he would not feel such an utter fool finally expressing these thoughts that were so close to his heart.

She smiled at him, clearly not privy to what was happening in his mind.

"I must go. I will call again . . . soon," he finally said, standing and giving a quick bow before hurrying out of the room, leaving cries of "Wait, Mr. Brougham!" in his wake.

March 16, 1814

Aunt Frances came into Louisa's bedchamber that evening to find Louisa tucked into bed, staring listlessly at the ceiling.

"Louisa, what was that all about today?" her aunt said abruptly as soon as she sat down on the edge of Louisa's bed.

Louisa frowned and sat up. "What do you mean?"

"With Mr. Brougham. Are you not in love with him?"

Louisa fiddled with the end of her long braid. "I do not know," she confessed.

Aunt Frances groaned. "Then what has all of this fuss been about?" she said angrily. "Why do you not simply marry the captain?"

"Mr. Brougham would be bet—"

"Not this again, Louisa." Aunt Frances closed her eyes and massaged her temples. "Louisa, you *cannot* do this. It is bound to cause a scandal. Marriage proposals, like milk, spoil very quickly when left unanswered."

"I would rather marry Mr. Brougham," Louisa said quietly.

Aunt Frances gave her a hard look. "That is not quite enough, Louisa," she said. "Mr. Brougham appears to have been under the impression that you are in love with him, as he has quite the *tendre* for you. When you did not reciprocate as warmly as he hoped, he grew embarrassed. As any man is likely to!"

"What should I have done instead?"

"You ought to express the fullest extent of your feelings! From his perspective you care equally about him and the captain."

Louisa silently chewed on a fingernail.

Aunt Frances shook her head. "As a matter of fact, I think the captain might be laboring under this misapprehension as well. Louisa, why can you not know your own mind?"

A tear slipped down Louisa's cheek. "I do know my mind," she said bitterly. "And I know that I don't want to get married at all right now."

Aunt Frances's face did not soften. "I heard you say that you wanted to be mistress of Hillside Manor."

"Yes," Louisa said. "And I have been trying to secure Lady Margaret's good opinion, painful though that has proven itself."

Aunt Frances shook her head and sighed again. "An estate is not enough of a reason to marry someone, Lou. Do you love him?"

The tears began to fall faster. "I care for him," she said. "But the word *love*, Aunt. I am still learning the meaning of it. Young society ladies toss it about so easily, first for one gentleman and then another! I have always promised myself not to do so."

Aunt Frances raised an eyebrow. "I think on the eve of your engagement to a gentleman you might be forgiven for a bit of sensibility." Her sarcasm was biting. "Poor Mr. Brougham. Poor Captain

Allen! Honestly, Louisa, I had thought you would handle yourself better than this."

Louisa covered her face with her hands and was wracked with noisy, shuddering sobs so deep her chest ached with the pain and fear behind them.

Aunt Frances sighed and reached out to catch Louisa into a firm hug, holding her tightly until the shoulder of her nightdress was damp from Louisa's tears.

March 17, 1814

Andrew was surprised to be interrupted the following morning by the arrival of a visitor. His mother was out conducting her own visits, so he had not expected anyone to stop by for her. When he entered the drawing room to greet his guest, he was even more surprised to see Miss Bickham, Louisa's aunt, by herself, looking out the window with her hands clasped behind her back.

"Miss Bickham," he said.

She turned and greeted him with a polite nod.

"I was not . . . please, do be seated," he said awkwardly, waiting for her to take a chair before sitting down himself.

"Thank you," she said. "I apologize for coming by unannounced, but I could not see how I could possibly do justice to what I need to say in a letter."

Andrew's head was spinning. He'd hardly slept last night, tossing and turning with Louisa's words to him replaying over and over again. He had gone back and forth between being embarrassed and angry and feeling humbly determined to win Miss Grenfeld's hand no matter the cost. Could her aunt shed a little more light on her feelings?

"Is something the matter?" he asked.

Miss Bickham sighed. "Yes," she said. "I have long been aware of your tender attachment to my niece."

Andrew could feel his ears getting hot at this pronouncement, and his mouth formed a stubborn line. He cleared his throat. "And?"

"She prefers you to any other young man she's ever met."

Andrew's heart skipped but he frowned and waited for Miss Bickham to continue.

Miss Bickham chewed on her lower lip for a moment. "But she is frightened, sir."

Andrew nodded slowly. He had of late, for the first time, tasted these same fears. Was he waging this war for nothing? Would they even make one another happy? What if they grew tired of one another, or even grew to resent each other?

He had finally realized, after his bitter disappointment at Miss Grenfeld's unenthusiastic response, that he didn't want only to marry Miss Grenfeld; he wanted to be placed at the first priority in someone's life. And he had hoped it would be hers. For the first time, he was realizing that he would not be happy with any young lady unless she truly loved, respected, and appreciated him as much as he did her. If Louisa's feelings for him were just as tepid as Lady Virginia's, he would be equally miserable with either of them. He wanted to build a life around someone willing to do the same for him, and not a lady he would constantly have to strain to please. That sounded exhausting.

He felt a sudden caution appearing. Walls being erected around his heart. He'd heard talk of heartbreak in poems, songs, and plays, but he had never experienced it himself and he was dismayed to find that he was no exception to the rule. But he had to at least try as long as there was a chance things could go his way. He sighed heavily.

"Is there anything I can do to help her?" he asked quietly.

"I do not know," Miss Bickham admitted, "but I know that if she wanted to get married at all right now—I do not believe she truly does—that it would be to you, sir. And no one else."

He nodded, somewhat comforted by this thought. "I think I understand. Thank you for letting me know," he said.

Miss Grenfeld's aunt stood, and he stood with her, exchanging a bow with her before bidding her farewell and returning to his study, a strange, diabolical plan creeping onto the stage of his mind like a ghost.

Chapter Twenty-Seven

March 24, 1814
Mrs. Folsham's card party

"Miss Grenfeld!" Lady Margaret called.

Louisa hurried to her side. "What is it, Lady Margaret?"

"We need your advice, child. We are all in uproar! Mrs. Withinghall says that lavender is in no way the color of this season, but I have seen you wear it *so* becomingly that I think I might redecorate my town house's drawing room all in lavender. What do you think?"

Louisa held back her grimace. The Broughams' drawing room was already beautifully appointed, with soothing tones of green and warm hues of gold lending both comfort and sophistication in perfect balance. Lavender would in no way be a welcome addition.

"Lavender is, er . . . a very lovely color for a ball gown," she said carefully. "Especially the very pale shades. However, curtains and ball gowns are not one and the same, my lady, and I would personally recommend against lavender curtains and upholstery in your drawing room."

Lady Margaret's expression suddenly grew colder. "I suppose you already have better ideas for redecorating my home?"

Louisa was by no means blind to the insinuation in the woman's watery gray eyes. She frowned, willing her cheeks not to flush. "I would never presume to advise you unless you should wish it, my lady," she said stiffly.

Lady Margaret nodded approvingly and returned to her former conversation, but Louisa was still infuriated. She had been suffering mild barbs like this one for months, and she wasn't certain how much more her pride could take, especially given Mr. Brougham's sudden appearance, confusing proposal, and subsequent disappearance a few mornings before. He had not been back to visit since, and she wasn't certain what to make of it.

She took part in the conversation with Lady Margaret's friends, gave her opinion when it was asked of her, and smiled and nodded when called for, but on the inside, she was ever on her guard against Lady Margaret, and felt herself growing dangerously short-tempered with the woman.

"What young gentlemen have caught your eye this season, Miss Grenfeld?" Mrs. Folsham asked innocently.

Louisa could've slapped her, but instead she smiled demurely and looked away. "I would rather not say," she said evasively.

"Hmmph," said Lady Margaret. "She turned down my nephew easily enough. Let us hope she does not chase away *all* of her available prospects!"

Louisa could've bitten Lady Margaret's nose off, but she remained silent. She was grateful when Mrs. Withinghall came to her aid. "Isn't your nephew Alfred Stanley?" the woman said. "Well, I would worry if she *had* encouraged advances from him. He's a bit of a loose screw if I ever saw one!"

Lady Margaret's glare was fiery, aimed at Mrs. Withinghall before turning toward Louisa. Louisa could not imagine a better time to escape. "I beg your pardon," she said, giving each of the ladies a nod and holding back a bemused smile. "I have seen another friend I must greet."

She hurried away from the trio, taking a slow, calming breath as she sought the company of someone else she knew. She was relieved to see Mr. Brummell, though she couldn't help but be surprised at his attending an affair like this one. She was surprised he wasn't yawning.

"Brummell! So very good to see you," Louisa said, holding out her hand to him.

He smiled. "Louisa! So taste hasn't completely abandoned this little gathering, has it?" He bowed gallantly over her hand.

"I must confess I am surprised to see you here. Glad, but surprised." He chuckled. "Well, you see, I'm promised to Allen for the evening, and he practically begged me to make a brief appearance, knowing that you would be here."

She prickled a little, but hoped she managed to hide it well from her perceptive friend. "Oh, is Captain Allen here this evening?"

"He is, and is most eager to claim your attention, miss," a voice said over her shoulder.

She whirled about to see Captain Allen standing there, resplendent as ever in a perfectly fitted navy blue jacket with cream-colored breeches. "I did not see you there! How are you, sir?"

"Much better, now that I'm standing before the prettiest young lady in London," he said with a smile, taking her hand and raising it to his lips.

She fought a sigh. There was something about Captain Allen's compliments that always made her cringe, especially once she'd realized that they were completely sincere. They chatted for a few minutes before she was able to excuse herself and greet the rest of the other guests. There were not many of her close acquaintance at this party—most in attendance were of Lady Margaret's set, and of a more advanced age. She had rarely felt so alone. Aunt Frances was speaking with a friend of hers at the far end of the room, but Louisa hoped she might be prevailed upon to leave early. Louisa was already tired.

"It seems there *is* a young gentleman who's caught your eye after all," Lady Margaret sang, almost gleefully when Louisa passed her way. "And a military captain with a reputation like his," she clucked her tongue. "You might want to look out to be sure your good name is not tainted."

Louisa had had enough. "Lady Margaret, that sort of ill-meant advice is precisely the sort I *don't* need from you."

Lady Margaret puffed up like an irritated hen. "How *dare* you speak to me this way!"

Louisa shook her head, her nostrils flaring. "I have no desire to toss about insults with you, my lady, but you have made it abundantly clear that you neither need nor desire further assistance from me. I will no longer burden you with my presence or frequent visits, never fear."

She dropped a quick, shallow curtsy and shot Aunt Frances a meaningful look before heading toward the door to request that their carriage be brought around at once. Not five minutes later, she and Aunt Frances were riding home, wrapped in furs and shivering—Frances with cold and Louisa with anger.

It took a moment for Louisa to notice that Aunt Frances was smiling cheerfully.

Louisa groaned. "Why do you smile, Aunt? You can have no idea what has just passed between Lady Margaret and myself."

"Actually," her aunt said, "I have a very good idea. I wish you could have seen the look on Lady Margaret's face when Mrs. Folsham and Mrs. Withinghall both scolded her for scaring you away and losing the opportunity of having you for a daughter-in-law!"

March 25, 1814

When Louisa paused on the threshold of her father's study, she saw he was peering down at a ledger over a pair of spectacles. He made a mark or two, closed the book, and sat back in his seat.

Louisa smiled. "Hello, Papa."

He glanced up, surprised. "Louisa. Come in, my dear."

Louisa entered and took a seat in a soft chair not far from his desk.

"What is on your mind today?" he asked cheerfully. "I have just finished going over my accounts and am now at my leisure."

"I am happy for you," Louisa said. "But I am . . . going to be frank with you, Father. Things have been a bit difficult for me lately."

"Difficult?"

She nodded. "Yes."

"Is this because of Captain Allen's proposal?"

"In part," she said.

"Have you answered him yet?" her father asked.

She shook her head, staring down at her hands.

Her father nodded, looking away. "I gave him my consent because he is a decent man with a decent fortune. A house in town—just as you wanted. And he seems to have plenty of address and conversation, which I know to be important to you."

Louisa smiled. "But you don't like him."

Mr. Grenfeld shook his head. "No, I do not. I could *grow* to like him, in time, but he would not be my first choice for you."

"And whom would you choose for me if you could?"

Louisa's tone was playful, but her father's expression was serious. "No, Louisa. I am not such a fool as to do that. If what I want is your future happiness, I doubt I would succeed in securing it by taking matters into my own hands. The pair of you chastised me enough earlier this season. This decision is yours to make."

Louisa sighed.

Mr. Grenfeld frowned curiously. "But may I ask what became of Mr. Brougham? I cannot seem to keep track of the man. One moment it seems he practically lives here and the next it seems he's abandoned us entirely. Is he here now, or gone?"

Louisa chuckled halfheartedly. "I do not know. He . . . expressed an interest in me. Just after Captain Allen's proposal."

"He did?" her father sat forward in his chair, trying not to look too excited and failing miserably.

"Yes. And I encouraged him, I think, but something changed, and he suddenly seemed unhappy and I worry he has since changed his mind. I do not know if he will return anytime soon. Perhaps I should have shared more of my feelings for him."

"Your feelings, my dear? Does this mean you have feelings for Mr. Brougham?"

Louisa could feel heat rising in her chest and cheeks. "Yes."

"Excellent!" her father said.

Louisa frowned. "Excellent?"

"Yes, he told me he was interested in courting you when we hunted at Hillside Manor. Seemed quite taken with you, Louisa. Assured me he could provide well for you."

Louisa was taken aback. "You two spoke of me again?" she asked, feeling betrayed.

Her father grew defensive. "Only when it came up in conversation."

Louisa massaged the bridge of her nose. She felt quite uncomfortable.

"What is the matter, my dear?" he asked. "Have I bungled things again somehow?"

Louisa shook her head. "I do not know," she said. "I do not know why he left in such a hurry, or what I ought to have done differently. I do not want to lose *both* my suitors for my inaction, but I do not know what to do."

Her father's forehead was crinkled with concern. "I did warn you, my dear, that failing to choose is a choice unto itself."

Her mouth opened, then closed. "I think I am beginning to understand what you meant."

"It sounds as though you would prefer to marry Mr. Brougham," her father said. "Ought I to go and visit him?"

"No!" Louisa said hastily. "No, no, Father, that . . . won't be necessary. I am certain he will come back again soon. I *hope* he will come back again. And in the meantime, his mother likely wouldn't take kindly to a visit regarding me."

Mr. Grenfeld's brow was deeply furrowed by his frown. "What do you—"

"Let us speak no more of me," Louisa said quickly. "What of you, Father? What are you going to do if you finally achieve your dream of having me wed and out of your home?"

Mr. Grenfeld smiled, but there was real concern behind his eyes. "I suppose I . . . will go back to Thorngrove," he answered. "Why?"

"Alone?"

"Alone? What do you . . . ah." A light seemed to flicker behind her father's eyes and the shine went out of them. "You mean Frances."

"I do," Louisa said. "Frances cannot remain in your home without a woman to care for and interact with. You know this."

Her father's face suddenly appeared much older. "I had realized that," he said quietly. "But I have been trying not to dwell on it."

"Why do you not marry her, Father?" Louisa asked gently.

His expression grew stormy. "Louisa you know that is out of the question. We are related by marriage."

"But not by blood," she insisted. "It is a silly law and I have told you so before. Besides, it has certainly been done."

Heavy lines etched themselves onto her father's face. "Louisa . . ." he said. "It would be a voidable marriage."

Louisa's eyes narrowed skeptically. "And who would void it, Father? I cannot think of a single person who might stand to gain from doing so. You already have an heir, and uniting yourself with Aunt Frances would not change that. Besides, Aunt Frances has been the only mother Charlie has known. He would never begrudge her such a place in our family, and no one else could stand to gain from doing so."

"The scandal, Louisa, would harm you both."

"It may harm my prospects," she admitted, "but not if I am already married. And I'm sure it would long cease to be a subject of interest by the time Charlie is seeking a wife. He has years yet."

Mr. Grenfeld closed his eyes, removed his glasses, and placed his forehead in his hand. He was silent for a long while, and Louisa held her breath as she waited, knowing that if her argument was to have any effect she had to wait patiently.

A few minutes later, he looked up. "Louisa, you are very stubborn, but you have made your point."

A smile stole onto her face before she could stop it.

"But," he continued sternly, "I do not want you to speak of this matter again until after your wedding day."

"Or what, Father?" she teased.

His eye twinkled. "Or I guarantee that I will find some way of embarrassing you at the next ball you attend."

Louisa bit her lip. She knew him too well to think this was an empty threat. With a smile, she stood and walked over to press a kiss on her father's forehead. "Fair enough."

Chapter Twenty-Eight

March 26, 1814

Once dressed that morning, Andrew jogged down the stairs and toward his study, near the dining room on the ground floor. But when he passed the drawing room door, he heard voices. He assumed they were just visitors for his mother. However, when he overheard the name "Grenfeld" as he passed by, he paused abruptly and stood still, listening.

"Whyever wouldn't you want Miss Grenfeld for a daughter-in-law?" one of the ladies was saying.

"Yes, why wouldn't you?" echoed another. "Lady Virginia is of noble birth, to be sure, but she's such a shy little thing! Miss Grenfeld would make a far better hostess, and her connections are at least as good."

He did not hear his mother speaking, and he could only imagine she was utterly dumbfounded. He grinned to himself.

"I suppose there's the fortune to consider, however," the first lady said. "Lady Virginia has a far larger portion than Miss Grenfeld does."

"Indeed," the second lady agreed, "but I had thought that Mr. Brougham's affairs were well in order and he could afford to marry whom he pleased."

"Perhaps he *prefers* Lady Virginia," the first lady said.

His mother still had not responded, and he could only imagine how furious and embarrassed she was feeling right now.

"Yes, does he?" asked the second lady.

There was a pause as they waited for Lady Margaret's response. "I am not certain whom he prefers," he heard his mother say. "I will have to speak with him."

Andrew ground his teeth and narrowed his eyes.

"Yes, but regardless, you ought to apologize to Miss Grenfeld straight away. You were quite rude to her, you know. You are fortunate that you two were able to visit so often up until now."

Andrew's mind was racing as he listened to the women's chatter. Miss Grenfeld had been visiting his mother all this time? Despite the awful way she'd been treated at Christmas? Why on earth would she? Perhaps she really did care for him. But then why would she continue to encourage the captain's attentions?

"She is indeed a valuable friend, especially considering she is still a single young lady. Encourage your son to pay court to her as soon as possible!" the lady said. "She would likely be far better for his fortunes."

"Better?" his mother said, "but you already said her fortune is nothing to Lady Virginia's!"

The second lady spoke again. "Perhaps not, but Miss Grenfeld has come as far as she has on quite a moderate sum!" she said. "I have heard it said that she spends less than a thousand pounds per year on new gowns. My sister's daughter Annabelle insists that less than two thousand pounds a season will have her looking beggarly, and she does not present herself half so well as Miss Grenfeld does."

"I've heard she spends less than *five hundred* pounds per season," the first lady said. "And I have it on good authority, as I've finally managed to find one of her dressmakers!"

"Oh, do tell me where I might find her!"

"Ladies, please," Lady Margaret said. "I can hardly control my grown son, can I? His will is his own."

Andrew shook his head disbelievingly at his mother's nerve. She certainly seemed to think she could control him in private. He grew tired of the conversation. He had been amused at first to hear his mother knocked down a peg, but he was in no humor to obey society's every whim. The thought of being tethered to Miss Grenfeld if she did not wish to marry him, or worse—only desired to marry him for his worldly assets, was miserable.

He fumed into his office and began going through the estate ledgers with a vengeance, settling shopkeeper accounts and going over household expenditures with violent scratches of his pen on the page.

He was still working at it busily a half-hour later when he heard his mother bidding her guests farewell in the hall. It was not until silence had reigned for several minutes that he finally heard a hesitant knock on the door.

He did not respond immediately, but knew his mother would simply knock until he was willing to let her in. "Yes?" he finally said.

His mother opened the door and shyly peered around the frame. "Might I speak to you for a few minutes, my dear?"

Andrew looked up at her and sighed. "Very well," he said, setting down his pen.

She sat down in the chair opposite his desk. "We haven't talked in a few days," she said quietly.

He frowned at her. The last time they had spoken she had withdrawn from their silly agreement about his courting Lady Virginia. He acknowledged her, but did not speak. He had learned the art of stubborn silence from her.

At last, she sighed. "I wanted to ask you how your courtship with Lady Virginia is coming along."

"We are still courting, as you wished," he said tightly.

"Yes. And I have every reason to believe a proposal would be very welcome."

Andrew forced himself to relax. "I will keep that in mind." His mother had almost certainly heard that from Her Grace, and not from Virginia. Virginia was, after all, not exactly herself at the moment. He highly doubted his mother was even aware of the deception, and he wasn't about to change that. He had no desire to see a young lady as pleasant and innocent as Harriet dragged through the mires of scandalous gossip.

"And are you . . ." his mother hesitated. "Have you given more thought to which lady you would most like to marry?" she asked.

Andrew's mind suddenly latched onto a terrible idea—what if he *did* become engaged to Lady Virginia just to shock his mother and Miss Grenfeld out of their own ambivalence? A smile twitched at the corner of his mouth as this awful, brilliant idea unfurled in his mind like a desperate but triumphant banner. His heart thudded in his chest at the thought of it. *It could ruin everything. But it could also solve everything . . .*

Time seemed to slow down as this absurd idea gained traction within him. How would they react? His mother may initially seem happy, but would grow to regret her decision one way or another. Perhaps she would learn to finally let him choose for himself. And Miss Grenfeld? If she still wasn't certain whether she wanted him or the captain, he'd make the choice easy for her by removing one of the options. His stomach lurched at the thought that she might simply choose the captain and move forward with their engagement, leaving him behind.

But he stiffened his resolve. He did not want her if he could not be sure she wanted him, too. He could, and would, begin the process of finding a young lady all over again after healing from Miss Grenfeld's loss. But he was not so desperate that he would ever want to marry a young lady who did not return his feelings.

This was one way to know for certain if she did, and although it was unkind of him, the side of him that hurt the most from her indecision was willing to let her fret a little.

The more he thought of it, the more it seemed just the thing to rid his mind of all of its present concerns. He already knew that an engagement to Lady Virginia under false pretenses could be easily dissolved if necessary, though he hoped the need to expose her publicly would never arise. But his mother's idea of a match between himself and Lady Virginia was so terrible that the best punishment he could think of for his mother was making it come true, at least for a time.

"Perhaps Lady Virginia," he finally said, breaking the silence.

"I . . . what?" the surprise on his mother's face was difficult to watch without laughing. "I had thought you wanted to marry Miss Grenfeld," she said innocently.

He did not respond immediately, his mind carefully analyzing the tone of her voice and applying every ounce of knowledge Miss

Grenfeld had ever taught him. This may be as close as his mother would ever come to admitting she was wrong about insisting on his pursuit of Lady Virginia, and he would enjoy this moment.

". . . Andrew?" his mother asked, when he did not answer.

He hastened to respond appropriately. "What do you wish me to do, Mother?" he asked.

Her brows were knit with concern. "I want you to do whatever makes you happiest," she said.

His mouth went dry. Could she possibly be serious? After all of her cajoling, controlling manipulations, and dismissals of his preferences, she only wanted him to be *happy*? He had wondered what changes this false engagement might effect, and was thrilled to see that it already seemed to be working to his benefit.

"I thought you wanted to marry Miss Grenfeld," she continued. "And I am prepared to wish you two very happy and be a good mother-in-law to her if that is still the case."

He stopped a smile from sneaking onto his face and replaced it with a serious expression, careful to keep the tone of his voice sincere. "Actually, I think you were right from the beginning—I want to marry Lady Virginia after all," he said. "Do you really believe she would have me?"

March 26, 1814

Andrew escaped to the club that afternoon because he did not trust himself not to laugh at his mother's various reactions to his sudden apparent change of heart. He did not return until after his mother had supped and gone to bed. The next morning, he took breakfast in his room and prepared himself for the day before skipping down the steps and heading toward his study.

"Oh, hello, Andrew. How are you?"

Andrew jumped as he sat down at his desk. His mother was never so quiet as she was then. She was sitting in a chair near the window and looking outside thoughtfully, her hands folded in her lap.

"Mother! I did not expect to see you . . . here. In my study. How are you?"

"Fine, fine," she said carelessly, waving a handkerchief. Her wrinkled forehead betrayed the half-truth, however, so Andrew came up to sit next to her, determined to keep from smiling or laughing at her expense.

"What is the matter, Mama? You seem a trifle glum."

She looked up at him with a smile. "I . . . oh, it's nothing, Andrew. Only I've just come from visiting Lady Virginia."

"Did you?" he said. "And how was it?"

She shrugged. "She was perfectly polite. Perfectly amiable. But I did not get the feeling that she cares for you very deeply. And I felt so very uncomfortable being around her! Perhaps because she seemed so uncomfortable herself."

Andrew raised his eyebrows. His mother sounded dangerously close to recommending he pursue a love match. Perhaps her sudden shift toward Louisa was due to more than interest in her social influence.

Andrew had trouble pulling his mind away from Louisa once it rested there. The way her face would light up when she entered a room filled with people she knew, and how very at home she seemed at nearly every party. She made everyone around her feel comfortable, too. It was one of her gifts. He sighed at the brief reverie and shook the memory of her from his mind like an unwelcome cloud of smoke.

His mother's continued talking gradually pulled him from his thoughts. "But I am certain that I could grow to like her more, since it is clear that you are fond of her, my dear." She sounded utterly miserable.

"What?" Andrew said, tugged rudely back to reality. "What did you say, Mother?"

"You are fond of Lady Virginia, are you not?"

Andrew's jaw had dropped and he fought to keep his eye from twitching. His mother's recent shifts in attitude had been so erratic that he was having trouble keeping his thoughts in order. "Of course," he said.

His mother nodded.

"She is a good match for you, I suppose. But both of you are rather quiet, you know. I do hope that, if you marry, you two won't disappear completely from society."

"I am certain we won't," he said vaguely, turning from her to hide his smirk at her growing discomfort. It was wicked of him to enjoy her unhappiness this much, but after all the misery she had caused him, he could not help himself.

March 27, 1814

Andrew hurried along the pavement to Curzon Street, his thoughts all a blur. He had thought he was allowed to see behind the charming mask Miss Grenfeld presented to the rest of society, but he was not certain he was after all. The thought of being tolerated rather than wanted was worse than being despised somehow, and his doubts rankled at him.

Frustration could change to admiration in an instant, but apathy was far more difficult to combat. He was not certain what he was about to do was a good idea, but he had to try. He'd regret it the rest of his life if he didn't. Besides, it would keep Harriet safe longer, buy a bit of time for Virginia's lover to return, and might just be enough to force Miss Grenfeld out of her apathy.

Slivers of memory jabbed at him. Memories of her embarrassment, her frustrations with him, of her smiling shyly at him over the fire at his home on Christmas, leaving her portrait for him. His heart thudded. Perhaps she wasn't apathetic toward him, but she refused to say she loved him, and seemed more eager to be mistress of Hillside Manor than the wife of its master. Besides, if she was still considering marrying Captain Allen . . .

He took a deep, resolute breath as he arrived at the duke's palatial home, ascended the steps, knocked, and entered before he could change his mind. Only a few moments later he was granted a private audience with the duke, in which he asked, with hardly any ado, for Lady Virginia's hand in marriage.

The duke had not seemed remotely pleased. "My wife will have my head if I refuse your suit," he said with a sigh. "So I shall accept it, since you are a thoroughly respectable young man. But I am really not certain you would make one another happy."

Andrew was glad the duke was as reticent as he was. It showed he was not completely indifferent to the fate of his poor daughter, who likely had no desire to be married to a man she had never even met. Andrew considered cheering the nobleman up by mentioning the efforts he'd overheard about reuniting his pregnant daughter with her lover. He suspected that telling him this was not a good idea, however, and so he thanked the duke before making a hasty exit.

As he left the study, he saw "Lady Virginia" and her mother walking through the front door. Harriet's face almost immediately paled when she looked at him coming out of the duke's study, putting two and two together. There was no sense in prolonging the inevitable. He straightened his shoulders, walked directly to her, and offered to lead her into the drawing room. "Lady Virginia, might I have the honor of a private word with you?"

Harriet's terror was easily visible behind her thin facade. Andrew bit back a chuckle as she forced a little smile at him and allowed him to lead her into the room.

He mentally ran through the speech he'd rehearsed to himself. Some of the lines were from his friends—William Cox and Michael Heron had both become engaged in the past month or two. He'd also determined that he needed to remain as formal as he reasonably could. After all, he had no actual intention of marrying either Lady Virginia or her double, Miss Harriet, and he was certain she had as little desire to marry him as he did her. He was determined to make the experience as painless—and innocent—as possible for the both of them.

She sat with trepidation on the pink sofa and looked up at Mr. Brougham.

"Lady Virginia, I . . ." He cleared his throat and looked down at her. He had remained on his feet. "You can be in no doubt of my intentions toward you. I have found you a most pleasant and lovely young lady since the moment that my mother introduced you to me. Remember? At Lady Gregor's ball, at the start of the season."

"Yes, I remember." Harriet's smile was almost genuine.

"I have wished to court you ever since that first day."

Andrew shifted a couple of steps at this small lie. It was a good thing he had practiced. He was more nervous than he'd thought he would be.

"Lady Virginia . . . might I simply call you Virginia?"

Harriet did not speak for long enough that Mr. Brougham began to wonder if his proposal would be denied. He would not want her to become the object of the duchess's wrath by refusing him.

"Yes, of course!" she finally said, "I should like that very much. And might I call you . . ." her eyes widened in panic, and he bit his lip to keep from laughing. She'd clearly forgotten his given name.

"Andrew?" he prompted, determined to help her feel more comfortable. "Of course! Virginia, you are the soul of propriety! You hesitate to call me by my Christian name even when appropriate. That is one thing that I do admire about you—your commitment to decorum."

Harriet's smile became so genuine for a moment he wondered if she'd start laughing. "And I you, Mr. Brou—er, Andrew."

Andrew smiled, holding back his own laughter. It wouldn't do for them both to burst into uncomfortable giggles now. "There now, Virginia. We are getting along famously already, are we not? I do like calling you Virginia. 'Tis a beautiful name."

Her expression flattened at this, her mind clearly wandering again.

"Virginia?" Mr. Brougham asked. She looked back at him.

"Forgive me, Mr—I mean Andrew. I was lost in my thoughts. You were saying?"

He came toward her and knelt on the ground before her, chastely grasping both her hands in his. "Virginia, will you do me the great honor of becoming my wife?"

Chapter Twenty-Nine

March 28, 1814

Aunt Frances had taken the news with surprising calm. "You were not exactly as encouraging as you could have been," Aunt Frances reminded Louisa.

Louisa's eyelashes fluttered as she came to herself and registered that someone was speaking to her. "Of course. Naturally. He wouldn't . . . he has his family to consider. His position."

Aunt Frances's eyebrows raised. "He has *Lady Margaret* to consider," she muttered.

The ghost of a smile passed across Louisa's face before fading. She stared out the window. It had not been easy to ready herself for the day that morning. The night before, after hearing the news of Mr. Brougham's engagement gossiped at a party, she had slept only fitfully. She wanted to feign a sudden illness that would allow her to escape and bind her broken heart in peace, but knew that would never do. If there were already suspicions in society that she and Brougham had fallen in love with one another, her suddenly taking ill as he became engaged would only confirm them.

She had to greet everyone who visited her—and there had been many curious visitors thus far that day—with a smile and her head held high. But talking cheerfully about Mr. Brougham's engagement throughout the morning had taken its toll and now she wanted nothing more than to hide away under a mountain of blankets until her pain subsided.

"Lady Margaret here to see you, miss," the butler said.

Louisa blinked a couple of times in disbelief. Lady *Margaret* was here to see her? Whatever for? To crow over her son's recent engagement? She had dismissed her rudely enough a week or so before, and the lady had seemed perfectly content to ignore her until now.

"Miss Grenfeld," Lady Margaret said upon entering the room. Louisa stood to greet her, suddenly as clumsy as a puppet.

"Lady Margaret, what brings you here?" She hoped her smile was genuine despite the surprise.

"Though it has not yet been officially announced, or published in the *Gazette*," she said hastily, "I am certain you are aware that my son has lately become engaged to Lady Virginia, daughter of the Duke of Dorset."

Louisa nodded. "I had heard," she admitted, struggling to seem happy as another painful ache seized her heart. "May I offer my warmest felicitations?"

"No!" The lady snapped, then threw a hand over her mouth, as if surprised by her own outburst. "That is . . . I am not certain how supportive I feel of the engagement myself," she said.

Louisa's mouth dropped open in surprise.

"It is a most eligible match," Aunt Frances said slowly, and gestured for Lady Margaret to take a seat.

"It is," Lady Margaret said as the three of them sat down. "But I cannot help but feel a certain hesitation . . . You see, I do not believe he truly wishes to marry her."

Louisa stared at her hands in her lap, not believing what she was hearing.

"But, as with most other truly eligible matches, affection can grow over time. And it sometimes does," Frances said reassuringly.

"Sometimes?" Lady Margaret asked, her brow creasing.

Aunt Frances was clearly enjoying herself. "I have heard anecdotes. Oh, there are stories of *cicisbei* and mistresses, of course. But there are also stories of sincere and heartfelt attachment born out of the ashes of the former desires of their hearts."

Lady Margaret stared at Aunt Frances in abject horror. It seemed as though her aunt were trying to make the poor lady uncomfortable. Louisa felt she had to help. She assumed a soothing tone.

"What my aunt means, I am sure, is that Lady Virginia and Mr. Brougham ought to deal very well together in time."

"In time," the lady echoed. She sighed a little. "I must admit, if you'd asked me not three weeks ago for my opinion on the matter, I would've agreed with you wholeheartedly. However, now . . ." The lady shook her head. "I ought not to discuss my son's personal affairs with others, I suppose," she murmured.

Louisa reached a comforting hand over to pat the lady's lap, and it was immediately grasped, with a heavy sigh.

"Forgive my impertinence," the lady said, dropping the rude self-importance she normally affected around Miss Grenfeld. "I've no right to ask your advice or be taken into your confidence after speaking to you as I did almost a fortnight ago. But was there not a time when you held affection for my son?"

Louisa felt warmth rising in her cheeks. "I do not know what to say," she said after a pause. "Expressing a preference for an engaged gentleman is not behavior becoming a young lady of decorum."

"Rubbish," Lady Margaret snapped. "I'm not about to tell anyone no matter what you say. Besides, if I wished to make up a rumor to harm you, I'm certain you could dispel it just as quickly as I could spread it."

Louisa smiled to herself. That the lady was finally recognizing the influence she held in society was significant. "I do have feelings for your son, my lady," she said softly, struck by the passion behind the words as she said them.

Lady Margaret's face brightened. "Excellent," she said. "Truly excellent. Because I'm *sure* he's still dangling after you, despite all this nonsense with Lady Virginia. All he needs to do is call off the engagement, as it's not yet been announced!"

Aunt Frances shook her head sadly. "That will never do, my lady. Even you must see that. For a young gentleman to make an offer to a lady and then three days later to unmake the same offer? It would cause a scandal, not to mention be dreadfully unfair to the young lady in question."

"But she does not even seem to care for him! She may even be relieved!" Lady Margaret cried.

Louisa shook her head. "I'm afraid my aunt is correct. If she wishes to end the engagement, *she* may end it without disgrace, but he cannot."

Louisa hated knowing that she and her Aunt Frances were right, but there was no way around it. There was nothing they could do to avoid an unbearable scandal, short of waiting and hoping against hope that Lady Virginia would find a way out of the engagement herself.

March 28, 1814

That night, Louisa went to bed early only to stare at the ceiling in the dark, unable to sleep. She sighed, turned over this way and that, and tried thinking of dull, ordinary things like needlepoint or knitting, sighing again when none of it worked.

The door clicked open and creaked on its hinges.

"Lou?" Aunt Frances said. "Are you asleep?"

"No," she said.

Aunt Frances tiptoed in and slipped under the covers with her for warmth. The ends of winter were holding on ruthlessly and it was nearly as bitterly cold that March evening as it had been in January.

"What is the matter, dearest?" she asked.

Louisa sighed. "I do love Mr. Brougham," she said, and a shiver shot down her spine even as she said it, for though she was frightened of both the words and the feeling, she could not deny they were true.

"Oh, Louisa," Aunt Frances whispered. "I'm so sorry."

A tear slipped down Louisa's cheek. "I had not thought . . . I suppose a little part of me thought him a sure thing. Arrogant of me, wasn't it?" She shook her head as another tear fell.

Aunt Frances was silent for a long time. "The captain wants to marry you, Louisa."

"I know. I do not know what to tell him."

"What do you mean?"

Louisa paused. "I do not wish to marry him. He is handsome and charming and has all that I need, but the thought of marrying him only makes me sad."

Aunt Frances nodded. "Because you are in love with Mr. Brougham."

"Yes." Louisa took a deep, shuddering breath and choked back a hopeless sob. Aunt Frances reached over and rubbed Louisa's arm comfortingly. They lay in silence for a long while.

"Mr. Brougham is engaged now, dear," Frances whispered. "You know what that means."

"Yes—it is over," Louisa said.

"Do not keep the captain waiting too long, Lou," Aunt Frances said.

Louisa let the air out of her lips with an undignified flapping sound. "I know. I will have to tell him soon."

"Tell him what? Aren't you going to accept his proposal?"

"I do not know. I do not wish to, and yet I must be married and settled by the end of the season. My fate, and any chances of you and Father being together, depend on it. It seems that Captain Allen may be my only chance."

"Oh, Louisa. Do not dare worry yourself on my account," Aunt Frances said. "I would be miserable if I knew you were making yourself unhappy for me."

"You would? But then perhaps you and Father could . . ."

Aunt Frances tsked. "Louisa, I will admit that I love your father, and marrying him would seem a happy dream. But I could never enjoy it knowing you were made unhappy in your match. You are so like a daughter to me—likely the only daughter I will ever know—and I love you completely. I am accustomed to being alone, and I am happy most of the time, but I am not accustomed to seeing you miserable, and I could not bear to."

"Perhaps I would do better to consider Captain Allen more seriously. And I had thought that I could. But even when other hopes are lost, I find I simply . . . cannot. Not when there is the least shred of hope. Brougham isn't married yet, and as long as there is a chance Lady Virginia will break off the engagement, I have to hope. Perhaps I could speak with her!"

"There would be a scandal to manage either way," Aunt Frances warned.

Louisa shook her head. "I don't care."

"You don't care?" her aunt echoed disbelievingly. "Louisa Grenfeld is no longer bothered by scandal?"

Louisa shook her head. "No. Not anymore. If Brougham loves me and marries me, that's all I could wish for."

"Hmm. Would you have *him* break off the engagement?"

Louisa paused. It was one thing for the lady to break off the engagement, but it was another entirely for a gentleman to do so after he had already proposed. The latter was infinitely more scandalous. She took a deep breath. "I do not know. I think I would still have him," she finally said. "But if I mustn't keep Captain Allen waiting, I will inform him at once that I do not intend to marry him. Thank you for helping me to see that, Aunt."

Aunt Frances sighed. "You are welcome, I suppose."

March 29, 1814

"Are you certain she wishes to marry you?" his mother asked him over breakfast for the fourth time that morning.

Andrew groaned. "She accepted my suit, did she not? Why do you not go and celebrate, Mother? Your fondest wishes for my conjugal success are coming true before your eyes."

His mother bristled. "I already told you, darling. I want you to be happy! Those are my fondest wishes!"

Andrew stood, unable to mask his annoyance any longer. "You told me countless times that you wished for me to marry Lady Virginia. You begged me to pass time in her company. You insisted that my affection for her would grow in time. And now that I am engaged to the young lady, you are suddenly of a different mind?"

The lady humbly looked down at her unfinished breakfast.

"I thought that it would make you happy," she said. "I . . . was wrong."

Andrew stared at her. "You thought forcing me toward a lady I expressed no interest in would make me happy?"

"It is an eligible match."

"Then why are you not happy for me now, Mother?"

"Because you seem so . . . you don't seem very happy to me. I am sorry," she whispered. "Perhaps it is all my fault."

Andrew quickly walked to her side. "Mother," he said gently. "I am certain all will be well. You said so yourself that Lady Virginia is a very good sort of young lady. I am certain my chances of happiness with her are as great as they are with any other."

"Greater than they are with Miss Grenfeld?" she asked doubtfully.

Andrew looked away. Even with his recent practice, he couldn't pass that off as truth. "Perhaps not," he admitted. "Though it is by far too late—I have already proposed to the lady, and now I shall have to marry her." Even speaking the words, though they weren't true, made him feel dizzy. It was true that he would never wish to break off the engagement himself—what a scandal that would cause! He was either relying on Virginia's rescuer to keep him a single man, or, if he were desperate, using the threat of a potential scandal to urge the duchess to withdraw from the engagement. And he also relied on Miss Grenfeld's willingness to accept the hand of a man tainted by some scandal. He was still a relative social novice, and his heart pounded whenever he thought of the delicate, sticky situation he had gotten himself entangled in. He forced himself to breathe slowly and calm himself.

"Perhaps I shall speak with Lady Virginia about this," his mother said.

Andrew winced. "Er . . . that may not be a good idea."

"Why not?" his mother challenged.

"It may jeopardize the good feelings between yourself and the duchess," he said quickly. "Was not this match a product of both of your desires?"

Lady Margaret puffed out her chest with a stormy brow. "If you think that I would place my own social aspirations above my son's happiness, you are sorely mistaken!" she cried, and then flounced out of the room.

As soon as she was gone, Andrew's head flopped to the table and he issued a groan. He felt like he'd just finished a long game of tug-of-war that had ended with his surrender and his mother landing on her *derrière* in the mud. "If only she could've undergone this transformation *before* . . ." he muttered, chuckling to himself at the absurdity of the situation.

Henry paused brushing the lint off Andrew's jacket the next morning. "Sir? I beg your pardon, but I had wondered if I might be permitted an impertinence."

Andrew raised an eyebrow. "You've never taken the trouble of asking me for permission before, Henry."

Henry chuckled. "I suppose not. But I know how little you like being the subject of gossip—especially gossip that isn't entirely true. And there has been more than a little bit of talk downstairs about your recent engagement."

Andrew sighed. "I would be surprised if there weren't. What is being said?"

Henry continued brushing, not making eye contact. "Some are saying that your attachment to Lady Virginia must be sincere, and wish you very happy, but others wonder about the time at the beginning of the season when you were visiting Miss Grenfeld so frequently and thought you may still be taken with her. Others, still, are saying that you are only engaged to Lady Virginia to please your mother."

Andrew nodded. "That all makes a fair bit of sense. What do you say, Henry?"

"I beg your pardon?"

"What is your opinion? You know me better than any of the servants do. What do you think is in my mind?"

Henry flushed, but he took the question seriously. After a moment's pause he said, "I am honestly not certain. You have been confiding in me less than you did at the beginning of the season. That is quite good," he added quickly. "You ought to rely on the advice of your peers. However, I know there was a time that you were quite taken with Miss Grenfeld, and I have heard from the servants of other houses that there are even a few bets at White's over which lady you would choose. But I do not know if your feelings have changed. If you sincerely wish to marry Lady Virginia, then I wish you very, very happy indeed, sir."

Andrew watched Henry begin to shine his boots and realized it had been a while since he had confided in his friends, and even longer since he had in Henry. He still had not told anyone about his lack of sincerity in proposing to Lady Virginia, and the deception was weighing heavily on him.

"I will be honest with you, Henry, but only to satisfy *your* curiosity and not that of the rest of the servants."

Henry nodded. "I understand, sir. I would never share your secrets."

"Thank you." Andrew took a deep breath. "I only proposed to Lady Virginia to demonstrate both to my mother and to Miss Grenfeld how foolish they were both being. I have no desire to marry Lady Virginia at all, and I have reason to believe she does not—and *will* not—marry me either."

Henry shook his head, trying to keep up with this narrative. "You . . . are not going to marry Lady Virginia, then?"

Andrew shook his head. "I have no intention of going through with it."

Henry was utterly flummoxed. "How will this false engagement solve anything, sir?"

Andrew allowed his scattered thoughts to tumble out of his mouth all at once. "Miss Grenfeld had seemed as though she were beginning to develop feelings toward me but then Captain Allen proposed to her and she seemed confused all over again and had not decided whether to accept or reject him and my mother suddenly realized, thanks in part to her society friends, that Miss Grenfeld was really a wonderful match for me after all and stopped encouraging me to court Lady Virginia and I was frustrated with the both of them for allowing society to dictate their desires and I decided to punish them both by proposing to Lady Virginia."

Henry blinked several times as he digested this rambling monologue.

Andrew chuckled and clapped Henry on the shoulder. "I know that all of this is madness. I am already beginning to regret my decision, but I must confess it has been rather fun seeing my mother agonize over finally getting her wish."

Henry looked him straight in the eye, a sympathetic smile twitching at the corner of his mouth. "This was all a terrible idea, sir."

Andrew gave a lonely bark of laughter. "You are not wrong, Henry! Now I must see if I can successfully extricate myself from this situation without harming anyone."

Henry shook his head. "I wish you the very best of luck, sir. As for me, I now regret asking. I think that I am not paid quite enough to be brought into this sort of confidence."

Chapter Thirty

April 1, 1814

Louisa's smile grew forced as she looked at the young lady sipping tea across from her. Her eyes carefully dissected Lady Virginia's appearance, as she had learned over years to do. The lady was holding her cup in a slightly awkward fashion, and as Louisa watched her closely she realized the lady was tense and anxious, though she hid it well. And she was really quite beautiful. Louisa was not so vain that she could not appreciate the loveliness of her competition.

She did not know when she would again have the chance to address Lady Virginia on her own—Aunt Frances had purchased their time alone together by asking the duchess for a private tour of the small gallery in the music room upstairs. She could not waste this opportunity.

"Lady Virginia, if I may speak plainly, may I ask if you are in love with Mr. Brougham?"

A look that closely resembled panic flashed for a brief moment in the lady's eyes before she calmly replied, "I do not know that I would say I *love* him, but I am fond of him."

Louisa nodded. "I see. When is the wedding to be?"

"In three weeks," she said, and Louisa noticed another nervous flash of fear in the young lady's eyes.

"I see," Louisa repeated slowly. "Well, I will leave you with only a word or two of wisdom, though the two of us have equal experience in society, I daresay! The first is that love can grow over time, from what I hear, and that many of the qualities we admire now may not be those we will want in the future."

Lady Virginia nodded and smiled, seeming relieved to speak no more of the wedding.

"The second word of wisdom is that you ought not to marry him if he is not the man you want to spend the rest of your life with."

Lady Virginia's smile disappeared, replaced by a look of confusion.

"That is to say . . . if you do not feel confident that Mr. Brougham is the right gentleman for you to grow old next to, the *honorable* thing to do would be to break off the engagement."

Louisa's heart was pounding and she heard her voice shake as she spoke. Lady Virginia frowned at her for a moment.

"I . . . thank you," she finally said. "Thank you for your advice, Miss Grenfeld."

Louisa nodded, feeling ridiculous. What sort of person advises a recently betrothed young lady to cancel her engagement? This was a hopeless business, especially as they were not exactly close friends. She sighed. "I am sorry if I have been too forward, Lady Virginia," Louisa said. "Sometimes my mouth runs away with me!"

Virginia nodded and smiled gently. "Of course. Do we not all feel this way at times?"

Louisa forced an uncomfortable smile and wondered to herself yet again why she had thought this might work. She took a sip of tea and waited awkwardly for her aunt and the duchess to return.

April 10, 1814

Henry's conversation had left Andrew feeling completely silly about his supposedly brilliant plan. Each time Andrew saw Miss Grenfeld that week, he ached with longing. He berated himself for continuing to feel this way, given her inability to commit to him, but then he recalled the many times she had looked up at him shyly with that warmth in her eyes that seemed reserved only for him. He had watched her closely at many parties and had never quite seen it duplicated, even for Captain Allen.

His heart lurched yet again as he thought of her. *Would she ever accept his proposal now*? He could not undo the scandal caused by a broken engagement, and he felt an utter fool. How could he have thought that someone as proper and refined as Miss Grenfeld would willingly embroil herself in scandal only to marry him? She was not exactly keen on marriage in the first place.

She had been seen at the park with Captain Allen multiple times in the past couple of weeks. It seemed they were rarely apart. He felt a complete gudgeon for having tested her affections in the way that he had. The most likely thing now seemed to be that she would marry the captain and that he would marry . . . either Lady Virginia or, God willing, *anyone* else.

But as much as Louisa's initial hesitation had pained him, he still wanted nothing more than to marry her and walk through life at her side.

This realization sat heavily on him for a day or two before he made up his mind. As soon as it was made, Andrew broke from his reverie and had Henry dress him for a morning visit immediately. Not an hour later he was sitting in Miss Grenfeld's handsome drawing room, waiting nervously for the opportunity to speak with her without so many other guests hanging about.

Lady and Miss Norbury were still there, laughing together about the latest *on-dit*, and he tried to smile along and act naturally, but when Mrs. Folsham and Mrs. Withinghall walked through the door with smiles on their faces, he nearly despaired. It was only after he recognized where he had seen the ladies so many times before—in his own sitting room at home, chatting eagerly with his mother—that he grew interested in the way the conversation began to unfold.

"We had been so *certain* that you would propose to Miss Grenfeld, sir!" Mrs. Folsham said, shaking her head. "But perhaps we were mistaken in the direction your affections lay."

"Not that it is any of our business," Mrs. Withinghall said quickly, "only you two would have made such a handsome couple! Ah, well. Dear Miss Grenfeld, *do* tell me where you found the fabric for these beautiful drapes!"

He waited impatiently for the two women to leave, his heart pounding, and after an agonizingly long conversation about fringe and tassels and crystal ornaments, he was finally left alone with Miss Grenfeld and her aunt.

Silence reigned only a moment before he blurted, "Miss Grenfeld, I've been a fool."

She looked up in surprise, her eyes meeting his and a flush rising to her cheeks. She was so lovely, and so obviously hurt by his actions, that he cursed himself all over again.

"What did you say?"

His courage fled. "Nothing. I . . ." He shook his head. "How have you been, Miss Grenfeld?"

She smiled sadly. "I have been well . . . And you, sir?"

There was a veritable chasm between them, and Andrew hated it. "Have you answered the captain's proposal yet?" he asked.

"Not yet, but I will soon," she said quietly. "I have kept him waiting far too long already, and he has been very patient."

His heart throbbed, though he had no right to hope she would refuse an eligible match on his account when he was no longer on the marriage mart. He took a deep breath. It was impertinent to ask what she intended her response to be. He was embarrassed he had not seen so earlier.

Their conversation dragged on uncomfortably for a few more minutes before he excused himself. He could not take one minute more of it.

April 10, 1814

Aunt Frances clucked her tongue as soon as Mr. Brougham departed. "Well this is a fine mess the two of you have made," she said, shaking her head.

"Can anything be done about it?" Louisa asked hopelessly.

Her aunt chuckled sadly. "I don't know."

"I already tried talking with Lady Virginia," Louisa said.

"And what did that accomplish?"

Miss Grenfeld sighed. "Nothing, but perhaps I ought to try again. I do not think that she will listen to me, but what else can I do?"

They were interrupted then by another visitor coming through the door. Captain Miles Allen, resplendent in a dark green riding outfit that complemented his lovely blue eyes, walked into the room with a cheerful smile.

"How are my two favorite young ladies in London?" he asked.

Aunt Frances chuckled. "You are incorrigible!" she told him, shaking her head.

He took the liberty of sitting down near Louisa and reaching for one of her hands. "I hope I find you well today, my dear," he said.

Louisa's skin tingled unpleasantly where he touched it and she drew her hand away.

His smile faded as he awaited her response.

"I am well enough," she said.

He searched her face for the answers he was hoping for and did not seem to find them. He took a deep breath. "I . . . see. You are looking well," he said. "As lovely as ever." There was a sadness in his tone that she could not recall having heard before and it pierced her heart.

She stared at her hands clasped in her lap. "I am so sorry, Captain," she whispered.

He took in another sharp breath.

She looked up at him only to see that he was staring down at his hands in tense thought. "I am so sorry to have kept you waiting so long," she said. "It was very wrong of me. I was waiting for my confused feelings to settle, for me to feel I could accept you. But they simply never did."

He frowned and looked up at her, a touch of anger in his expression, though he kept his voice calm. "You did keep me waiting for some time."

She hung her head. "I know. And it was very wrong of me. You deserve far better. You deserve a lady who grows weak in the knees each time you pass by! A lady who cannot wait to answer your every desire. A little part of me is very sad I cannot be this young lady for you. You are a good man, Captain Allen."

She watched him swallow. He grew calmer and nodded. "That is kind of you to say," he finally said.

They sat together in silence for a long moment. Finally, the captain spoke again, shaking his head. "I . . . am not accustomed to losing," he said, laughing ruefully. "But this is a battle unlike any I've ever fought before."

Louisa could have cried. Part of her was pained at the loss of the captain's faithful courtship and delightful company and wanted to accept him in the face of Mr. Brougham's recent engagement, but she had to be honest both with herself and with the captain if she was to have any peace. She could not marry him feeling as she did, and to keep him waiting even a moment longer for her answer was unfair.

She sighed. "Again, I am so sorry, Captain."

He nodded. "I . . . understand. I must leave you now."

He stood abruptly and Louisa rose from her seat to see him to the door.

"I will gladly welcome you the next time you see fit to visit," Louisa said quietly.

He nodded again, and attempted a smile that looked more like a grimace. "I will return when I can," he said gruffly. "I do not know when that will be. I . . . wish you all my best."

Louisa winced as the door closed behind him with a very final-sounding *thud*.

Chapter Thirty-One

April 17, 1814

Andrew stared again at the missive inviting him to Jackson's boxing club to spar with Captain Allen. The less civilized part of Andrew had wanted to throw Captain Allen's invitation directly into the fire and ignore it, but he knew that he could not do that. What did the man want from him, though? Did he wish to gloat? That seemed the most likely. Could he possibly be jealous of his friendship with Miss Grenfeld? Would he tell him off and bully him into leaving her alone? He could not think of a *happy* reason Captain Allen would want to meet him, and at Jackson's boxing club, of all places. He was a terrible boxer and did not present particularly well when not fully clothed, so he would be at a decided disadvantage.

He sighed as he reached the club's Bond Street entrance and ascended the stairs. He had only been there two or three times before, at Miss Grenfeld's encouragement—all the pinks of society aspired to land a facer on the great Jackson, though precious few ever did. The times he'd visited he had felt embarrassed enough by his lack of natural talent and his lean frame that he had not been eager to return. Reluctantly, he dressed down to spar and nervously waited for Captain Allen to meet him.

When the captain arrived in the boxing gym, he was difficult to miss. His dark hair was immaculately coiffed, and his bare chest had a handsome amount of hair to match. His muscles were easily visible, rippling gently whenever he moved. He was a natural athlete who had plenty of practice at nearly every sporting endeavor and was a decorated war hero as well. Andrew forced himself to stand up straight and meet the captain instead of cowering in the corner or sneaking out of the room.

"Brougham!" Captain Allen said. His jaw was tight when he smiled.

Andrew swallowed. "Captain Allen," he said, bobbing a polite nod.

"I hope you have come prepared for a good sparring match," the captain said. "I have been . . . eagerly anticipating this."

"I will oblige you if you insist, but I really am not—"

"Excellent. There is a good bit of space to practice over there." He clapped a hand on Andrew's bare shoulder and led him to an area near the edge of the large room. Then he put up his fists and assumed the stance made famous by Gentleman Jackson himself—his fists up and his stance lithe, bouncing on the balls of his feet with his knees bent.

Andrew reluctantly mirrored his posture as best he could, and the two men began circling one another. "I have not had much practice," he confessed.

Captain Allen merely smiled and shot forward with a quick jab that Andrew barely dodged.

"There," said the captain. "That was practice."

"That was practice?" Andrew said weakly. He had felt the force of the captain's fist as it whistled past his face, so he was not looking forward to a *real* hit if that was only practice.

"Are you ready now?" the captain asked.

No. Absolutely not. Never will be, Andrew thought to himself. "Ready as I'll ever be," he finally said.

The captain began circling, looking for openings. He lunged forward to catch Andrew in the ribs and Andrew needed to fight to catch his next breath. He looked frantically for an opening to return a hit and could not find one. He wasn't even certain he remembered how to block a hit properly.

Andrew tried to punch the captain but his hand was batted away harmlessly. Before he could return to a defensive stance, the captain's fist made direct contact with his gut and Andrew doubled over in pain.

"Are you all right?" the captain asked, a hint of mockery in his tone.

"Yes," Andrew said quickly. "I . . . yes, I am all right." He stood up straight again and held his arms in front of himself. The next hit he was able to dodge successfully, twisting out of the way. But the one after that hit his unprotected face.

"Oh, I'm afraid that will leave a mark!" the captain said. "I am sorry, sir."

Andrew forced a pleasant look onto his now bruised face. "No matter," he said.

"You will have quite the story to tell the ladies at the next ball," the captain said, smiling cheerfully. There was a glint of something mildly malicious in his eye, and Andrew once again fought the urge to run in the opposite direction.

"I think it obvious you have the advantage of me, Captain," he said.

"Nonsense," the captain said. "I am certain you will be able to get a good hit in. Give it another go!"

Andrew took a deep breath and resumed his unpracticed boxer's stance, ignoring the pain from the captain's blows and looking desperately for a good way to get a hit in on his opponent. He ducked a hit to the head, dodged a hit to his midsection, and focused with all the intensity he could muster. Immediately after dodging that second blow, he managed to punch the captain in the chest, only to feel his hand cry out in agony and to see the captain hardly wince at the contact.

As he massaged his sore hand, the captain dropped his arms from their stance. Captain Allen hardly looked winded, and disappointment radiated from his countenance. He had likely never attempted to box with someone as pathetic as Andrew before.

"You really *weren't* made for boxing," Allen said.

Andrew could not help but laugh as he continued nursing his injured hand. "Not at all," he said. "I could never be the athlete you are."

The captain frowned, took a deep breath, and turned away for a long moment, before saying, "Then how did *you* manage to best me?"

Andrew chuckled disbelievingly. "In what way do you think I have bested you, Captain?"

The captain shot a look of intense frustration at him. "Certainly not in any way that can be *measured*," he said sharply, giving Andrew a quick glance up and down that left him feeling utterly exposed and humiliated.

Andrew folded his arms over his chest and pursed his lips. There was only so much self-deprecation a man could stomach at once. "My talents lie firmly in the realm of the natural sciences." He felt foolish even saying it.

The captain laughed. "I . . . forgive me, sir. I have simply never . . . I've never attempted a contest that I did not stand a chance of winning until now."

Andrew frowned. "What do you mean, sir?"

The captain could not meet his eyes but was staring ahead with intensity. "She would not have me," he said.

Andrew's heart thudded behind his ribs. "Miss Grenfeld?"

The captain chuckled humorlessly. "Who else could possibly bring me up to scratch?"

Andrew's mind was racing at the implications of Allen's words. Had she refused him, then? Without another engagement in place? Did that mean she cared for Andrew, after all? His heart pounded.

"I am sorry, Captain," he finally said.

The captain eyed him suspiciously for a moment before nodding and clapping a hand on his shoulder so hard that it stung, although Andrew would never admit that.

The captain was thoughtful. "Whatever it is you have that I don't appears to be what she wants. I do wonder what would have happened if I had met her first. If she hadn't already known you. But it's pointless to wonder. There are other fish in the sea, as they say, though no one else quite like her."

Captain Allen turned then, shaking his head once more, and walked away.

April 18, 1814

The weather was still brisk, although spring was beginning in earnest and Andrew felt the familiar desire to travel back to his estate where it was green and birds and animals were more plentiful. But he was more determined—and more hopeful—than ever before that he would have Miss Grenfeld with him the next time he went. His home had felt so desolate as soon as she had left it after Christmas.

He hurried up the road and knocked on the familiar door on Park Street without pausing to catch his breath. He kneaded his hat in his hands as he waited to be allowed entrance, and hurried into the drawing room as soon as the door was opened to him.

Miss Grenfeld sat on her usual settee, sketching away in her notebook. She wore a soft gray-green morning dress and auburn curls framed her perfect face.

He bowed. "Miss Grenfeld," he said.

She looked up at him and smiled, setting her drawing to the side, sadness and hope mingling in her eyes. "It is good to see you, Mr. Brougham."

He sighed as he took the seat next to her. "I am so sorry," he said.

She looked down at her hands, clasped tightly together.

"I cannot hear you, sir," Aunt Frances said. "What did you say?"

"I've been a fool!" he repeated loudly, shaking his head. "I should never have put you into this position, Miss Grenfeld. I should never have proposed to Lady Virginia."

"You do not wish to marry her?" Miss Grenfeld asked quietly.

"Do you wish to marry the captain?" he retorted and regretted it almost instantly when she winced at the question.

"No," she said.

"I know," he said gently. "I am sorry to cause you distress. I saw the captain and he told me so."

"You saw him?" she seemed surprised.

"Yes, he . . . challenged me to a fight."

Miss Grenfeld paled. "He *didn't*."

Andrew chuckled at the panic in her eyes. "He certainly did, but it was at Gentleman Jackson's and he only relieved a few of his frustrations on me. I think he will be all right, poor fellow."

Miss Grenfeld grimaced again. "Your face," she said, just noticing the bruise on his cheek where Captain Allen had struck him. She reached up gently to touch the injury and he seized the opportunity to cover her hand with his.

"I've been truly wicked," he whispered.

Miss Grenfeld's large brown eyes were sad. "What do you mean?"

"I meant to punish you," he said, taking her hand in his and lacing his fingers with hers, relishing each sensation. "I was proud and angry. I . . . I thought perhaps you would accept my proposal regardless of the scandal that breaking my engagement would cause, but I do not know what I was thinking. That is an impossible burden to ask you to bear."

"No, I am to blame," she said quickly, squeezing his hand. "I should never have encouraged the suit of the captain when it was only yours I wanted."

He sank into her gaze, feeling warm to his toes at this confession. It was the first time she had said anything so direct regarding her feelings for him.

She looked away. "But why did you have to propose to Lady Virginia?" she asked miserably.

"Because I thought that she would back out of the engagement herself," he said with a sigh. "I fear I was wrong."

Louisa pursed her lips. "It will cause a dreadful scandal if you end it, you know."

He nodded. "I know. But there is only one person's forgiveness and good opinion I care about."

Louisa met his eyes again. "Oh?"

"Louisa, if you would have me, I would marry you in a heartbeat." His voice was little more than a whisper. "I have wanted to for months, from almost the moment we first met, but there have been . . . obstacles. I am determined to remove the last of them," he said earnestly. "And I'm done with the stupid pride and doubt that has kept me from rushing to your side so many times."

Louisa finally let out a breath. "I am too. I very much hope you know what you're doing, Andrew, because I would have you—scandal or no scandal, fortune or no fortune, and with or without your mother's approval. I finally see that now. I suppose it took your becoming engaged for me to see that clearly, but I will not change my mind."

"I love you, Louisa," he said, squeezing her hand.

Her eyes widened and shone with sudden tears. "I love you too," she whispered.

Aunt Frances sighed and her hand flew to her heart.

Andrew's lips twitched into a disbelieving smile for only an instant before he leaned forward as if to kiss her. He paused an inch from her lips and released a frustrated sigh, instead pressing a brief kiss to her cheek.

"Louisa," Andrew said, pulling away. "I do not know if your father will grant me an audience, but I intend to beg him to as soon as I am again a free man, unworthy though I am."

Louisa laughed, a tear spilling down her cheek. "I certainly hope that he will, for I won't have anyone else!"

Aunt Frances sniffled loudly. She was openly sobbing now, smiling broadly all the while.

April 18, 1814

Andrew had refused to talk with Louisa's father until he was freed from his engagement with Lady Virginia. Cancelling the engagement immediately was the best hope that he had of receiving a favorable response from Mr. Grenfeld. Still, he was not looking forward to ending the engagement, and he hoped he would not force poor Harriet into an awkward situation by crying off. He did not dare confide in her the whole lest she confide in him—and he had no desire to bear the weight of a perfect understanding of her predicament. She had problems enough without worrying about her secrets being aired to the *ton*.

He was anxious when he knocked at the door and awaited a response. Andrew did not recognize the footman who answered. He must have been new to the place.

"May I see Lady Virginia, please?" he asked.

The man frowned. "I am afraid my lady is not available," he said. "May I inform her of your visit?"

Andrew frowned. "Not available? What do you mean?" *Is she well? Has the baby arrived?*

"I have not been informed," the footman confessed.

"Hmm. I'm afraid this is rather urgent," Andrew said. "Do you know when I might speak with her?"

"I will see that she is informed of your visit as soon as possible."

He sighed. "All right. Tell her that Mr. Brougham came by. Andrew Brougham." He held out a card to the footman, but the footman's eyes widened and he shook his head.

"I beg your pardon, sir! You are Lady Virginia's fiancé. I have heard your name but had never seen you before."

Andrew smiled and nodded. He did not exactly enjoy being called "Lady Virginia's fiancé," but it was true enough until he could make it otherwise.

"A man ought to be able to visit his own fiancé," the footman said firmly. "Or at least know where she is! If you are willing to be seated in the drawing room, I will ask after her and as soon as I know where she is I will inform you directly. *Someone* here ought to know."

"Thank you," Andrew said, following the footman into the drawing room and taking a seat on a comfortable chair.

The man rushed off, promising to hurry back. Andrew glanced at the pictures on the wall around the room and stood. He was too nervous to sit and wait. He walked about the room. What would she say when she came? Would it be Harriet coming to greet him or Virginia—the real Virginia? Were they both all right? He still had countless questions about their unusual arrangement, but his roiling stomach could easily answer for what he wanted the most—to have done with this whole pretense and to see both Harriet and Lady Virginia safely married off. To *other* men. He sighed to himself as his anxiety made him quicken his pace about the room.

When the door finally opened, he immediately leaped to attention. But when he saw that the young maid opening the door was *not* Lady Virginia, he was puzzled.

"I'm afraid I *must* speak with Lady Virginia. It is rather urgent."

The maid gave him a smile laced with sympathy as she closed the door behind her and began to speak quietly. "Mr. Brougham, you are a fine chap. But you've been caught in the middle of . . . an unusual set of circumstances."

His heart began racing. He refused to allow his hopes up and tried to school his expression into something neutral, but it was difficult. He tried to assume a look of innocent concern. "Is something the matter with Lady Virginia?"

The maid grimaced. "Not exactly. To arrive at the point—Lady Virginia cannot marry you."

Andrew grinned before he could stop himself and let out the breath he hadn't realized he'd been holding. "Really? Oh, that is capital news!"

The maid blinked a few times in surprise. This was clearly not the response she had expected of him. "You . . . aren't upset about this?"

He was speaking too quickly but couldn't stop himself. "Upset? Why, I'm delighted! And relieved, ecstatic . . . I only courted Lady Virginia to make my mother happy and—" Louisa's face was all he could see in his mind, but he managed to avoid saying her name somehow. ". . . to prove to her that it would never work." He let out another little sigh. "I was worried Lady Virginia would never call it off and that I would be forced to go through with it."

The maid burst into helpless giggles. "That is the best news I've had all day, Mr. Brougham! I am so happy to hear you aren't disappointed."

He smiled. "Far from it, I assure you." His mind wandered to Lady Virginia and Harriet, and he hoped this turn of events was as much in their favor as it was in his. He stood. "In fact, I must be off directly. I have a . . . friend I need to visit."

The maid raised her eyebrows and smirked, clearly impressed and relishing the mild scandal of his having elsewhere to be right now. "Mr. Brougham! *Already*?"

Mr. Brougham flushed. He had not done a good job of concealing his emotions, it was true. Perhaps he ought to try harder. "Is that so very terrible of me? I suppose it is. But . . . you say Lady Virginia is well? Is she happy?"

The maid nodded and smiled. "Very much so. Married. And with a beautiful baby boy, too."

Mr. Brougham tried to look confused for a moment, which wasn't easy when all he wanted to do was loudly cheer, but he wasn't willing to let on the fact that he knew anything further about the situation. "I wish her very, very happy indeed," he said sincerely.

"Harriet is happy, too. She's engaged now."

He tried to appear utterly bewildered at the mention of Lady Virginia's double, and hoped he was convincing. "Who is Harriet??"

"Harriet is—"

Andrew held up a hand to stop her, laughing. He couldn't hold back his relief that both Lady Virginia and Miss Harriet had found the happy endings they deserved. But he would never be able to keep a straight face through the whole of it if this maid insisted on telling him the story there and then. "No, no! I . . . I have heard enough. I am not entirely sure what drama was playing itself out in this household, but I am happy that it all appears to have ended well."

The maid smiled ruefully. "You, of all people, are entitled to a full explanation, Mr. Brougham. If you won't sit and hear it, I shall write it to you in a letter."

Perfect. Andrew chuckled. His cheeks were beginning to grow sore from smiling already. "Very well. Thank you very much, er—?"

"Mandie."

He nodded and turned to walk out the door, but Mandie stopped him again. "May I be so impertinent as to ask what friend you are off to visit right now?"

Andrew grinned. "I hope you'll see our engagement in the society papers soon enough." He tipped his hat, gathered his cloak, and tripped cheerfully down the front steps with an added bounce to his gait.

April 18, 1814

Louisa's father had not done particularly well at masking his pleasure at the sudden dissolution of Andrew's engagement. He was clearly trying as hard as he could to remain stern and intimidating, assuring Andrew in no uncertain terms that he was not a man to be trifled with, and demanding his daughter be treated with the utmost respect. Andrew had been relieved to make it through the entire interview without smiling or laughing once.

As soon as the door opened, he hurried to the sitting room, where Louisa was rushing into a seat, a smile on her face. It was as obvious as anything that she had just been eavesdropping on their conversation.

Andrew smiled at her and allowed himself a luxurious moment to stare at her lovely face and enjoy the warmth of her gaze. He was less nervous than he had thought he would be, though his heart was pounding a triumphant rhythm in his chest. He felt a curious peace, knowing he was looking at the most important part of his future life. He took a deep breath, suddenly feeling there wasn't enough room behind his ribs for all he felt.

"Is anything the matter, Mr. Brougham?" Louisa asked.

"Yes," he said, trying to sound stern.

Her face fell.

His lips twitched into a smile and he said, "Please call me Andrew."

Louisa laughed. "Of course . . . Andrew."

He walked straight to the chair where she sat. He knelt before her and took her hand. "Darling Louisa," he said with a grin. "Forgive me?"

"Of course I do!" she said with a laugh. "Do you forgive me?" she asked.

He shook his head. "There's nothing to forgive."

She smiled and took one of his hands in hers, placing it gently against her cheek.

He leaned forward and gazed into her lovely eyes. "Marry me?"

Louisa blinked back tears and smiled back at him. "Yes," she whispered.

He stood and grasped her hands, pulling her up toward him and into a kiss. She clutched his lapels tightly and he smiled, one hand cradling her face and the other holding her close against him. Her lips were soft, the taste of her delicious, her gentle scent intoxicating. He would never, ever have enough of her. It was not possible.

He wasn't certain how long they kissed, but he never wanted it to end. They broke apart only when the door opened to Aunt Frances's happy squeals and Mr. Grenfeld loudly saying, "Now, see here!"

He and Louisa both laughed and stepped forward to accept their felicitations.

All was as it should be.

May 7, 1814

Andrew and Louisa decided to marry in London, where their friends could attend and celebrate with them. The day after the banns were all read, they walked to a chapel near their homes in town and were married.

Louisa's wedding clothes were, of course, much talked about. The lacework on her gown alone set off a trend that was all the rage for two full years afterward. But Louisa's attentions were fully focused on her handsome new husband, who wore a smile from the moment they arrived until the moment they climbed into the waiting carriage and departed for Hillside Manor.

Philip had clapped Andrew on the back after the ceremony and the rest of his friends had nothing but effusive praise and surprise over the turns of events that had led to his and Louisa's engagement. Louisa's friends squealed over how perfectly well suited the couple was and how flawlessly her hair had been styled.

Louisa's favorite moment had been seeing Aunt Frances and her father speaking quietly to one another in a corner, their cheeks flushed with something like embarrassment or anticipation. She had high hopes that Aunt Frances would never need to leave her father's household at all.

"Are you eager to return to London for the next season, Louisa?" Andrew asked.

"Yes and no," she said. "I am far more excited for what will precede it!"

"You mean our wedding trip to the North?"

"Of course!" Louisa said. "I have thought of little else these past three weeks. London can wait."

Andrew pressed her hand. "Oh, really? London can wait?"

Louisa smiled. "Yes, it can. If you were to tell me I could never have another season in London, I would still be perfectly contented—as long as you and I are together."

Andrew's eyes shone with tears and he blinked them away. "I thought you only wanted a house in Town to be happy."

She shook her head. "That was only before I knew what real happiness was," she insisted. "My greatest happiness is with you."

"Oh? Should we forsake London entirely, then?"

Her cheeks turned pink. "No! That is . . . I would choose you over London every time, but I hope that, at least sometimes, I won't need to make that choice."

Andrew laughed. "Only sometimes? It won't bother you to hide away in the countryside every now and then?"

Louisa grinned at him. "Not at all. I'm looking forward to it."

Epilogue

September 1814
A honeymoon cottage in Scotland

Louisa walked into the little room they both used as a study for their work, clutching a letter to her chest. Tears were flowing down her cheeks.

"Bad news, Lou?" Andrew asked, leaving his work and coming up to wrap his arms about her.

She shook her head and looked up at him, her eyes shining. "No, no. The very best. I've just had a letter from Aunt Frances."

"And?"

"And she and father are very, very happy together."

"Excellent! I wish you could have attended the wedding. I know you wanted to."

Louisa shook her head. "It was better to keep it very private. The fewer people aware of their marriage, the more likely it is to remain valid."

"It has always seemed odd that cousins can marry but widows cannot marry their in-laws. After all, we've seen what has happened to the royal family and poor King George."

Louisa shrugged. "I am only happy that they have found a way to be together. Now that I know they are so happily matched, my own happiness is complete."

Andrew smiled and pulled her into his chest, gently resting his chin on top of her head. She sighed and leaned into his embrace, her hands comfortably resting in her favorite crevice of his back. After a long while, she looked up at him.

"Now, what do you think we should do about decorations for the ball I mean to host in London this October? Red satin? No, no. Too wintry. I think we had best keep with blues and yellows."

Andrew smiled. "Whatever *you* think, Louisa. I am certain you know best."

She smiled at him and walked back over to her desk to adjust some of the notes and designs she had jotted down about the ball. "There," she said. "I think it will be the highlight of the season!"

He chuckled. "You could likely throw a ball in a dirty alleyway and half of the *ton* would join you there, my love."

She shook her head. "You overstate my influence!" she said, "but I do think that this party will be quite a success, and I am certain your mother will like it as well. I will send copies of these plans to her directly to see what she thinks."

Andrew nodded. "It is still incredible to me that you managed to bring her so thoroughly onto your side, my dear. She was so irrationally determined to dislike you at first! And I will never forget her reaction on hearing of our engagement."

"I wish I could have seen it," Louisa said.

Andrew chuckled. "She gave a loud *whoop* of delight and began bouncing up and down, her hands shaking in front of her. I had to fetch her smelling salts."

Louisa laughed heartily, throwing her head back. Andrew smiled.

"I knew I could never secure *your* happiness by upsetting your mother," she said, taking both of his hands in hers.

He grimaced. "She does have her ways of making herself unpleasant when disobeyed. Still, though. For you, Louisa, I would have."

"I know, but having her approval makes you *happier*."

"I won't deny it," he admitted. "I am not one to look for a fight—that much you know."

She laughed again, and his hands clasped hers a little tighter.

"You really care so much for my happiness?" he asked.

Her cheeks pinked and her eyes glowed. "I do," she said. "I couldn't be truly happy myself without it."

"You need me to be happy in order to feel happy yourself?"

She nodded. "Yes. Is that so very odd?"

He smiled, and shook his head. "Not to me. I feel the same way about you. Why do you suppose we feel this way?"

Louisa looked into his familiar green eyes until her heart swelled in the happy way it did when she was around him. "You know?" she said playfully, "I think it is because we are in love, Andrew."

The corners of his mouth lifted in a crooked grin. Before she could say another word, he had stopped her mouth with a kiss. His arms wrapped around her, pulling her closer, and her fingers found their way into the curls at the nape of his neck. After another breathless minute or two, he pulled away, resting his forehead against hers. "I love you, Louisa. So very dearly."

Louisa smiled. "And I you. And I *like* your Mother, you know. No one is irredeemable," she insisted.

"Even me?"

"Especially not you," she said, kissing the tip of his nose.

He seized the opportunity while he was so close to grab her about the waist and sink into a chair, pulling her onto his lap. "I cannot believe my good fortune," he said, nuzzling against her neck.

She giggled—her neck was quite ticklish. "What makes you so fortunate?"

"I don't have to choose between what I want to do and who I want to be with."

"You mean studying birds?" she asked. "You had better not be leaving me behind on your expeditions—you know I like them just as well as you do."

He kissed her again, and she smiled against his lips and pulled him closer. "We've had a lovely holiday here," she said, "I will be so sad to leave."

"Holiday?" he said indignantly. "We've been hard at work!"

Louisa smiled. "It doesn't feel like work to me, but we have created something pretty remarkable together so far, I think."

Andrew glanced at his desk at the half-finished bird she was drawing in exquisite detail, from memory, right next to the research he had written on the species thus far. The pile of papers and notebooks strewn about was a sight to behold. Their ornithology manual would be magnificent, that was certain.

"You've made me so impossibly happy, Louisa."

She sighed in his arms and held him tightly. "Good. I've made *me* very happy, too!"

About the Author

Mary-Celeste Ricks earned a BA from Brigham Young University in Humanities with an emphasis in English and minors in editing and Italian. She finally dared to imitate her hero Georgette Heyer after studying abroad in London, taking Romantic period literature courses in both English and Italian, and sneaking peeks at 19th century manuscripts while working in the archives. She has two darling children, loves to learn, and enjoys cooking and eating delicious food. She loves love and is currently living happily ever after with her handsome, nerdy husband playing board games, D&D, and video games.